THE
PARAMOUNT
DIMENSION

JOSEPH CALEV

ISBN: 978-1-7362617-0-5 (Hardcover)

ISBN: 978-1-7362617-1-2 (Paperback)

Library of Congress Control Number: 2021901352

This is a work of fiction. Names, characters, places, and incidents either are the product of the author's imagination or are used fictitiously. Any resemblance to actual persons, living or dead, events, or locales is entirely coincidental.

Cover design by: Damonza

Space Needle Photo https://commons.wikimedia.org/wiki/
File:International_Fountain_with_Space_Needle.jpg

First edition 2021

Publisher:

Joseph Calev

Bellevue, WA

www.josephcalev.com

To my wife Nelya and sons, Eitan and Nathan, for letting me travel to the Paramount Dimension.

1

THE CITY WAS sleeping when the Guardian Drums awoke.

Dum-dee-dum-dum-dum-DA-dum-dum they roared over and over again.

A gargantuan troll manned each nearly hundred-foot-tall daiko drum, and pounded them with enough force to split a mountain. The thumping beat reverberated from every hilltop around the piercing spires of the city. It rattled every house, sent every pet into hiding, and woke an entire region.

The drumming was not without cause. Far above the emerald city, a flotilla crept forward through the deathly silence of space. Its bulky cuboid-shaped crafts were not built for beauty. Each sparkled with the lights of hundreds of fighters firing their engines. The reptile troops knew the drill; in a few hours the planet would be theirs.

The flutter of lights ceased and the dark-gray crafts aligned in rows. Then, with the deathly grace of the most professional of killers, they began their descent. Their gentle trip through the atmosphere was calm compared to the subsequent annihilation that awaited the inhabitants below.

The drumming got louder.

The sky turned red and the gigantic beasts pounded forth with even greater fury. Every human in the city had to be awakened. This was not a drill. The massive Last Shofar called out to the scurrying citizens from atop Cougar Mountain, which loomed over the metropolis of Seattle, in a desperate attempt to reach everyone.

Jason jumped from his bed and flew to the window. How had he slept this late! Everyone had known the lizards were coming. He'd always told himself the drums would waken him. Yet here he was, only pulled up by the Last Shofar. Its purpose and signal was well known, even though this was its maiden use.

The message was simple: Get up and fight, or die.

Jason gasped. The captain of his cruiser, the *Ravager*, would not wait for a lowly yeoman. There were no courts-martial for missing one's ship during wartime, only executions.

He pulled on a shirt so quickly that he tore it, then covered it with his uniform jacket. Maybe this was humanity's end, but he would still do his tiny part in giving these reptiles hell.

To his relief, they were still priming the wooden ship's wings for launch, so he jumped through the door and took his position at the bridge. The captain, a gruff man who walked with a limp and had lost two fingers, gave Jason a snort but otherwise said nothing. They were all about to die anyway.

Jason hurriedly checked his comms while dozens outside struggled to lift the hundred-foot-long wings, which had no purpose given the hydrogen engines, up and down. The *Ravager*, like the thousands of others in the fleet, was never designed for wartime. It was a pleasure craft, meant for scenic cruises over the Cascade and Olympic Mountains, or jaunts to the San Juan Islands. Its intricately carved wooden hulls were stunning to behold, but also made it a defensive tinder box. For some reason it mattered how elegantly firewood could fly.

A few hundred feet away, a ship Jason recognized as the *Gallant* ascended. With one hundred and forty-three crew aboard, these things moved more like overweight bumblebees than war craft, and

Jason gulped at the thought of battling at several thousand feet in this thing. A few seconds later, the entire bridge shook and the death trap that was the *Ravager* lumbered into the air.

Little time had passed since the evil Mordriss, who led the lizards, had made his demand. "Surrender to enslavement, or be annihilated," he had ordered.

Yet never could they give up their freedom. So, this peaceful city along the Puget Sound went to war. Every window in these pleasure craft was replaced with a gun turret, and men and women alike were drafted into a new navy. The administrative side of the operation had functioned like clockwork. Combat efficiency was a different matter: The guns tore the canvas wings to shreds on the first practice runs. Jason couldn't help but realize how hopeless this was.

The drums ceased, and the trolls replaced the massive sticks with rocket launchers. From above, Jason noticed one aim his tube the wrong way. These were not soldiers. This was set for a slaughter.

The crew's eyes wandered and hands fidgeted on the *Ravager*'s bridge. Thousands of similar cruisers struggled to the air over Lake Washington, creating a sea of slow butterflies with wings now gleaming from the golden sunrise.

The silhouettes of the invading force took shape in the clouds. Their perfect formation resembled a tremendous game board, and he immediately thought back to those simpler pleasures. Jason turned to the captain, whose eyes glanced from side to side with a nervous twitch. And then he knew: There were no orders for the individual ships, no formation, and no strategy for the city's defense.

He couldn't help but consider whether their rockets and bullets would even affect these gleaming crafts. These reptiles were savage beings, world destroyers. A bunch of flying coffins with rusted guns wasn't going to stop them.

The oversized, unit-block-shaped crafts left the clouds, and the battle commenced. Jason shuddered as a blast ripped through the *Gallant* in front of them. The crews of the two ships had trained together. On board was a certain Angie, whom he had been mustering up the courage to ask out. He would never have the chance.

A dozen other ships met similar fates, and then, just when everything seemed only mostly hopeless, each attacking ship pulled open its iron doors, and a plethora of pill-shaped fighters spilled forth.

The lizards clearly wanted this genocide finished before lunch.

The captain screamed and Jason echoed him for the gunners to begin firing as the horde of spinning crafts buzzed around them. As they all suspected, the machine guns' volleys just richocheted away. The cannons, though, gave them a sliver of hope. Briefly he saw the gleam of an enemy's windshield with all four blasters aimed at his heart, before a cannon blast clipped its side and sent it plummeting.

At least a few lizards wouldn't survive this encounter.

Never before had he felt so completely helpless. This was no strategic battle. Around him their fleet was disintegrating like a swarm of flies swiped with an electric net. The *Ravager*'s captain was sweating profusely on the same realization. The gunners kept firing, but almost everything that fell was wooden. There was no goal of victory, only temporary survival.

Outside, a lizard fighter tore through one of their wings, but no one paid heed. There would be no need to land. They would not return.

And then they saw it.

Gently floating through the medley was a singular black craft. Shaped like a stiletto, with no hints of windows or turrets, the sleek craft ran unopposed through the chaos. In a moment, a lizard fighter was on it, peppering it with a rain of lasers that disappeared completely in its sides. The dark ship continued unhindered.

This was no ship of theirs, but if the lizards wanted it down, it couldn't be too bad. After attempting to obliterate it from every side, the pesky fighter collided straight into the sleek craft and not even the paint was charred. Fragments of burning reptile wreckage fluttered to the ground, but the black ship showed no sign of caring.

In stunned appreciation of a potential new ally, every gun on that side of the *Ravager* went silent. Immediately the captain ordered them to resume firing, just only at the reptiles. As two more kamikaze lizard craft were obliterated, one thing became clear: Whatever this thing was, its needle shaped front was aimed directly at them, and it was closing fast.

Was this any better than being incinerated under the lizard fleet's guns? Jason stood at attention, awaiting the order to fire. The captain didn't give it. There was no use. If the lizards' weapons had no effect, theirs would be even more embarrassing.

The *Ravager's* entire crew gasped when the black vessel came close enough to split their craft in two, then paused inches away. A door slowly materialized from its top and a black-shrouded figure emerged. Roughly human sized, it proceeded to stand on top of the thin nose, then calmly opened a side door on the *Ravager*.

"Whatever it is, don't let that thing in!" the captain barked through the intercom.

Yet it was no use. A moment later, a soft voice said. "It's not a thing. Looks like a woman."

"Well . . . tell her to go away," replied the old man.

Jason somehow knew how unlikely that was.

"She wants to see you," said someone after a lengthy pause.

Before their captain could fathom a response, they heard another voice. "Right this way. I'll show you."

Outside, dozens more of Seattle's cruisers were perishing every minute. Evidently tired from making aerial bonfires, the reptiles were beginning to direct their wrath on the city itself as explosions popped from everywhere. After all, annihilation meant everything had to go.

The door opened and a young girl, perhaps seventeen years old, waltzed in. While Jason stood tight in his red button black uniform, she carried herself in jeans, a loose pink sweater, and a worn pair of cowboy boots. He instinctively removed his cap in the presence of a woman, then dropped it on recognizing that she was the single most beautiful thing he'd ever seen.

Her long brown hair moved like a wave down her back, while her soft brown eyes gave no clues of someone who'd just outshone the entire lizard fleet, but instead disarmed him as the childhood friend he never knew. While Jason mentally avoided looking farther down than her v-neck, she casually pulled out a chair, sat down, and kicked her boots up on a desk.

"Hell of a party you're throwing here," she remarked.

The captain turned his back while Jason shook himself out of staring dog-eyed at her.

"Sit down," she said playfully but with a flash of seriousness in her eyes.

"Look," their chief grump started, "I don't know who you are—"

She shook her head. "I'm not going to ask you again."

The entire crew gasped at this young girl speaking to a man who had once tossed a crew member out the window for smirking. Jason backed away slightly, aware that he was closest to the window and to the captain.

Their captain turned sharply, then held his three-fingered fist in a threat that he wouldn't mind striking a girl.

She didn't hesitate. After one brush of her hand the captain had but a brief second to realize his situation, then he was gone.

Desperate to escape this demoness' wrath, Jason immediately dashed toward the end of the ship, but after just three steps something made him halt. No one else had budged. They weren't frozen, but it was as if she'd stuck an invisible pacifier in each as they now stood with heads admiring the floor, and arms listless by their sides. A few wandered around the bridge like zombies.

She swiveled in her chair to scan the remaining misfits, and Jason began to study the contour of her lips. Then she leaned back and crossed her arms.

Everyone on the *Ravager* was quiet.

"What the hell are all of you doing?" she asked out loud.

Jason glanced out the window, just to ascertain that they were in fact in the middle of a battle for survival. Over half of their fleet had been destroyed. The Space Needle had collapsed and a hole burst from the Columbia Tower. A troll took a direct hit.

"We're defending ourselves from annihilation by the evil Mordriss," said the first officer in a monotone voice while still admiring the floor.

She lifted her hand in a halt sign and he stopped speaking, then she sighed.

"And what do you know of Mordriss?"

A cricket could have given a soliloquy across the ship given the silence. Even Jason admitted that, despite owning a uniform and knowing his place on the ship, he couldn't recall ever having any military training.

"And when did he threaten you?" she added.

Everyone stared at the floor while contemplating. When Jason paused to think of it, this was the first time he'd ever seen a troll. He also couldn't recall ever hearing of drums that large, or the Last Shofar.

She stood and strode across the room while pausing to eye each person. Jason lowered his head like the rest when she reached him. He caught a heavenly scent as she stood but inches away. It was as if plumeria, gardenia, and the most fragrant of roses were blended together, then multiplied by a thousand. For her part, she ignored him.

"And have these flying . . . whatever these things are . . . ever existed in Seattle?" she yelled.

"I'm sorry, ma'am," said the first officer with his hands clasped together half between a prayer and a beg. "But we're all the city's got. Could you please let us continue?"

The girl shook her head, then plopped herself back in the seat and leaned back.

Jason again glanced outside to witness his beloved city crumble underneath the lizards' assault. The Columbia Tower was now leaning over, while Rainier Tower had been completely destroyed. Soon there would be nothing left.

She laughed quietly. "You know . . . you're right." She tucked her hair back. "These lizard things are obviously a problem, so let's take care of them."

She grinned, then turned toward the bow and waved both of her arms to create a sudden wind that blew effortlessly through the *Ravager's* walls. Just outside, a lone reptilian fighter burst into a white oblivion. Within moments, those beyond it suffered the same fate.

Like a great wall sweeping across the land, the gusts flew across the battlefield, obliterating every lizard craft they met, while sparing every cruiser, troll, and building. Even the fires were extinguished and the handful of enemy wreckage was removed.

Above them, the now startled mother ships turned to flee. With another wave of her arms, every one disappeared in blinding flashes, and what little remained fluttered as dust below.

She had their full attention now. "As I should have said, you don't need an armada. You just need *me*."

The crew broke out of their trance to shout in unison while a roar of cheers broke across the city. Had they just won? Jason couldn't believe this. Whoever this girl was, she had just saved them all. The first officer moved to hug her, but she backed away.

"How did you do that!" the officer shouted, then paused to admire the disintegrated lizard armada. "You've just annihilated the most feared fleet in the universe!"

"Don't thank me yet," she remarked with a glare in her eyes. "Play time's over. You all need to go home."

What did that mean? A cold howling wind took his breath and Jason suddenly was staring up at the clouds, which were growing more distant. Surrounding him in midair were now thousands of bodies. He turned frantically to see the Seattle armada disappearing into dust and the metropolis rapidly approaching. Jason flung his arms and legs while straining to scream, but there were no options. He closed his eyes while the ground rapidly approached. Everything would be over soon.

2

JASON'S BODY HURTLED into the ground and instantly he was flailing and thrashing until his feet and arms became so entwined in something that he could barely breathe. Yet he should have been scattered remains rather than hopelessly wrapped up.

He awoke to find two sheets completely constricting his legs, to the point that he tumbled from bed untangling himself. His arms were sandwiched between three pillows, which themselves were wrapped in quilts. After finally freeing himself, he stood and laughed. Everything had seemed so real. Jason paused to smell his forearm, and swore that it smelled a bit like plumeria and gardenia. Yet it was nothing more than a dream.

He canvassed his room, the floor covered in comforters, quilts, pillows, and layers of blankets. No wonder he'd felt that he couldn't move. He couldn't recall ever owning this many.

"Mom?" he yelled hearing footsteps outside. "Did you buy more blankets?"

She sprung open the door and examined the mess while the underwear-clad Jason dove for cover.

"Can't you knock!" he screamed.

"Yes," she replied in a monotone voice. "I thought you were a little cold last night, so I brought you these."

He shook his head. "You bring one blanket, Ma. One blanket! What the hell?" He looked at the pile of layers. "I nearly suffocated. Had some crazy dream."

"Don't be so dramatic. There was a good sale," she replied, then left.

At times Jason seriously wondered whether his parents were embedded aliens from the Planet Zorg, where an advanced civilization thrived whose members lacked a single bit of empathy or common sense. Their standard response to everything, whether it was spilled milk or a severed artery, was "That's very nice." Now there was this tidal wave of bedding.

After struggling to shove enough comforters away so he could open his bottom drawer, Jason dressed and made his way to the kitchen. His father was there, a frail man with a thin layer of black hair that had been permanently bonded together with nearly as much hair gel. He wore his standard buttoned up white shirt complete with pen holder and gray slacks. His attention was absorbed by something on his tablet.

"Hey, Dad," Jason called, who knew it was useless to wait for a response.

He poured some cereal while his mother screamed that he hadn't folded the mountain of blankets that filled his room.

"So, what's the news?" Jason asked. It was just small talk. He really didn't care.

"There's a new pancake house in Renton," his father said without looking up. "They found that dog that's been missing for the last two weeks in the Cascades."

Jason had no idea what any of these had to do with the other, or why he should care. His father spent endless hours watching videos on that tablet, and very rarely made any sense. "Good news about the dog," he said while his mother called for him. He downed the rest of his cereal and grabbed his bag. It was still a few minutes before the bus, but he desired anything outside of dealing with that mess.

"Oh," his father said again without glancing from the tablet. "I almost forgot. Ninety-seven thousand people died last night from lightning."

Jason nearly regurgitated his cereal. "What? Where?"

"Here," answered his father without a thread of emotion. "Seattle. Bellevue. Tacoma. All over. Biggest lightning storm in years. Lots of people unhappy. Be careful when you go outside. They're still cleaning up bodies."

After wracking his head and wiping his face, Jason looked for proof from his father's tablet, but he'd already moved on to a kitten video. His father had long been incapable of joking. Was this his first feeble attempt?

"Ninety-seven thousand," Jason questioned out loud in a calm voice.

"More or less," said his father, then smiled at a cat falling off a shelf.

Jason started to pace. "This is a major distaster, then." He thought back to the battle, then shuddered. "Should we go out to help them? And I take it there's no school."

"And why would they cancel school?" asked his mother incredulously.

Before he could even consider an answer, there was a honk from the street where a familiar yellow bus stood. Instinctively, he bolted through the door and made it just as it was starting to head away.

Was his father serious? After all, how could lightning kill so many people? His parents rarely made sense, but this was a new low for them.

Inside the bus, a few students moaned while others cheered as Jason found his seat.

"That's three now!" shouted one of them. "Told you Jason

wouldn't be hit. I've never seen him outside. With Angie fried that makes it thirty bucks! Forty if Arnold's dead."

Jason suddenly felt sick. How could they be so light about this? Thousands seemed dead, and they were taking bets? Why was there even school? Why was no one crying? And why had that destruction he dreamed about felt so real, and then mysteriously a similar number of people actually died?

Further shouts accompanied Arnold's vacant house. There, a body lay sprawled on the street. It was an old lady, together with her equally dead dog. The bus had slowed to divert around them. Two other corpses lay across a distant lawn, next to which was a dump truck halfway filled. How could they be treating it this way? Such a disaster was a full emergency complete with lengthy mourning, yet to everyone else it was just an annoying clean up.

His eyes paused on a very alive homeless man as the bus sped up. He walked with a limp and waved a three-fingered salute as they passed. His scowl was uncanny, and Jason shrunk down his seat until the bus jumped from hitting some obstacle in the street. He grew sick. There were no speed bumps here.

The rest of the bus ride was a blur. By the time he reached his classroom, Jason was ready for the day to be over. Perhaps there were some interesting schools out there, but this wasn't one of them. Here, the teachers were more adept at torture than at any form of teaching.

"Pay attention in class, Bezna!" a deep voice barked from the front, and Jason knew that it could only be his sadistic history teacher, Mr. Flemence.

If ruining lives required a degree, Flemence would have a PhD. They'd covered in nauseating detail for the last month the Mongol conquest of the world, and more than ever Jason wished to be back in that time. The Mongols at least would have killed him quickly.

Half of each class was spent reviewing mistakes on the previous days' homework, with the victim often made to stand while his work was publicly ridiculed. The other half was spent reading verbatim from the textbook, with every third word specially enunciated, as if that made any difference.

Jason Bezna lifted his head, but withheld a groan. While his homework was often a prime choice for Flemence's ridicule, he desperately hoped he'd receive a reprieve today. That aspiration was short lived.

"So, Sleeping Beauty, let's see what you did."

This was an invitation for him to retrieve his homework from his bag, then walk to the front and hand it over.

A greasy hand ripped it from his fingers, and Jason retreated back to his seat. He canvassed the room and saw five empty seats. There had been no mention of their names, and during morning attendance the missing had been calmly marked "probably dead" instead of tardy.

Yet just when his hastily finished work was plastered on the projector, a fleeting vision of brown wavy hair and unforgettable piercing eyes grabbed him. The seat diagonal from him was normally occupied by the designated class bully, who often tripped him on his many walks to the front. This stunning sight was most definitely not him. He stole a glance. She caught it and smiled. This wasn't just any girl. This was *the* girl.

She looked exactly like the one from his dream. She had that slight hook to her smile, and the same perfect gleam in her hair, this time in a ponytail. She wore a white sweater, the same jeans, but sneakers instead of the boots. He looked again, and when his eyes met his reflection in her brown irises, he quickly faced forward.

"What was the birth name," boomed Flemence, "of the first Great Khan?"

Jason had clearly written, "Genghis Khan," but his teacher scanned the classroom for volunteers.

"That's wrong," replied the class brown-noser with a smug look toward Jason. "It was some chick. Her name was—"

"No it wasn't," answered another clear voice near him. It was the girl. "Does it really matter if he can't remember Temujin?" she continued.

Jason inched his desk away from hers.

"And why have you been studying him for the last month? Does it really matter that much? Or are you so stupid that you forgot the rest of the curriculum?"

She said the last words with a wide smile, and Jason cringed in anticipation of the nuclear explosion.

"You're absolutely correct!" was Flemence's stunning response. There wasn't a hint of anger in his voice. "I did forget it."

"Let's be honest," she continued. "All his answers are more or less right. You're just pissed that you haven't dated in fifteen years, your cats abandoned you due to the smell, and the biggest love of your life is your left hand."

The entire class broke into raucous laughter, and Jason winced in anticipation of this huge man bulldozing through the aisle, desks flying in every direction, then smacking that smile from her with their fifteen-hundred-page history book.

"You're absolutely correct!" he instead replied gleefully. "Every bit of that is true. Now let me tell you some funny stories about our principal."

Jason leaned forward, unsure whether he was more stunned about his placid response, or that Flemence might actually say something interesting. Instead, he was staring into those all-knowing brown eyes. She moved her desk right in front of his. The screeching of her chair against the tile floor cracked his ears, but no one else seemed to mind or even notice.

"I'm Raynee," she said with her hand outstretched. She had a perky smile.

Jason looked from side to side, worried what others would think and expecting Flemence's full wrath.

"Don't worry about them," she said. "I could shove pliers up their noses and they wouldn't care."

"Who are you?" he whispered.

"Like I said. I'm Raynee," she answered loudly, her hand still outstretched. He took it. Her skin was the softest he had ever felt.

"I'm Ja—" he started, but she shushed him.

"That's a pretty stupid name you've got there. Let's think of something better. Hmm." She tapped out loud while Flemence continued talking and the class ignored them. "I've got it!" she shrieked over Flemence's lesson. "I'll call you Turnip."

He shook his head. "Um, not really."

"Sorry. Decision's been made. You're Turnip now."

"Were you? My dream?"

"Ninety-seven thousand are dead and you still think that was a dream?" she answered and poked his nose with her finger. "I thought you were a smarter turnip."

He paused to consider that. How had he been lulled into the same state of ignorance as everyone else?

"So, that actually happened?"

"You tell me," she said, looking up at the ceiling tiles. "You were there, Turnip."

"Why am I a turnip, and how are you doing this?" He was beginning to get used to the fact that no one was paying them any attention.

"Well, am I a girl?"

He blushed more than slightly. She wasn't just a girl. She was the absolute perfection of one. "Um, yeah."

"Then you're a turnip," she said in a pointed voice. "And as for your fellow vegetables here . . . . As I said. That's not for turnips to know."

It occurred to him just then that he had to know more about this girl. It wasn't simply because she was the only link between his dream and sanity. There was something more real about her than anything he'd ever noticed. Sure, none of this was likely happening and he was bound to wake at any time, but right then he desired nothing other than to be near her.

"Funny," she said while he gazed at her. Her eyes were squinting and she seemed to be concentrating on something. "I can't read you, Turnip."

"Can you please just call me Jason."

"Nope. You're not a Jason. You're a Turnip."

"Am I dreaming? Why are you here?"

She laughed and he nearly fainted when she hooked her lip in a smile again. "I think you're the only one *not* dreaming. And I'm here for answers. Ninety-seven thousand turnips are gone. These other brain-dead vegetables don't care. Would *you* like some answers?"

Jason so desperately wanted answers that he had yet to consider the questions.

"Listen," she said after looking around for the first time. "You're not so bad. How about we discuss this over a date?"

"A date?" His respiratory system was shutting down while his heart jumped on a treadmill.

"Yeah, a date. Since you're a boy and I'm a girl and you obviously like me. I believe it's custom for you to ask me to accompany you somewhere, so I can refuse."

"Why would I ask if you're going to refuse?"

She snickered, then leaned forward so much that he inched back. "Well, you don't know that. Do you?"

Jason puffed up his shoulders while she withheld a laugh. "So, would you like to go out with me sometime?"

"That's more like it. All right. It's a date."

She stood to leave and he immediately jumped. "But wait. I haven't said where—"

"Go somewhere at seven o'clock," she replied and then shoved another student's desk out of her way. "I'll be there."

3

NO SOONER HAD Raynee slid her desk back, did Jason cast a dreamy glance forward and met the outstretched middle finger of its original inhabitant. He shook his head. Was he going crazy? Up front, Flemence had chosen some other unfortunate soul for homework display. The story was over.

In the hallway, someone shoved him against his locker and Jason was a little bit thankful. Perhaps that was the jolt he needed to wake from this stupor. He spent the rest of the day searching for her through every class, but the only thing he found was normality. There were only the usual uninteresting lessons.

There was a peculiar physics lesson that day. It covered the four elemental forces: gravity, electromagnetic, strong nuclear, and weak nuclear. The material went quickly over his head, and he couldn't recall that ever being on the lesson plan. But he hadn't read the syllabus since the first day of class. And also, there was no Raynee.

When he returned home, his father was in the same spot he had left him, staring at his tablet. Supposedly he worked as a computer programmer, though Jason had never witnessed him use a keyboard.

"Good evening, son." This was the same thing he uttered every day. "How was your day?"

"It sucked—" he started. "Actually, it wasn't that bad. I met a girl. We're going out in a few hours."

He had no idea why he was telling his father this. Jason wasn't even sure if it was true.

"Well, that's very nice." His father didn't even look up.

"Don't get her pregnant!" his mother yelled from the other room.

"What the hell, Ma!" he shouted back, but she didn't respond. He found her in his room. Circling his bed were five piles of bedding, each nearly as tall as he. Every single one was neatly folded. She had just finished the last pile. Jason shook his head and walked out.

"Is Mom going crazy or something?" he asked his father. "I feel like I'm living in a yurt with all her damned blankets."

"That's very nice," answered his father.

Jason groaned and plopped himself in front of the television. He glanced at his backpack, with a full night of homework, then kicked up his feet and clicked the remote. Anything to get his mind away from the recent events was welcome. To his disappointment, the news appeared.

"Millions are dead in New York City after category six hurricane Sa'ira devastated the city and the surrounding region."

He flipped the channel forward, since he didn't care for far-fetched disaster movies. Immediately another calamity appeared. This one seemed to be Moscow, with that funky-looking church and backward letters. People were running and screaming while fires emerged from everywhere. Was some lame movie appearing on the news channels?

"Ma! What's with the news?" he shouted.

"World disaster," his mother said calmly. "Hurricane in New York. Buildings toppled like dominoes. Some deadly disease in Alaska from mosquitoes. One hundred-thirty degrees in Australia, and Beijing is negative forty."

Jason shook his head. "But isn't it winter in Australia and summer in Beijing?"

"I don't know," his mother said from the other room. "All this science stuff is too complicated, so I just stopped paying attention."

"It's all very nice," added his father.

He flipped the channel back to New York City, but now there was a blurb about some new waffle house. They spent several minutes extolling the waffles, then moved on to the weather. When they started a section on "This date in Mongol history," he turned it off.

Hurriedly he turned to his computer and confirmed everything his mother had said. There were more disasters. Unbelievable things were happening all over the world. Millions were dying in calamities far worse than a lightning storm, but without much fuss. In fact, the largest headline had something to do with physics.

Jason shut his laptop then squeezed his head with both arms. The entire world was collapsing, and all anyone cared about were waffles and physics.

His parents were no help now. They were as brain dead as the rest, but there was Raynee. It seemed no coincidence that everything started when she arrived. What exactly was she anyway, and why did he cease caring the instant he recalled those fiery eyes?

There was no escaping this. His only hope for sanity was to meet her. Jason's entire conception of world order now depended on a date. Yet what would she do to him if he chose the location poorly? If what happened in the air wasn't a dream, then she was just toying with him. She could do very bad things.

His mother entered the living room. "Um, Mom," he said with trepidation. "Where's a good place for a date?"

She shook her head. "I can't tell you that. It would be cheating."

Jason didn't know what to make of that. Yet after some thought, he decided that this merited a conservative approach. They would meet for dinner. An attractive Italian restaurant was only a bicycle ride away. Though old enough to drive, he owned neither license nor car. The answer to both questions, of course, had been "That would be nice." Since she was meeting him there, a bicycle would have to do.

He arrived with five minutes to spare, and half expected to find a table and wait for her to magically appear at seven on the dot. To his surprise, she was already seated by the window. She wore a simple black dress, with her back nearly bare and her front mostly clad up to her neck. How did she know he would choose this restaurant?

A waiter in a tuxedo caught him at the entrance. Jason canvassed the dimly lit room, decorated with Tuscan sunsets and bottles of Brunello. A single rose and short candle adorned each table. Jason wore jeans and a black hoodie. He smiled, but the waiter didn't.

After an anxious few seconds, the waiter fixed his tie then pointed toward Raynee. Her attention was engrossed in the menu, and she didn't notice him approach until he sat across from her.

He started to ask how she was accomplishing all this, but she shushed him while still admiring the menu. "You seem in a rather good mood considering your world is falling apart," she said.

Jason just stood there with his mouth open so wide an owl could fly in. How could he respond to that?

"Listen." She didn't look up. "We need to start with a few ground rules." She folded her hands together and put them on the table, then leaned forward. "First, don't get attached. There's no happy ending here. Someday, likely quite soon, I'll be gone and you'll never see me again. I'm here for information, and you're here to provide it. Accept that."

He nodded, but when he started to ask what information she needed, she cut him off again.

"Second. I'm sure you have tons of questions. However, you're a turnip. You won't understand the answers, so I'm not going to bother. You want to know where I'm from, and as far as you should know I'm from somewhere not as far away as you'd think.

"Third. No touching unless I say so. I'm made from a different kind of stuff than you. If I don't expect it, your touchy-feely will be the last thing you do. I'm being serious. You try to grab me and chances are you'll die."

21

"Are you a witch?" he blurted out.

Her head moved backward. "A witch? Fuck no. That's kind of an insult, actually. There's no such thing as magic. That's just what people call science they don't understand."

"And what you did in the classroom?"

"Bits and electrons, Turnip.

"But these were people," Jason muttered. "Flemence?"

"What? You think your brains are special? They're just neurons and synapses. It's easy to mess with them."

She leaned forward and brushed her fingers against the side of his head. A strange static seemed to caress him as she did.

"But don't worry. I'll leave your head alone, Turnip."

"Could you please call me Jason?" he nearly shouted until stares reached him from the other candlelit tables.

She laughed. "Let's see, Jason Bourne, Jason Statham, Jason and the Argonauts . . . Jason Voorhees. Nope, you're not a Jason. Relax."

He remembered back to her initial question concerning the lightning storm. "Was that you? In the air? Did you kill all those people?"

She waited a beat. "No," she replied in a soft tone. "But now you're asking the right questions." She gently grabbed his hand, though he tried to hold it back given her earlier warning. "I just put everything back. Something did kill them, and has caused everything else gone bad in this world, and I need you to . . . help me . . . find out what."

She had to force out the last words. Jason considered leaving right then. How could he possibly help? As far as he remembered, that night he was a lowly yeoman defending Seattle against the lizards.

"But why me?" he asked.

She smiled. "You're concerned that your world is disintegrating?" He nodded.

"You're the only one," she answered. "Everyone else is a happy little turnip, but not you. Don't ask me why, because if I knew then we wouldn't be here."

Jason breathed in. "So, what you're saying is last night really happened, and that all these people didn't die from lightning. They died in the attack."

She moved forward and that intoxicating scent returned. It wasn't just heavenly. It awakened senses he never knew.

"Not bad for a turnip."

"Why doesn't anyone else remember it? And how did you just wave your arms and everything disappeared?"

He wanted to ask if that was her intention with him, but held back. Something told him if she didn't want him around, he would already cease to exist.

"Because you're turnips," she answered plainly. "For the same reason you still had school today, and no one mourned, and they still assigned homework, and there's no concern about how lightning could kill so many. You simply aren't capable of understanding."

"Well that's a bit harsh. If we're just turnips, why are you here? Why do you care?"

For the first time, she hesitated. Then she sighed. "Because *I* have to know. There's . . . there's something evil out there, and I need to know if it was behind this."

Of course there had to be something evil in all of this. Jason thought back to all the movies he had watched. His odds of survival weren't high.

Raynee shook her head as if reading his thoughts. "I wouldn't expect you to understand," she said. "But what you imagine to be bad, to be evil—you have no idea." She looked toward the window at their own reflections. "You have no idea how dark and twisted this thing is, how it feels to face true evil."

"His name is Mordriss, isn't it?" Jason asked, remembering her questions on the airship.

A tear formed by her eye, then she recollected herself. "That's not a name for turnips."

The thought suddenly occurred that upsetting someone who

could disintegrate him so easily wasn't wise, so he moved to change the subject. "What do you need me to do?"

She wiped away the tear. "Do? Just follow along. Don't worry. I'll get what I need from you."

That was the least reassuring thing he'd ever heard. "So, have you interviewed other turnips?"

"No," she replied with a flutter of her hair and a perturbed look. "You're the first turnip I've talked to. They're not very interesting. Pretty stupid actually. But you . . . ." She leaned back and examined him briefly. "There's something different about you. You're not as stupid."

Jason also leaned back, slightly impressed with himself, when a waiter stopped by. He ordered a spaghetti Bolognese, while she asked for only an ice cream.

"Ice cream?" he asked incredulously.

"I can't eat your food," she answered. "If you start boring me, I'll just watch it melt."

"You keep kosher?" he said mockingly.

"No." She smiled. "It's just—"

"I wouldn't understand because I'm a turnip."

"Yeah." She grinned, wide. "You're getting it now."

"I don't think I'm getting anything."

She shook her head. "Just accept that you're a moron, and everything will be fine."

His spaghetti arrived, and he hesitated to dip his fork in it, seeing she really did only have a melting plate of ice cream in front of her. Outside, the sun was setting, casting the entire sky in a fiery red.

"That's a nice sunset out there." She eyed his unmoving hand, still holding the fork. "Okay, noodle boy. If this ice cream melts before you've finished, you won't be happy. We're wasting time now."

Jason devoured the Bolognese so fast that he unexpectedly burped after swallowing a large clump of noodles. Several restaurant patrons shook their heads.

"If I could smell, I'd probably be running for cover." She held her hand toward his mouth. "Now give the waiter some of those money thingies and let's get out of here."

"You can't smell?" he asked.

"Not here. Haven't learned yet. *Garçon!*" She waved her hand at the waiter, who approached with a sigh and handed him the bill.

Jason half expected her to have some trick to handle the check, but she only admired the transaction with bright eyes. With no transportation, he hadn't been able to procure a part-time job, so what little money he had came from mowing a few neighbors' yards. Regretfully, he handed over a fair portion of his life's savings.

"Now, to get started," she exclaimed upon exiting. The sun had finished setting, leaving a quickly darkening cloud line. Jason stood transfixed by her figure cut across the evening light. A single slit provided a hint of her entire leg, while the tight fit of her dress showed every curve. Then he remembered his bicycle. This would be a disaster.

"There's something I want to do. But how to get there?" She glanced at his transportation and shook her head. "The things a girl has to do around here. Fine."

She turned the other way, stuck out her thumb, and instantly a city bus arrived.

While Jason was quite sure there was no stop here, nor could one hail a bus that way, he asked no questions as they boarded. To his surprise, it was nearly full.

He paused as she scooted to the window while her hair glistened from the remnants of the sunset. When her glance caught his admiring her legs along the contour of the seat, he winced in fear of disintegration. She gave him half a smirk, then patted the next seat.

"Sit down. If I wanted to hurt you, I would have."

He sat while evaluating that statement. "Where are we going?"

"To experiment," she answered in a cheerful tone.

He briefly considered jumping off the bus for fear of becoming

25

a lab rat, but after he found himself again studying the intricacies of her face until she blushed, he no longer minded.

The bus left them on a dead-end street at the foot of the mountains. They had climbed far enough that a thin coat of snow covered the grass, and Jason was very cold. Ahead was a steep incline through the evergreens that disappeared into the dark.

Raynee handed him a heavy fur coat and pair of boots; he had no idea where she found them. She remained in her thin black dress and stiletto heels.

"What about you?" He tightened the cozy hood over his head.

"Your temperatures don't affect me," she remarked, then calmly traipsed up the hill, heels and all.

Only minutes after they started up the hill he was already lagging behind her. It was difficult climbing, and he was exhausted.

Multiple times she ran back down to check on him, then encouraged him to speed up. After two hours of unending incline, she finally let him rest by a stump. The stars were now in their full glory, providing a light outline of the twisted forest that surrounded them. Her back was still completely exposed, but the dress didn't even flutter from the roaring winds that made him huddle even deeper into his thick coat.

She produced a flask of water and some crackers, but he was no longer surprised. Raynee checked a watch he hadn't seen before.

"We're making good time. Just another seven or eight miles."

Jason groaned. "How many have we done?"

"Three."

She sat next to him, and instantly a wave of warmth overcame him. Yet just when he felt comfortable, something stirred from the darkness.

Raynee herself paid no heed. Her attention was on her new watch. A twig broke and an unseen bird fluttered away. Then came the unmistakable sound of snow crunching; something was approaching. Raynee now was paying attention and turned on a flashlight to reveal two twinkling eyes only thirty feet from them: A cougar.

Raynee sighed in relief. "For a minute I thought it was something dangerous." She turned her back to it as she took Jason's hand and pulled him to his feet.

"But that's a cougar!" he exclaimed, then frantically looked around in the dark, since Raynee had extinguished the light.

"Relax." She started forward. "It's just here to scare any wandering turnips. You should be more concerned about what's ahead."

That provided little confidence. The cougar kept its distance as they ascended, but it didn't go away. He heard the occasional snap or footstep from the shadows. Twice the moonlight illuminated more than one pair of eyes. It had friends.

Yet after another two hours, their companions lost interest and the forest became far too quiet. The wind stopped completely, but the air grew colder. Jason's muscles now ached with each step, and Raynee had to help him up the steepest parts.

His eyesight had slowly adapted to the starry night. The snow before them was pristine, without even the trace of wildlife. As they ascended the trees grew sinister with their barren branches grasping at them, as if preparing for a strangling. Through the trees' winding limbs, the Milky Way never appeared brighter. More than once he paused to admire it, and wondered what other worlds were out there. Was Raynee from one of them?

The farther they went, the more the limbs began to brush his throat. There was still no wind, but every mouth of these burned-out trees was aimed directly at him. He wasn't welcome in this place. He stopped his quick pauses to admire the stars and trudged on. The trees would not tolerate him long.

Raynee stopped. Though every bit of Jason now ached and sweat poured across his chest, her skin reflected perfection from the myriad galaxies. Her long hair flowed undisturbed, and her stiletto heels had suffered not even a scratch.

"Now, I need to warn you about—" she started, but to Jason's horror the branch above her snapped.

"Look out!" he shouted and shoved her away. They landed in the clean snow beyond, Jason entangled in the branches' long snares. No sooner did he pull himself out than a dozen creatures emerged from the forest.

Jason's terror subsided upon recognizing they were just rabbits. They hopped with such softness that not even a track was visible. He wiped his forehead and was searching for Raynee when they struck.

His body was flung back into the snow from their combined assault, and he cried in pain as their teeth bit into him. As he wallowed in the snow a pair of whiskers grazed his cheek, and he knew it was over.

Then there was nothing. The forest was again silent. The branch had disappeared, as had the rabbits.

Raynee loomed over him. "Very stupid. Brave, but stupid." She lifted him so hard to his feet that he flew several feet into the air.

"You're very lucky I saw you coming," she said. "Otherwise, there wouldn't be anymore of you."

Jason glanced around for more rabbits. Only the indentation in the snow where the branch had fallen remained.

"As I was about to tell you, they're here to get rid of random turnips, just in case one of you wanders too far. Stay close from now on."

As she instructed, he took several steps forward until their eyes locked under the stars.

"Nothing can harm me here," she said softly. "But that was very nice of you." She looked away. "I like you, Turnip. You're a quality vegetable."

Neither the rabbits nor the trees bothered them the rest of the way up. At even the hint of a stir or paw, Raynee held out her hand and the shadows disappeared. After a distance, the forest gave up and they walked in peace as the sky turned to a deep red.

They had walked so long that the sun was teasing an appearance. Jason himself was so exhausted he considered just making a bed in the snow despite whatever Raynee would say. Just when he was about to collapse, the trees ended and Raynee stopped.

"I need you to see this," she said, and he walked forward.

The sky was now a brilliant yellow with the sun in full pro-manance. Jason was so entranced with its beauty that he nearly stepped off the edge.

Raynee pulled him back as his foot dangled in midair thousands of feet high. Yet in that brief moment of terror, Jason noticed something odd. At its very edge, the cliff didn't seem to exist. It was as if he had stepped into a sea of blue air.

Raynee pointed, and far away was the unmistakable gray bustle of human habitation. From nowhere she produced a large telescope, then invited him to look.

Whatever this city was, it was huge. As far as Jason looked there was urban sprawl: shopping malls, office buildings, traffic, and billboards. He couldn't recall any such city anywhere in Washington. He had learned in school, that Seattle was their largest city, but this one appeared much grander.

"Look farther," Raynee said, with a smile.

Then he noticed the smoke. Past the sections where business appeared as usual, vast piles of dust permeated the air. She increased the magnification, and he clearly saw a swath of destruction. What once must have been massive buildings were now an indecipherable jumble of beams and debris. A river ran alongside that pile, and farther out he glimpsed a vast sea.

Jason shook his head, not sure what he was looking at.

"It's New York City."

That couldn't be. From every map he'd seen, New York was nearly three thousand miles away. It was not possible to walk there overnight.

"Not where you expected it to be, is it?" she said.

Jason backed a few feet from the edge, then sat. "So, Beijing . . . Moscow . . . Australia?"

"A day's trip by boat," she said.

"But why?" This made no sense. Why had he grown up expecting these places to be farther apart?

She sat next to him, and he so desperately wanted to hold her.

"Your planet here, your entire universe, is changing, but I'm not sure why. I know this must be warping your little mind, but some of this makes no sense to me, either. Who would do this?"

"Mordriss?" asked Jason, remembering their earlier conversation.

She turned to him with fierce eyes. "That's a name I never want to hear from you again. You have no idea the danger. You need to wipe that from your mind."

Jason nodded. He wanted the friendly Raynee again.

"If he did this, then things are worse than you can ever imagine," she continued. "But from your side, pretty soon you won't care."

Jason frowned at the suggestion.

"You're going to die very soon," she added, then pointed to her watch. "This world's time correlation is changing. It used to be one-to-one but is now much faster."

He just stared at her with empty eyes. He had no idea what she meant.

"Forgot that you're a turnip," she said with a laugh. "As you've probably noticed, your world is collapsing. Everything's heading somewhere. Soon it will all stop."

"And then?" Jason asked sheepishly, though he already knew the answer.

"Then you and everything else here will cease to exist."

4

WELL, THAT SUCKED.

Jason was rather fond of living, and though his parents were robots and his school was oppressive, he preferred them not to be destroyed.

They made their way back home in silence. With her focus always down, Jason couldn't tell whether she was deep in thought or simply not talking to him because he was about to disappear. Whichever, it made him uneasy.

At his driveway, Raynee was still frowning but faked a cheerful tone. "If it makes you feel any better, we can go on another date . . . before you disintegrate."

When Jason unlocked his door and collapsed onto the couch, he saw his father awake and in the usual spot, while his mother sat next to him staring into space.

"You're home late from school," she said.

Jason wanted to scream. Hadn't they noticed his absence?

"I didn't go to school. I was on my date. We walked up the mountains, then saw New York City on the other side. Oh, and our planet's going to blow up soon."

"Well that's very nice," his father said without looking up.

"That's so funny," added his mother. "I just assumed you took her to your room."

"Mom! What's wrong with you?"

She shrugged.

"Do you even care about anything? Does your brain actually function?"

His father had found a kitten video, and his mother was now looking on. Jason groaned, marched to his bedroom, and promptly tossed every blanket but his original into the hallway. He retrieved his bag with homework from the living room, but given the pending end of everything, that no longer seemed a priority. He had a better idea.

Who was this Mordriss? He opened his computer and navigated to a search engine. There was only one way to find out.

He stared at a blank search engine screen.

"Mordriss," he typed.

There were several pages of hits, but every single one was some form of gaming tag. He typed other versions, but there was nothing. He looked around. Could this be dangerous itself? Raynee could reprogram people's heads. Any computer would be easy game if she was paying attention. What if Mordriss himself was listening?

He typed a few more sentences, but again there was nothing. This was hopeless. Whatever Mordriss was, it knew how to cover its tracks. He spent another half hour searching for random things, then called it a night. As he drifted to sleep, he thought about Raynee's comments. That put a damper on his existence.

⁊

"What did I warn you not to do?" called out a male voice, which shook Jason awake.

To his surprise, he was no longer in bed but instead at the end of a wide bathtub. Staring at him from the opposite side of the tub was a cleanly shaven man perhaps in his mid-twenties. His body was muscular, but more like a basketball player than a body-builder.

He was lying comfortably with a towel supporting his head and sported a broad all-knowing smile that made Jason more than a little nervous.

The man's feet bumped into his and he grinned.

Jason huddled up on the other side of the tub. "Who are you?" he screamed.

The man laughed. "This is Raynee," he said.

"Umm, I don't think so." Jason put one arm outside the tub.

He shook his head. "I'm in the form of my brother, Val. I bet you would've loved naked me in here, wouldn't you?"

Jason paused, then considered this statement relatively tame compared to other recent events.

"So what did I *order* you not to do?" Val revealed a long paper. "Search queries. Mordriss. Who is Mordriss. Reptiles Mordriss. Mordred. Mordriss bad guy. Demon Mordriss. Mordriss New York City. Mordriss destruction. Mordriss evil guy. Mordriss can you hear me. Screw you Mordriss."

Jason moved to respond, but Val shushed him.

"There's also Raynee Mordriss, Raynee brunette, Raynee brunette nude, hot brunette nude."

He glared at Jason, who sank lower into the bubbles.

"I feel a little violated by those last ones," said Val, who moved to stand until Jason begged him to stay.

Jason looked around. Come to think of it, this wasn't his bathroom. The floors were polished white marble. Three gold-plated sinks adorned one side, while a water-jet massage table occupied another. His bathtub was easily ten feet across, and beneath an equally-sized arched window that looked onto the Bezna's small backyard.

Val smiled while Jason scanned the room. "That shower of yours was so narrow. No way the two of us were fitting in there. Funny thing is, you didn't even notice it. You just slipped into the tub. Sometimes turnips amaze me. You expect one reaction and get a completely different one."

The bathroom was not the only thing that had changed. A jungle now occupied his backyard, complete with impossibly tall trees and a dozen types of foliage. Two eyes peered in at him from what looked like a large, climbing mutant hamster.

"I rescued it from Australia. It's a tree kangaroo. I named it Boongarry."

Given the events of the last two days, having a jungle in his backyard wasn't so bad. Jason thought back to Mordriss. The computer searches had obviously been a bad idea, but he had a much better source now.

"So, who is he? Mordriss?"

"Someone you don't want to mess with." Val threw a pile of bubbles at him. "What's wrong with you?"

"I just learned that my entire planet is disappearing, including me. Aren't I entitled to at least some information?"

"No."

"So does Mordriss come from where you're from?"

Val sighed. "Yes."

"And where is that?"

Val stood for the soap to drizzle down his chiseled body, and Jason looked away. "Look, Turnip, I'm being nice to you. This is for your own good. Stop searching for things beyond you. If I catch you again, I'll-I'll . . . ."

It occurred to Jason just then that the last thing Raynee would ever do was hurt him, at least physically.

"I'll take Boongarry!" he shouted, then was gone.

Jason returned to his room, which now shared the only door with his new master bathroom. He opened it twice more, just to make sure it was still there, then went outside to check out his jungle.

Several shapes looked at him as Jason attempted to make his way through the thick foliage, then decided against it. Each tree kangaroo was at least fifty feet up except Boongarry, who looked on with lazy eyes from near his level. Jason fumbled through the bushes to reach him.

As he approached, Boongarry slowly slid down the tree. His head leaned forward, and he didn't flinch when Jason reached him. Above, two tree kangaroos were munching on green, golfball-sized fruits. Several had fallen on the ground, and Jason picked one up and placed it before Boongarry's nose. The tree kangaroo slowly moved its head toward the fruit, opened its mouth, then fell from the tree.

Jason immediately rushed forward and caught the animal. Its paws barely held onto him, while its nose nudged his cheek. Boongarry was not doing well, and Jason had no idea what to do.

He considered just putting the animal down. After all, the world was ending. Both he and Boongarry were doomed, so why do anything?

Boongarry's paw rested on his hip, while his nose snuggled against Jason's neck and his breath moved in and out across his ear. Jason carried him back into his room. If his last actions were improving the short life of this creature, then so be it.

He half expected Raynee to be there to help, but when she failed to appear, he searched for veterinarians, then called the nearest one.

"A tree kangaroo?" was the receptionist's reply. "I'm sorry, but dogs and cats only."

Jason shook his head and looked for the next number. Before he could dial it, his phone rang.

"Raynee?" he replied.

"Umm, no," a man said. "I do apologize, but I believe you just called my office about a tree kangaroo. Our receptionist accidentally told you the wrong thing. We *only* work with tree kangaroos."

So, Raynee was still paying attention, Jason thought.

Boongarry looked up at Jason with dreamy eyes, then fell asleep. Jason carried him to the living room. For once, his father wasn't watching his tablet. His parents both stood with their eyes transfixed on nothing in particular.

"I'm going to take this tree kangaroo to the vet. The world's supposed to end soon, but if not then I'll be back for dinner."

"That's very nice," his father said.

Before he stepped out the door, Jason couldn't resist asking "By the way, what are you doing?"

We're waiting," replied his mother.

"For what."

"We don't know," his father answered. "If we're patient, we'll find out."

They did this every once in a while. From his experience, they would remain seated for most of the day. As a child he'd thrown toy cars at them, without a single word.

Jason carefully cradled the animal into his arms, then set out for the bus stop. He was not surprised when the bus driver paid no heed to the three-foot animal that was growing heavy in Jason's arms, and let him aboard. Other than a young girl who asked to pet Boongarry, no one else paid attention through the thirty-minute ride.

"EMERGENCY TREE KANGAROO CLINIC" read the sign in bright red letters. Two clinicians waited outside, their eyes fixated on the poor animal barely clinging to Jason. A small gurney had already been rolled out.

Three clinicians and two veterinarians surrounded the helpless tree kangaroo while Jason looked on. They had an IV running in seconds and were quickly measuring every vital. Photos of tree kangaroos adorned the entire office, but there was a dog calendar in the corner Raynee must have missed.

"Hey, there," a female voice called out while they rushed Boongarry into a room. It was Raynee. She wore jeans and a blue sweater and, with so much he wanted and needed to say, Jason just stood there.

"Hey."

"I can't do biologics," Raynee said, her head toward the floor. "That's why I couldn't fix him. I can warp simple minds, but I can't change bodies."

Jason was both relieved and worried about her comment. On the one hand, that meant she wouldn't be turning him into a lizard or newt anytime soon. On the other, even she had her limits.

"But I have good news," she offered with a forced smile and half a tear.

He could really use some positive news. It wasn't just Boongarry. Jason had grown fond of living and rather liked Planet Earth, even if it was a bit smaller than he'd thought.

Raynee took Jason's hand and held it close. A strange buzzing sensation overcame him that spread throughout his body, until his eyes shut and the ringing hurt his ears.

"And I have some news myself," added a white-clad woman who had just entered. She seemed to be one of the vets.

"That's wonderful!" Raynee shrieked and dropped his hand.

He wrung his head, having heard nothing.

"He's going to be okay," the vet said. "It's good you didn't wait longer, though. I think the toxoplasmosis could partially be from the journey. It must have scared poor Boongarry to be transplanted so suddenly from his home."

Raynee jumped up and down in glee. She turned to Jason and hugged him, then hugged the vet.

"We'll need to keep him overnight. But don't worry. I'll have staff seeing to his needs every minute."

"That's amazing," Raynee said, and she again grabbed Jason's hand. The sensation returned, but this time didn't block his ears, as if he were growing used to it.

"You need some of those money things, right?" Raynee said. She produced a suitcase out of nothing. "Here's two million dollars. Will that be enough?"

The vet's eyes opened wide, then she calmly took the suitcase.

"Yes, that should do," she answered with a quick breath. "Would you like to see Boongarry?"

A broad smile appeared on the animal's face when they entered, and Raynee rushed to his side so he wouldn't exert himself. Jason followed and petted his head while Raynee double checked the vast array of medical equipment that provided vitals. Jason doubted even the President would have as much equipment.

They bid Boongarry goodbye, then headed down a small alley to a main street. Although Jason wasn't sure how much time he'd be in existence, at least for now he was with Raynee. She moved close and the plumeria scent overcame him.

"About that good news," she said as his thoughts raced in every direction. "Your planet may not end so soon."

Jason perked up. The day was getting better.

"Remember how I told you about time correlation?"

He did recall this, but still had no idea what she meant.

"Back then it was around one to a thousand, but now it's like one to twenty. I have no idea why. Never seen it before."

"So . . .?"

"So, I have no idea. On the positive side, you'll find the news much happier now. The lightning storms and hurricanes seem to have stopped, and Beijing and Australia have returned to their normal temperatures."

"And all of the people?" asked Jason incredulously.

They were only steps from the main street.

"They're still dead or picking up the pieces. But hey, it's getting better."

The good feeling didn't last long. Just as his mouth opened, a fist knocked him to the ground, then an impossibly strong arm held him against the pavement. A knife grazed his ear.

"Everything! I want it! Now!" the assailant yelled. "Hello, beautiful," he added in a mocking voice, presumably at Raynee.

The man's grip softened and the next instant he was helping

Jason to his feet. He was rough-shaven, had a poorly healed cut by his cheek, and reeked of booze and garbage.

"I'm so sorry, sir." The man dropped his knife in stunned disbelief he was holding it. "We're putting on a theater production and I do so hope you'll come see us."

Jason shook his head, then saw that Raynee was smiling. Unfortunately she didn't notice the other one, with hunting knife drawn, approaching from behind. Jason had no chance to warn her before he struck.

"Aaaaah!" the attacker screamed at the top of his lungs while Raynee turned toward him in confusion. She was perfectly fine. The knife was gone, as was the entire hand.

Blood spewed out of his limb and Jason could see his bone peeking out among the red flesh. The man looked at the wound and screamed so loud faces popped up from every window and corner.

"What the hell happened?" Jason asked.

Raynee was lost for words. "I warned you not to touch me . . . " she said at last.

"Then fix him!" Jason demanded, but Raynee shook her head. "I can't. I couldn't even help Boongarry. How do you expect me to fix that?"

The attacker was running in circles while the blood poured out of him. His friend took a stunned look at Raynee, then took off.

"Do you mean if I touched you that would've happened to me?"

"Well, I warned you didn't I? If I see it coming, I can prevent it."

Aware now that neither was going to do anything at all, the man continued to scream, then ran into the street until the front wheels of the next bus plowed into him.

The driver and every passenger jumped off while he writhed in pain, then gave out one last gasp. Raynee pulled Jason away from the oncoming crowd.

"This is bad," she said.

"Yeah, but you can fix it. Just mess with their heads like you did before."

"I can't do that with this many turnips. I'm just learning." She sat down and began to cry. "I finally thought everything was going to be fine, and you're an interesting vegetable."

Jason sat and moved to embrace her, then considered otherwise. "Yeah, but the planet's still fine," he said in an unsteady voice. "Just he's not."

She shook her head. "No. This is very bad. I can't hide this. They're going to know."

"Who's going to know?"

She looked up and turned his face toward hers. "It doesn't matter. I tell you to keep quiet and then I screw things up. There's nothing I can do. They're going to destroy everything."

5

JASON PEERED AT the man's remains amid the nearly hundred people crowded around. Someone was attempting to wrap a tourniquet on the arm, while another was trying CPR, but Jason knew it was no use. The ground everywhere was coated in red, and more than a few onlookers were eyeing them suspiciously.

He winced when Raynee grabbed his arm. One mistake on her part and he would end up the same, but she only pulled him away. "I'm going to try to fix this," she kept saying.

"So, first our world was going to be destroyed, then you said we're getting better, and now because of this we're doomed?" For some reason, he could spare no pity for the dead man who lay near them. The end of everything else, however, was a different matter.

"Because there's an order to the turnip patch," she said. "It's beyond turnips, but to put it simply, there are things that can happen and things that can't. This is most definitely something that can't."

"You mean peoples' hands usually don't just disappear."

"Right. And that causes ripples. You turnips don't see them, but others do. They'll notice."

"Who will notice?"

"It's beyond turnips."

Jason groaned.

"But bad people."

"Unless you fix it." Jason smiled. He moved to nudge her, then stayed back.

"Yeah," she replied with her head down. "I just need to think for a bit."

She shoved him on the bus along with the driver, and sent him home. None of this made any sense. Jason was sick of being a turnip.

"The grass is a bit high. Could you mow it?" his mother asked the instant he entered.

"That's not grass, Mom," he said. "It's a jungle. You did also notice the huge new bathroom, right?"

"Yes," his father said. "It's very nice."

Jason shook his head, then retired to his bedroom. He spent some time staring out the window at the ninety-foot-tall giants that now inhabited his yard, complete with tree kangaroos, then returned to the living room to watch television.

The news was already covering the man's death. Sketches of Jason and Raynee were next to the words "Persons of Interest." Jason gulped. They were close enough that someone would recognize him soon. Even though he truthfully had no idea what happened, he doubted the police would see it that way. Before his parents noticed, he turned off the television and spent the evening figuring out his water-jet massage bed in the new bathroom. If the world ended that night, it would at least be in comfort.

❦

Jason awoke to the coo-coo-coo-ka-ka-ka of some strange animal in his jungle. With no sign of Raynee, he decided to explore his new backyard. His father was already on his tablet when Jason passed him on the way outside.

"I wouldn't go out there," stated his father while continuing to stare at his tablet. "There'll be a lizard invasion in a few minutes."

Jason halted. "Lizards?"

"Yes," his mother said.

"They're coming for you," his father remarked, "and that's not very nice."

"They're coming for me? Why the hell me?"

"No time to explain," his father said, and for the first time looked up from his tablet. "Besides, you'll know soon enough."

Jason shook his head. At least they didn't call him a turnip.

His father walked to him and put his hand on Jason's shoulder. "They're going to be here any moment," he said with the first tear Jason had ever witnessed from him. "But before they arrive, I need to tell you something very important. I know I haven't been the best of fathers. I've never said much of use to you, but what I'm about to say will make up for those faults."

He kneeled and looked Jason straight into the eyes. Jason leaned forward, ready to receive the first piece of fatherly advice in his life.

"You need to have some waffles."

"What?" Jason asked, incredulously.

"That new pancake house in Renton. They have amazing waffles, too."

"You want me to eat waffles."

"Yes."

"The world's going to end, and you're concerned with waffles."

"Yes. They're very good waffles."

There was no time for further questions. A scream came from outside, followed by two loud roars. Jason's parents moved to either side of him, ready to serve as shields against the onslaught.

"Who are you guys?" he asked just when the first lizard burst through the wall.

"We're turnips," his mother answered, her arms drawn back and her stance wide. "Just a little better than average."

The lizard lunged and she grabbed it by the head. Despite the two-foot height difference and her miniscule frame compared to the behemoth, his mother had little trouble prying open the struggling creature's mouth, then pulling apart its jaws until the lifeless reptile slumped to the floor.

"Is this because Raynee distintegrated that guy's arm?" yelled Jason when three more appeared through the windows.

"No," his father replied. "We knew this would happen. It was only a question of when."

All three creatures lunged at once and Jason had no chance to run. Immediately, his father pounded his first straight through one, while his mother tore the arm off another, then lifted the huge body without effort and broke it in half. The third stood back and snarled while it contemplated the fate of its comrades, until his mother jumped on its back and snapped its neck.

Jason yelled in joy as the last thirty seconds seemingly made up for a lifetime of boredom. Though he had no clue how his parents suddenly became so powerful, he wasn't going to complain now.

"They're not so tough," he remarked with a broad smile. "Why didn't you ever tell me this would happen?"

His mother shook her head. "We just learned ourselves, and these are just lizards. Same dimensional, replicated creatures. Worse things are coming."

Before he had time to consider how she knew this, the floor began to shake apart and every window shattered. The ground was trembling while some gigantic engine roared. A house across the street collapsed, then dozens of footsteps echoed from behind it.

"We can't stay here; they'll surround us," his mother said. One sweep of her arm was all she needed to destroy the wall so they could easily exit. Their new enemy appeared only a few meters outside.

Adorned in black armor and nearly twice as tall as the average human, the soldiers sported shining visors with nothing behind them. They had the shape of humans, but a whirr with every movement revealed well-oiled machines. Each carried a five-foot-long rifle.

"Well, this sucks," admitted his father. "I didn't know they'd have lasers."

There were thirty of them now, a horde of hell-bent robots running in unison.

His parents understandably looked worried.

"New plan," his mother stated. "Jason, you make a run for it and we'll hold them off as long as we can."

"They'll kill you!" he protested. He had never been close to his parents, but he certainly couldn't take losing them. They'd always treated him well, even if they weren't active and placed an imbalanced importance on kitten videos and waffles.

The soldiers marched forward, while the three stepped back. Every robot raised its gun.

"The honor has been ours," his mother said, then somersaulted into them.

"Take care," was the last he heard from his father.

Before the soldiers could fire, his parents were on top of them. His father punched one of their heads so furiously it tipped straight back, but these were tough customers. One tumbled to the ground from his mother's blow, but then stood back up.

"Run! Now!" they screamed, and Jason took off.

Of course, he had no idea where to run to. A cascade of blasts landed all around him, and Jason was thankful that these things, despite being huge and powerful, were no better shots than in the movies. The lasers scorched the grass everywhere and kicked up enough dirt to make him choke, but amazingly not a single one hit him.

He considered running into the jungle, but then thought of the tree kangaroos. A blast might hit them. In the absence of any better ideas, he made for a nearby park. On his last trip there he'd been knocked unconscious by a soccer ball, but there weren't any real options.

Jason took off at full speed, and behind him the ground shook. He'd forgotten. At twice his height, these untiring machines could run a lot faster. He'd barely made any distance before a huge hand swatted him off his feet. He looked up. Over a dozen blank visors now loomed over him.

"Howdy," said a most welcome voice. Raynee was lying on the grass next to him. Her arms were sprawled out, but not from agony. Instead, she was staring past the robots to the blue sky and admiring the foliage.

"We have to get out of here!" Jason screamed.

She stood and brushed off some grass while every soldier trained its sights on him.

"You mean these things? Right?" she said and waltzed over to one. Three followed her with their guns, while the rest remained aimed at Jason.

"Raynee! No!" he yelled.

She walked straight through the nearest one's leg, which promptly disappeared in a fuzz in the same manner as the assailant's hand. Now unbalanced, the rest of the robot collapsed on top of her. The instant its armor touched her, it too burst apart. She skipped back to Jason, obliterating another robot in the process. Now every gun was directed at her.

"I think these are sad robots," she exclaimed with fake pouting eyes. "They need someone to play with."

She whistled and Jason swore all of reality turned into a single pane of glass, then a dozen pink spotted leopards came trotting out. With each step, the grass beneath them turned pink. The robots aimed their lasers and the leopards roared. Yet Jason suspected these weren't normal cats.

A barrage of lasers turned to the leopards, but the leopards were too quick. Instantly, they leaped dozens of feet and landed directly on the black armor. But instead of tearing them apart, the leopards snuggled against the gleaming metal, which turned pink, and the machines morphed into gigantic pink trolls, complete with lasers. Both trolls and leopards then moved on to new foes

Jason walked toward one of the leopards, ready to pet it.

"Don't do that!" Raynee warned him. She turned her attention from the fight and threw him back. "They don't have the shields I use. One touch and you're gone."

He nodded. He just hoped there were no little girls around who loved cats.

The last soldier was barely morphed when a cuboid ship popped in from nowhere in the sky. Briefly, it appeared that the world had been crushed to a single dimension, then the ship roared downward. Lightning flew from every side of its gray exterior. A hatch opened and a hundred more robots appeared.

The field exploded with lasers and robots, charging against other robotic trolls. Elsewhere, the huge machines were crumbling to the grass while leopards snuggled to make new trolls. When Raynee's troops finally began to falter from the laser onslaught, she sent another set of growling allies into the fray.

Jason looked back to where his parents had held them off. Their lifeless bodies lay next to each other. Tears fell down his cheeks as he remembered those endless days as a child when he'd danced around his father, who even then was deep into his tablet. His mother had spent a few minutes each day rapidly cleaning, and the rest seated on the couch face forward, her eyes wide open and never blinking. He had danced around her too. In retrospect, he should have noticed they were different.

"I'm sorry about your parents," Raynee said in a soft voice.

"They died protecting me." He thought of taking their bodies home and burying them, then considered a much better idea. "I need your help."

"What would you like? I can help you bury them."

"Not yet. First, I want some vengeance."

She smiled. "As you wish." She curtsied, and the world collapsed again until a house-sized spaceship slid into existence. Its silvery body nearly blinded them with its reflection, and two massive guns adorned each side of the pod-shaped craft. Another cannon projected from the middle, and a gun turret hung from the bottom.

Jason grinned. "You fly and I shoot?"

"Exactly. Only eat this pill first."

She handed him a moldy gray peanut.

"Umm, no thanks." He tried to push her hand away.

"It's a reverse decombulator. You touch that ship and it'll disintegrate you. Take this pill, and everything will be fine for an hour."

"And after that?"

"Then your quarter's up."

He gulped down the pill, then nervously approached the ship. A door appeared and he barely nudged it with his pinky. A dull electric pulse rolled through his body, but left his finger in one piece. Satisfied, he jumped aboard and climbed down the turret hatch.

The leopards and trolls had been overrun, and the instant he and Raynee took off a dozen ships appeared. Lightning burst from the ships' sides while Raynee did a loop and headed straight toward them. The first enemy was in his sights and he didn't leave it unscathed. The turret was simple to aim, and the moment the crosshairs turned red he fired and the entire enemy craft burst into an orb of fire.

Lizards fell from its sides and he locked down the trigger so a stream of blasts picked them off. Jason screamed. This was fun. He unleashed his fury on three more ships, while Raynee used the side cannons to finish off several more.

Yet with each enemy they destroyed, three more took its place. Soon they were soaring over downtown. Below, thousands screamed with each craft that teleported into existence. Their lightning bolts incinerated everything they flew near. Jason winced as one collided into the Space Needle, removing its base and causing the saucer to tumble into the buildings below. Another flew directly through the side of the largest building, releasing a tremendous fireball in the process.

He had destroyed perhaps fifty of them already, but over two hundred now dotted the horizon. Below were the *nee-naws* of ambulances, cars sliding off the road, and entire skyscrapers collapsing. His finger left the trigger. He wiped the sweat from his forehead.

"This isn't working," he said through the com. "We need to do something different."

"Yeah. They're awfully persistent."

He thought back to what his father had said. There was only one proper thing to do. "We need to go for waffles."

"What the hell? Your entire world is being destroyed and you want waffles?"

"Yeah. There's a place in Renton; a pancake house, actually. My father kept telling me to go there. I think it means something."

Raynee groaned, but soon they were hovering above a simple structure with three walls of windows and a sign with the words:

RENTON PANCAKE HOUSE And Now Waffles Too!

To his surprise, the patrons were oblivious both to their ship's presence and the carnage that surrounded them. Jason opened the ship's hatch.

"Care to join me for a waffle?" he asked.

She rolled her eyes. "You know I can't eat your damned food. Listen Turnip. I'm just feeling sorry for you. I can't hold them back forever."

After tossing him a com, she turned her attention back to the ships, every one of which was heading directly toward them. "Go eat your stupid waffles."

Music from the 'fifties played softly at the entrance. From every window was death and destruction, but the clientele here was just calmly chowing down on breakfast. There was a mix between pancakes and waffles, he noted, but his father had been specific on the waffles.

A hostess showed him to a booth where he had a great view of Raynee commanding the battlefield. She was constructing waves of pink armored drones, each with rotating lasers that annihilated rows of enemy ships. Still, with each casualty, more enemies appeared.

The waitress was slow to stop by for his order.

"I'll have the waffles," he said, then looked through the menu again and added a side of eggs with some hash browns. She recommended the fresh orange juice to accompany it, and he agreed. Outside, the restaurant next door was obliterated where a damaged cuboid crashed. He folded his fingers together and tapped on the table in anticipation of his order, while several robots almost grasped the window until Raynee finished them.

"I'm getting really sick of this," Raynee said through the com.

He smiled at her through the window and she frowned back.

She was tiring now, but the waffles finally arrived ten minutes later. They were missing syrup, so he waited another few minutes before it was delivered. He doused his waffle, then cut off a piece and tasted it. There was no revelation. Though he was no expert in waffles, it tasted fairly average. He downed it with a gulp of the orange juice, which felt a bit tingly but otherwise was unspectacular.

Why had his father ordered him here? Perhaps he was simply crazy? Maybe he was just a waffle nut? His breakfast was nearly done and Raynee was now sweating profusely. Seeing him with his fork dripping with syrup, she blasted the nearest robot and stormed inside. Jason gobbled up the last of his food before she reached his table. Several feet away, though, she stopped. She stared behind him.

"You dumb shit!" she yelled, then stepped forward and forced his head to look back. The entire back wall was covered in a mural of a park in downtown Seattle. The Seattle Center fountain was directly in the middle. Next to it lay the remains of the Space Needle. Everywhere on the image were people screaming, and the gray cuboid ships covered the horizon. A column of water was erupting from the fountain, whose center had been torn off.

"Seriously, all you had to do was look at that picture," she said and shoved his nearly empty plate to the side. "To hell with the waffles."

Jason calmly turned to look at the scene, then nodded. "I think you're right."

"Of course I am." She pulled him to his feet. "Listen, I'm doing you a favor here. I could just as easily have left them to kill you, but instead I'm here. So, stop screwing around and let's go!"

When they reached the skies again, the enemy had increased tenfold. Downtown Seattle now resembled more of a pixelated hodgepodge of death and destruction. Every building was missing some part, having been disintegrated by the alien crafts, and fire roared from many of the pockets. He winced as another building tumbled into a mushroom of dust.

The fountain was mostly spared, but not much remained of the Space Needle and other structures. A trove of lizards was dismantling the Museum of Pop Culture, and still not one came to tear off the fountain's center. Other than the missing water column, the scene resembled exactly that shown at the pancake house.

"Strange," Jason remarked from the seat next to Raynee. It seemed pointless to destroy any more ships, since three replaced each one that fell.

Raynee nodded glumly, and a slight tear formed in her eye. There was something she wasn't telling him.

She quietly landed the ship and sent it away. No sooner had they stepped on the concrete did every ship aim their way. The ground trembled from the march of thousands of robots and lizards.

Somehow, Jason felt that the answer to everything resided in the mural from the waffle house being complete. Within that column of water was the answer to why Seattle was under unceasing attack, why everyone behaved so oddly, and why he seemed to be in the middle of it. He gulped. It was time to know.

"We need to remove the center," he said.

She gave him a bewildered look, but finally nodded. With one swipe of her arm the fountain center was thrown to the side and the picture was complete. Jason jumped back as the basin around the geyser got deeper. He'd never been crazy about water, and something now made him even more afraid.

Raynee held out her arm and rocketed a blast that took out a dozen of the shining black robots. Twenty more took their place. A flotilla of craft moved in to hover over them. She reached her arms out and a hydra of fireballs poured out to devour ever ship in sight. And in seconds, the sky was a patchwork of new ones.

"I'm sorry," she said, then dropped her arms to her sides. "I can't stop them."

Deep within Jason's stomach, his waffles seemed to come to life and proceeded to tear at every one of his organs. He looked directly at Raynee and attempted to utter something, but was incapable. This was far different from any previous ache. His entire intestines felt like they were tightening, while every piece of food he'd ever eaten now wanted its way out.

"You're a great turnip," said Raynee with sad eyes. "I wish it didn't have to end this way."

Jason took one step forward and stooped over. The water was nipping at his feet, but there was something coming up in its midst. The shape was difficult to decipher, and even after a prolonged stare was nothing more than an amorphous white patch.

"Can you hear me?" she shouted, but he was no longer paying attention.

Something jolted through his body and Jason glanced down in expectation of a direct laser hit, but his body was intact. His insides, though, most definitely weren't. His body went limp, then he collapsed into the rising tide.

The last thing he saw was Raynee's blurred silhouette through the water. Her dark hair flowed like a painting and her light skin looked perfect. Something about the fading vision made her appear even more beautiful.

"Oh, shit," she shouted.

6

NOW, IN RETROSPECT some may think that this was when everything turned to color for me and there was a glittering yellow brick road complete with singing Munchkins. That would've been true, had the road been the I-5 Interstate and every Munchkin was prodding me with cattle irons.

One moment I was watching a menacing robot army devour the only city I'd ever known, the next I was cast into this vortex of confusion. Before Raynee, I'd never been beyond Tacoma, but here I was. Did I even exist? Had I died?

A moment later I was back in the fire and the chaos and a bunch of huge robots with a perplexed Raynee in the middle. I puked right onto one of their visors and that was enough to know that I was still alive, at least until I felt like a pancake held between irons. The world went blurry again.

I'm not sure what concerned me more at the time. On the one hand, my eyes were going completely buggy as if the optometrist went crazy with that puffy air thing. On the other, I suddenly couldn't breathe, though not for lack of air. My lungs simply forgot how to do it, and my nose and mouth had also called it quits.

My ears buzzed like a heavy rock concert, jackhammer, and the

1812 Overture all played simultaneously. Yet the weird thing was I could hear a caterpillar munching on a newly sprouted leaf and a feather landing on the floor at the same time. My nose probably couldn't breathe because it was being overwhelmed with every scent unknown to mankind. I smelled something like a banana that was put in the blender, dashed with cinnamon, next day aired to Vanuatu, then slowly roasted over a volcano. Yet my sense of smell was so strong that I felt able to predict which island and side of the volcano.

I felt like a revolving door had closed in on me, then spun off its bearing like a gyroscope on a tabletop. Every bit of my stomach was ready to reappear as I was slammed from side to side. Then I was falling.

I was above some field. At least I think it was. My eyes still couldn't focus, so I barely made out some distant grass and lots of clumps in the dirt. Of greater concern, though, was that my body was hurtling toward it.

The ground was approaching so quickly that I barely had time to close my eyes. Only nothing happened. There was no thud, nor even a whiff of fresh dirt. I opened my eyes to see the thick earth moving by. I was now deep underground, but somehow, I was passing straight through it. I wanted to scream but was worried that my mouth would be stuffed with fresh dirt, though my skin felt nothing but coldness.

A force pulled me in one direction, and then I heard her voice. It was Raynee, screaming for me. I tried to will myself over to her, but I had no idea either how to move or where she was. I didn't even know where I was, but her voice was louder, so she was closer. At last I felt her soft grip on my arms. Her touch felt strange, so smooth and gentle that I swore I'd never felt anyone before. Yet this wasn't the calm and controlling Raynee I knew. She was panicking.

"I'm so so sorry!" she kept yelling, but I was in no position to respond.

Then a light breeze hit my face and I was lying down, with hard dirt underneath me. My vision was still fuzzy, but I sensed some bright white light above. Everything else was black. She was shaking me, but that only made things worse. My body began to convulse. Electric shocks rippled through my toes up to my nostrils.

"Somebody! Help!" she screamed at the top of her lungs.

There was some mucous on my eyes preventing me from seeing her clearly, but her warm hands tried to stop my convulsions without success. She seemed to reach down and take out some device.

"This is an emergency," she stated through quick breaths. "I've no idea what happened, but I have a turnip. He's here. I have no clue how."

She leaned her face inches from mine. Had my arms not been shaking faster than a rock tumbler, I might have held her.

"Hang in there, Turnip. That reverse decombulator must've messed with you somehow. We'll get you somewhere safe."

She lowered her head to listen for my heartbeat. Suddenly my head felt like it had landed in a pile of defibrillators and then I shot up so fast that I nearly knocked her over. Every sandwich, breakfast cereal, and burger that I'd ever eaten wanted out at that very moment. I leaned over and threw up. Though I felt everything spew up my throat, nothing came out.

Four white lights were hovering over us now, accompanied by the steady hum of some vehicle. It was landing near us, with the pitch of a large aircraft. Dust particles hit me for the first time and my tongue lapped them up like it had never tasted anything before.

"What happened?" a gruff voice next to Raynee asked.

"I don't know. I was in the turnip patch, then he fell through."

"That can't be," replied another voice.

A bright light peered into my pupils. Someone else grabbed my hand and placed a device on my wrist. Every part of me started to convulse quicker. Then I was either on a stretcher or levitating. I couldn't really tell with every muscle not cooperating and my eyes only showing me a fuzzy mess.

Then everything was bright and I heard the whirr of engines. Raynee sat next to me. I could recognize her bright eyes and shape anywhere. I felt the warmth from her hands, but she didn't touch. She smelled like every fragrant flower in the world: rose, gardenia, plumeria, and a bunch of others I'd never heard of, mixed into one. It was intoxicating.

"I gave him a reverse decombulator. We have to get him back! It'll wear off."

They placed some heavy black device on my head. A tube slithered down my throat; I gagged and fought it. It felt like a dozen centipedes were crawling loose in my stomach, though there was nothing left. I'd puked everything else out.

"You gotta see this," said one of them to the other.

My arms were now moving straight up and down with my legs, as if they intended to march off that gurney. They only succeeded in knocking away some equipment.

"He's dying!" Raynee cried.

"It *is* a decombulator," muttered the second technician. "But how?"

"No," Raynee shouted. "I said a reverse decombulator! So, he could touch a higher dimension."

"He's not dying," one of the technicians said.

That brought relief, though my body was no better.

"It' a decombulator. Only I've never seen one like this."

"What are you talking about?" she asked.

"He's one of us. Only he had one heck of a decombulator. Even allowed him to eat and drink. Covered every single system."

Her hand grasped mine. It felt small, but more real than any grasp I ever remembered.

"So, you're screwing with me?" she said to me.

Of course, I couldn't reply. My teeth were chattering in between my mouth opening and closing like a fish. I still have no idea how I didn't split my tongue into two.

"I don't think so," one of them replied. "This is professional stuff. This kid probably had no idea."

The engines whirred down and I felt the craft landing. Again, I was floating somehow. This time I couldn't feel anything underneath me. My limbs were wailing in the air with nothing to harm.

Raynee's sweet scent grew dim. She was leaving. I tried to beg her to stay, but my mouth only uttered gargles with that damn tube down my throat. I tried to move my hands to rip it away, but arms on either side caught me. Still, I was relieved that I managed to move them myself.

The last thing I remember were several needles plunging into my skin. I attempted to gargle the start to a question, but never finished. Everything went dark.

∾

I awoke to a dim room. Tremendous breaths left my lungs like they'd never been exercised before. I could discern objects for the first time, though there wasn't much to see. The walls were bare and the only things of note were the bed I was lying on and a small light from the corner, where someone sat.

There was only a silhouette, and when I tried to pull myself up to get a better look, Raynee raised her hand.

"You're one major asshole," she said.

I didn't pay much attention to the words since her voice sounded so *real*. I paused for too long just listening to the air move in and out of my lungs.

"Nothing to say?" she demanded.

"Where am I?"

She sighed. "I'm the one asking the questions. Where do you think you are?"

"Seattle? Actually, am I still in Bellevue, just at the hospital?"

"Try again."

Everything in my body buzzed the moment I moved. Nothing

felt like this back home. My entire previous life felt like watching a 3D movie without the glasses.

"I'm where you're from."

"That's better. Now where are *you* from?"

"But where is here?"

She groaned. "Stop screwing with me. You never were from stupid little Bellevue, on insignificant Planet Earth, in the Milky Way galaxy of an unspectacular universe. You've always been beyond the third dimension."

"Dimension?"

"Yes. One of trillions. Stop playing stupid."

I was royally confused. "So . . . there are more dimensions?"

She stood and I sensed that I was really pissing her off, though I really had no clue what had happened. "But, I still don't know where I am."

"You really have no clue? You're here."

"That's not helping."

She drew a deep breath. "You're playing with me, but fine. The universe where we met was a simple three-dimensional one. We're way more than that."

"I have more than three dimensions?"

"Yes, you idiot."

"Then why can't I see my own eyeballs?" I tried to sit up again. This was becoming one extremely involved joke.

"You tricked the medics. They're all like 'never in history has this happened,' but I know this was all you. The only reason I'm still here is curiosity. How did you do it?"

I so desperately wanted to reply "Do what?" but I knew that would infuriate her, and she was all I had now, so I stayed silent while she fumed.

My fingers rolled over the blanket that comfortably but firmly pinned me to the bed. Every fabric I'd ever caressed was plastic compared to the simple hospital sheets over me. Every fiber jolted me.

The current of this entire place sent vibrations everywhere. I'd never felt such things before, or had I? There was that buzzing sensation when she held my hand.

"Did Mordriss do this?" I asked.

She shook her head. "Now that's a real bullshit move on your part. You know what he did here. How dare you insert him into your little world."

I was completely lost now. How could I insert whoever he was anywhere? What was she accusing me of? And then I knew. "The waffles," I blurted out. Their syrupy remains were now the only thing remaining in my stomach. Everything else had been hurled. "I think they did something to me."

"Congratulations, genius."

I pulled myself up, but then felt immediately dizzy and collapsed back down.

Raynee stood and waltzed over to me. "You have them fooled, but not me," she whispered, and a sudden force began to constrict my neck. "Now I don't know if you're just a joker, or someone more serious, but I'll find out."

My arms tried to reach for my neck as my throat shut. Raynee only glared at me with knowing eyes. "And if you do have anything to do with Mordriss," she said in a seething voice, "you'll wish I'd never found you."

7

RAYNEE WAS GONE by the time air resumed circulating through my lungs. In her place was an orderly, who calmly injected me with something that knocked me straight out. Before that, Raynee's comments about the medics echoed through my brain. Even they didn't know what happened.

Wherever I was, this was new for all of us.

I awoke in a white room this time, complete with an old woman. She had the wrinkled skin and long grayish hair, but wasn't so old that I couldn't fear that she'd beat the daylights out of me if need be.

"You must have a lot of questions," she said, in the understatement of the year.

I lifted my arm, and after my previous travails with bodily control, thought that was pretty neat. I smiled.

"I'm sure you want to know where you are," she said with a sweet voice.

I nodded. It was about time someone explained this.

"Before I tell you, we need a basic physics lesson."

I tried desperately not to roll my eyes. Physics certainly wasn't one of my stronger subjects. Ever since that professor had booted me from his class when my mother, rest her soul, had left me there, it had stained me with a black mark. The police had spent the entire day figuring out where I lived, until my mother arrived to pick me up and they had a little talk with her.

"There are five fundamental forces," she began.

"Yeah, I know," I said. "Gravity, electromagnetic, strong nuclear, and weak nuclear." Please don't ask me how I remembered that, though I couldn't recall the fifth one.

"Not really. Those are from your old world. Here, they are different. I won't bother you with their names now, but those forces you mention only exist within the three dimensions, or four if you include time, where you previously existed. They don't apply here, or in any other dimension set."

"So, I'm in another dimension set?"

"Yes," she said with a smile.

I felt like a genius, though later I realized she was treating me like a moron. This was baby stuff to them.

"Because objects in a dimension set exist from their basic forces, objects from one cannot interact with another. That's why we have decombulators and reverse decombulators. They're kind of like shields that prevent one set of forces from completely annihilating others."

"So, I had one of those decombobulator things in me this whole time?"

"Decombulator. Yes."

"But now I don't."

"That's correct." She forced a smile, but I knew it was the damned waffles.

"So why was I there?"

"We simply don't know." There was sadness in her eyes, and something told me she wasn't lying.

"Where's Raynee?"

She shook her head. "She seemed most unhappy when I saw her."

That kind of burned me a bit. Here she'd popped up in my

life, ruined my preconceptions of the entire world, sliced off some stranger's hand, invited lizards and giant robots to destroy my world, and then blamed me for it. My life right now, compared to hers, was pretty fucked up. Still, she was hot, so I forgave her.

"So, what about my parents?"

"I assume you've figured out by now that they never were your parents. They weren't even from the same dimension set. If you were on one, and are now in three, then they were in two."

I nodded, though felt a bit sad about it. They weren't bad guardians. They were just incredibly weird. The thought, however, that my real parents were still out there, occurred just then. Maybe they would even pick me up, and for the first time I'd be part of a real family. Yet, based on how serious these people were, I doubted that.

She stood and looked down at me in my hospital bed. "And about your real parents . . . no. We have no idea. You're quite a mystery to us."

I pulled my neck up and scanned the room. It was completely white. There wasn't even a door. Just this bed and white walls, and a chair. The ceiling was white too, but contained no light fixtures. There was no indication how the room was lit, but it was.

"This world looks kind of boring." I laughed a little.

"I'm sure you think that, given what we've showed you so far." She smiled. "We felt that full exposure to this world would be a bit of a shock to you, so we designed this room to bring you along gradually."

"When will I see it?" I asked politely, though underneath felt that all this caution was ridiculous.

"Your lungs have never been used before. Every part of your body has to relearn. There are great medics who will help speed that along, but it'll still be a couple of days. When the time comes, I'll be back here to pick you up. You'll be living with me. My name's Annie."

Annie said her farewell, then left me alone in that empty white place. My stomach gave a terrible thunder, and it occurred that the easiest way to both see more and obtain some grub, was to find a way out of this room.

As practice, I kicked my legs up and down. They worked. I did the same with my hands, and was delighted to see they were fully functioning. My toes wiggled just fine, and my fingers felt ready for a piano concert. This was easy! I tried to sit up, but other than tilting my neck, I was stuck there. This was only a slight setback. Since everything else worked, all I had to do was slide from the bed and push myself up. I grasped both bed rails and threw myself off.

And plastered my nose to the ceiling.

The prospect of getting off the bed and falling up instead of down was new to me. It probably would have hurt too, had they not installed some form of soft shield that stopped me a few millimeters from the plaster. Evidently, they figured I would do that. Now, of course, my primary issue was that I was floating horizontally eight feet in the air.

My natural instinct was to push off the ceiling and try to pivot my body down, so I went with that. This promptly flipped me upside down and threw me against the back wall. My situation had not improved.

"I see you're practicing!" a male voice called from behind me. It frustrated me that I couldn't turn to see him.

"Why am I upside down and against the wall?"

"Well, your body has habituated to a force in your old universe called gravity. We don't have that. You've just met our first force, called resonance. Basically, every object in our universe, yourself included, exchanges particles with every other. The math is probably a bit complicated for you right now, but just understand that it's kind of like a handshake. You and the wall need to come to an agreement on where you are in relation to it."

"So, when I got off the bed, why did I fall up?"

"There's no such thing as falling. You likely hurtled yourself too quickly at the floor, which got scared and sent you the other way."

"Got scared?"

"Well, not really. I'm trying to keep this simple for you."

I was worse than a moron. Literally, the only difference between me and a farting, shitting, baby right now was the fact that I could construct coherent sentences.

"I'll leave you to your negotiations. But don't get too flustered. Your body will remember."

There was no door shutting again, but I knew he was gone. So, it was just me and the wall now. I greeted it, but that was unproductive and quite stupid. When I lifted my hand and placed it nearby, I felt the same static from earlier. That was probably the resonance stuff he mentioned. Great, so now I knew the answer to that trivia question. Only, I hadn't moved at all.

I stayed there for ten minutes trying to negotiate with that obstinate wall. I exclaimed that I was the boss, it being just a wall, and that it was high time it listened. Finally, I lifted my arm and swung at it, only to immediately get flipped over, but still upside down.

My stomach was about ready to jump out of my torso and help itself, I was so hungry. At the very least the hospital workers could've fed me, upside down or not. But no. Like it or not, this was my first lesson. I screamed out for my real parents. Who in the hell puts their kid somewhere that has completely different basic forces! There was no way I was going to get this.

"Need some help?" asked a little girl who had just materialized in front of me. She had long braids, bright blue eyes, and looked all of six years old.

"Yes," I admitted. This is what I'd been reduced to.

"You can't talk to the walls, silly."

I nodded.

"Put your hand against the wall," she ordered, and I did it. A slight electrical pulse reverberated across my hand.

"Do you feel that? Now move it away a little bit. Do you feel that?"

The static-electricity-like thing I felt lessened somewhat when I moved my hand away.

"Now relax and let that go through your whole body."

She looked like a smart little girl, complete with a stylish yellow top. She was also making a lot more sense than anyone else so far, so I closed my eyes and every bit of me started to buzz. It was somewhat like when I first arrived and my hands and arms couldn't stay still. Could that have been why? Somehow, they'd figured it out.

"Now, you need to make your body feel less of it. Like when your hand moved away, make your body feel less energy without moving it."

I took a deep breath and concentrated on the static. It slowly decreased a slight amount, and I opened my eyes to witness myself moving away from the wall.

"I did it!" I exclaimed, and was promptly on the ceiling again.

She giggled. "When you're like me, you'll do it without thinking. But for now, you need to concentrate."

Great. So now my biggest aspiration was to be just like a six-year-old girl. Still, she was a very clever girl. If I closed my eyes, I was able to move away from the ceiling and after a good five minutes I was back on my bed. Well, sort of. I was on the edge. When I looked up, she was gone. There were obviously limits to her patience.

To my great relief, the guy returned with a plate of food. There was a bright yellow fruit, perfectly spherical in shape. Next to it was some brown muck, so I decided on the mutant orange. When I reached for it, the thing flew across the room until the man caught it. He gave me a bright smile that I knew meant "You're a complete moron," then hand-fed spoonful of the brown stuff into my mouth. I was glad the little girl wasn't there to witness it.

Despite looking like steak that was freshly shit out of a chicken, the stuff wasn't that bad. It tasted rather like chocolate raspberries combined with walnuts. My stomach didn't complain and I kept my mouth open like a good baby. A bit of it fell across my face, but

I was pleased that my hand knew how to wipe it off. Finally, only the fruit remained.

"This is a lamma," he proclaimed, but I didn't care.

I opened my mouth wide.

"No, no," he said, and for the fiftieth time that day it was painfully obvious how stupid I was. "This'll be a bit of a game. You need to learn to deal with objects. The goal is simple. Grab the lamma and eat it. You'll find that it's soft and particularly delicious."

I returned that same kind of smile to him that outwardly appeared nice but inwardly meant, "The instant I somehow grab this thing I'm jamming it up your ass until that fake smile disappears."

So, he left me again with six walls and one fruit. Remembering what the girl had said, I reached out my hand and felt the signals between myself and the fruit of torture. It promptly rebounded across the room and ricocheted off every wall, before settling in midair, completely unharmed. I sighed, and was immediately back on the ceiling.

I was able to move away from the ceiling, then navigate the other walls to have the yellow thing in my mouth after just five short hours of effort. Of course, I'm not counting the six hours I spent crying and screaming that I couldn't even eat a simple fruit, but after everything the effort was worth it.

One bite was like spending an hour on that water-jet massage table, eating five chocolate ice cream bars with a fudge filling, then ending with an exhilarating jump off a swing straight into a swimming pool. It was just a fruit, but I didn't care while I chomped that thing to a pulp. I even tried gnawing on the wooden core, but then spit out splinters.

Now feeling literally the best I'd ever been in my life, I walked circles around the bed. I jumped and touched the ceiling. That miracle girl was right. Once my body learned, I no longer needed to concentrate.

This world wasn't so difficult after all.

Satisfied that I'd cracked this universe, I walked forward straight into the wall where they had materialized. My nose bounced off the force field.

"Glad that you're getting the hang of it," said the guy from behind me.

He had a more serious look now, and I only guessed that he'd lost a bet with his colleagues on how quickly I'd finish.

"So, what's next?" I asked.

"Now," he said with that same evil grin. "We blow your mind."

8

MISTER BLOW ME, which is the mental name I gave that condescending prick, calmly walked through the wall and I only assumed waited for me to follow. Figuring that this must be some magical barrier, I promptly walked straight into it. I reached my hand out and felt the resonance, but other than being able to move forward and back, I couldn't move through it.

Blow Me, this time failing to withhold his laughter, appeared from the side wall.

"It's still resonance. Only this time you need to negotiate passage."

I really wished the little girl was here, because she would've made some sense of it. Being used to a world where floors never got scared and walls never negotiated, I really wished they had cut me some slack. When I approached, my entire body felt the static, but I was utterly incapable of reasoning with this inanimate object. Yet when I turned side to side, I felt a slightly different buzz. This wall was only loosely attached to the others.

With a glance at Mister Blow Me, I proceeded to slide my arms and knock the wall on its side. I turned and gave an evil grin. He had his resonance, and I had mine.

Yet in all my self-satisfaction, I neglected the view just beyond. We were on the edge of a canyon.

How deep it was I couldn't say, but my eyes weren't focused on the height but were instead directed at the unfathomable waterfall-like thing at the other end. It must have stretched a mile long and its roar was defeaning, but the amount of water was nowhere near as impressive as what it was doing.

It was going both up and down at the same time. While various channels collapsed to the floor far below, others proceeded straight up to the clouds. In between, they weaved and dashed between each other like traffic on a terrifying highway. Paths traversed the canyon and went straight through the waterfall.

Well, they were more like stones floating in the air every two to four feet. People calmly hopped along them, going to and from the waterfall without any heed of the certain death that awaited one missed step.

"Welcome to our lobby," Blow Me said.

My sole desire at that point was to give him no reason to gloat at my idiocy. I'd learned enough resonance to get by here. Of course, there was the added danger that I was just as likely to fall up to the clouds, never to be seen again, as I was to become a pancake on the canyon floor.

Blow Me gave me a smug grin while his eyes motioned back to my little white prison, but I would give him none of that. I lifted my foot, felt the resonance of the first platform, and stepped onto it. That was easy. I hopped over to the next one, and it started to wobble.

Way below I made out what seemed to be a river on the floor. It was just this thin hair of blue I was so high up. I could've finished a novel on the way down. Then my stone, upon which my life depended, decided to be an asshole and flipped upside down.

Immediately, I lunged for the rock and barely grasped on as my legs dangled in nothingness. I attempted to hang on with every muscle, but I'd always been lazy in gym class and now my grip was slipping. Desperately I screamed to the others walking around to help me, but they only stopped and stared as if I were some mutant chicken. Then came something I never would have suspected.

"May I help you?" a woman on the cliff face asked.

She was dressed in white and was literally standing next to me on the cliff wall. Only it wasn't a wall at all.

It was more of a forest, over which random wooden blocks had been stacked by a three-year-old. In the center of it ran a creek, complete with a few waterfalls of its own, though their sounds were drowned out by the roar of the tremendous flow that now formed our ceiling. The woman continued to stare at me, with little surprise that she was standing perpendicular to me.

Since sitting in a forest was a lot calmer than dangling over a canyon, I used the resonance tinglies flowing through my body to toss myself onto the path before her. By my face was now a small pond, and before I picked myself up some squirrel-mermaid looking thing flew into my hand. It wasn't so cute, with bug eyes and huge flat teeth.

"You need to learn to control resonance with other things that manage their own resonance," said Mister Blow Me, having appeared by my side.

No shit, I thought while I tried in vain to shake the critter away. With what seemed like glee, he tossed the critter, which seemed to enjoy basking in my hand, back into the stream. Another one immediately took its place.

"You're very silly," came a sweet voice from next to me. It was my savior in the form of a little girl again. "What's your name?"

I had to pause on that one. Just the day before I was certain that my name was Jason, but now my confidence was eroding. Was that really my name, or was it false like everything else that I used to believe?

"You don't have a name? Mine's Sareya."

"Jason. Or at least I think it is."

"Why are you holding a squimmer?"

I looked down at the furry creature with its paws held wide, its tummy sticking out, and its broad eyes and buck teeth grinning at me. She laughed, then calmly threw it back in the stream and pushed me away so no replacement came.

"Do you need help?" She didn't have the condescending look of Mister Blow Me. "I saw you wrecked the wall."

I nodded profusely, just like a little kid.

"You know how you make the buzzing a little more and less?"

I again nodded.

"This time make it a lot more. If your mind makes it a lot more, and it happens, then you can walk through it. If it doesn't, then the wall said no."

Well, that made sense. I promptly placed myself in front of a different wall and felt the slight buzz. When I focused on making it increase dramatically, my entire body shook. With some trepidation, I walked straight through the wall, then stuck my tongue out at Blow Me.

"The squimmers like us. So, when you feel the buzzing increase from them, just stop it. Then they'll stay in the water."

I could've hugged her, but instead I strolled up and down the path while triumphantly shooting down squimmers.

Annie arrived just in time to witness me running over the path as it went above and around the forest. While it still seemed weird to be suddenly walking upside down, or sideways, or in midair, it was admittedly the coolest thing I'd ever done. I even collapsed into the stream and threw squimmers from one small pond to another. Sareya giggled the entire time.

"I see you're learning," Annie said, and Mister Blow Me used the opportunity to take off.

Just for fun, I walked up a palm tree, then balanced upside down from one of the leaves.

"Very cute. I think it's time to take you home. There's school tomorrow."

To be honest, the thought hadn't yet occurred to me that, regardless of the universe, there still had to be school. For some reason I figured that everyone here must already know everything.

"Are you excited?" Sareya asked.

"I think so." That was the truth. Though back on Earth, school and especially Flemence were unbearable, I had a feeling the subjects were a bit different here.

"Will you be in my class?" I asked in a half parental, half serious tone. After all, I really did need her help, even though I was eleven years older.

"Of course not, silly!" She smiled. "I'm in the first level!"

I bowed. "Thank you for your services, ma'am. I am most obliged."

She didn't know what to make of that, but after some confusion she returned the bow. She probably had no idea what I meant.

A tuft of wind caught my shirt and I turned to find an airline-sized shimmery craft parked right next to us. For a hundred-foot interstellar ship, it sure was quiet. True to form, there was no door, but Annie led me through the right spot to resonate. This whole walking through walls thing was beginning to freak me out a bit. What if I accidentally walked into the engine?

While I'd hoped for the prototypical space vehicle Raynee had treated me to, complete with laser cannons and a turret, this one resembled an overfed Volkswagen Bug. The interior was spacious, though, and Annie and I both had enough room to kick our feet out.

"It's not too far. I hope it works for you. My son's old room will be yours."

She had a slight tear in her eye.

"Does he have a family of his own now?" If there's anything grandparents love talking about, it's their grandkids.

"No." She looked down. "He died, during the troubled times."

I felt it best not to press more, though I desperately wanted to know if Mordriss had had anything to do with it.

"So, I'll be attending school?" Since Raynee wasn't about to see me, I was determined to run into her. I had to explain my side of this, now that I could at least move around.

"Of course." Her face brightened. "You start tomorrow. The first few days will probably be tough on you, but you'll do just fine, honey."

Her home was a fair-sized square pod in the middle of a wide meadow. Beyond it lay an endless patchwork of forest, and on the other side were several waterfalls complete with squimmers. In the far distance were the hints of a few other houses, but she had no real neighbors.

When we landed, Annie held out her hand and the entire craft shrank to the size of a thin business card, which she placed in her pocket. There was, of course, no door to her house, but an engraved niche suggested where to resonate.

Inside was a quaint dining room, with what I assumed to be a kitchen next door. The living room resembled ours from Seattle, except the couches were spread over every wall, the ceiling, and the floor. Jutting awkwardly from the side was a small rectangular room with countertops and cabinets. A plaque with the word "KITCHEN" hung by the entrance, though in place of the sink and appliances was a silvery six-inch box with a red button. Only the two rooms were visible.

"I added that room for you. Just push the button and ask for anything you desire to eat or drink."

She pointed up and we resonated into a small room with bare walls and a four-poster bed.

"I tried to make the bed familiar."

I nodded in approval.

"Also, feel free to decorate as you see fit. My son had every inch filled, but I had to remove all that. It was time."

She showed me where her room and the bathroom were. Though she mentioned a way to prevent walls from allowing others to resonate, it involved some math and I quickly lost focus. Given there were neither doors nor hallways, I made a note of the orientation. The last thing I wanted was to wake up half naked in the morning and accidentally resonate into her room. Even thinking about it gave me the shivers.

"Well." She sighed. "It's been a long day for the both of us. If you don't mind, I'm going to sleep. I suggest you don't stay up too late. Tomorrow's a big day."

I looked out the window to the grass flowing with the wind. It didn't look much different from Earth, though the forest with its three-dimensional terracing and strange plants was completely foreign.

"May I take a walk around? If it's safe?"

"Of course, it's safe." She laughed. "Just don't stay out too long and don't go too far. You may get lost."

"I'll stay in the meadow."

"And don't forget to turn the suns off when you're done."

I shook my head. "Turn the suns . . . off?"

"Yes. There are two of them." She slapped her head. "Oh! I'm so sorry, dear. Your planet was probably lit by a flaming ball of gas and plasma, correct?"

Admittedly, until then I thought that was the norm.

"Ours is a bit different. You'll study them in school, but I have them set to a signal. Top one is two claps. Bottom one is three."

"So, when I turn them off . . . they go off for everyone?"

"Of course not!" She smiled broadly. "I'm so sorry, but I'm very tired. Remind me tomorrow and I'll explain."

I nodded and returned to the living room, then resonated outside. It occurred to me that I could've just gone from my bedroom. There was no longer any reason to do a tour of the house on the way out.

Though the blades felt more like plastic straws, the grass was the most similar thing I'd seen yet. They even grew up, instead of down and side to side like everything else. They were a bit prickly to the skin, so I sat just beyond them and admired the view of the dueling suns. More orange and less blinding than Earth's, they still looked ordinary.

As I was sitting, a strange bulge from my pocket caught my attention. I pulled out something that resembled a police badge, but had only the engraved letters ORECA with lots of stars surrounding it. On its back, instead of a fastening pin, was a rough rod. When I turned it over, I recognized some sort of key. It folded out to unlock something.

While examining the object, I moved to resonate back up to my room, then remembered Annie's request and clapped twice. The top sun immediately disappeared. Three claps later it was midnight. I shook my head and retired to my bed.

From outside there was nothing: no crickets, tree kangaroos, birds, or even the rustle of the wind. I cradled my new-found key as I struggled to sleep in this deathly silence. With the same resonance as everything else here, it was clearly from the paramount dimension. Someone had slipped it into my pocket. Somewhere, there was something important I needed to open.

9

ANNIE TUGGED AT my sheets in the morning.

"Time for school!"

For the first time I remembered, I was actually excited. Going this long without Raynee's hooked smile was killing me. I hoped we had at least one class together.

Breakfast was a lamma fruit and some polka-dotted green soup. Since I knew the lamma was awesome, I devoured the soup first. It tasted like gingerbread, even though it was a soup. While I expected a school bus, she instead flew me there.

"It's overkill to go this way, but we'll use it until you learn."

I had a feeling, unlike school back on Earth, that they may actually teach some useful stuff. By the time we arrived, every student was already there and classes had just begun. The building looked familiar, with its single floor, many windows, and multiple playgrounds outside. One of them had what resembled a three-hundred-foot rollercoaster, so that was a bit different. High-schoolers, of course, had no need for the lame stuff.

Annie left me outside, and a tall principal with a white shirt greeted me.

"Greetings, Jason," he said.

He might as well have added "Earthling," but he was being friendly about it.

"We're so glad to have you here."

"I'm glad to be here." I didn't lie.

He led me inside and smiled upon noticing that I already knew how to resonate. Sure, there was a lot to learn, but I was making quick progress. My highest desire, though, was to show Raynee what I'd learned.

We resonated into my classroom to the faces of twenty barely five-year-old kids. Each had a wide smile and shouted "Good morning, Jason!" when I entered.

I looked around. Save for the teacher, a rather attractive blonde in her mid-thirties, no one was taller than four feet. They were evenly divided over five of the six surfaces of the room.

The principal gave me an affable smile and pointed at a tiny seat on the ceiling. When I resonated over to it, the chair was barely large enough for my foot. With more than a little confusion, I stared at the teacher, who was making wave motions with her hand at me.

Finally, she sighed, walked over, and laid her hands flat over the table and chair. Instantly they increased threefold and I was able to sit.

"Now, class." She stooped down with a wide grin that really gets little kids. "We're going to have an easy day today, in honor of our new student in level zero. So, let's begin by solving a basic equation. Jason, I did some research and on Earth it's called the Riemann Hypothesis."

Every one of those brats held out their hands for a screen to materialize, then all sorts of lines and funny symbols appeared. Apparently, their minds controlled it, because the numbers flew through their screens faster than any video game I'd seen. The teacher smiled at me and held out her hand. Evidently, she expected me to somehow follow.

"Create a screen." She opened her hands like the kids had just done.

I held out my hands, but there was no screen.

"You need to synthesize it."

"Uh-huh."

"You didn't synthesize your own screens on that planet?"

"No. We had computers."

"How quaint. Well, our new student has some homework for tonight, but we shouldn't leave him out, should we?"

Every kid shook his head. "No, Alina!" they shouted. They'd all solved the equation anyway.

"Let's do some differential equations in our heads."

She wrote gibberish in midair, and every kid blurted an answer before she even finished. I remained with my mouth open.

"You of course had differential equations, right?"

"Well, we had them, but that's kind of a college course, I think."

Several kids fell off their chairs, laughing.

"So, what did you learn? The uncertainty principle . . . ?"

"Uncertainty principle! We talked about that one."

"Very good." She sighed in relief. "Kids, let's each make a wormhole."

A little girl next to me, who stood a good six inches below Sareya, twirled her arms to create a whirling hole. While its front consisted of swirling silver, from every other angle it was invisible. Within seconds, there were twenty of them.

"I think they left that part out," I said.

The teacher gave a fake smile, then calmly twirled her hand to create one in front of me. To my relief, she then ignored me for the remainder of the class. There was a mathematics lesson, or at least I think that's what she discussed. With the amount of symbols and graphs, it could've been art or Greek literature for all I knew.

At the end of the day, each of us jumped through our wormholes. I'd wondered for several hours what this portable whirlpool did, so I was excited to finally test it out. At first it felt like I'd put my face in a cotton candy machine that battered me through a multitude of dimensions, but I was soon transported back to exactly the same spot. It was the most spectacular yet thoroughly disappointing thing I'd ever done.

"We're glad to have you here," she said to me when every kid had left. "I'm so sorry they didn't teach you the basics where you lived. I can stay after class to help, just not today. But you'll need to put in a lot of effort, too."

I nodded. Never before had I been so hopelessly destroyed. There was no possibility of meeting Raynee. She was finishing her last level at school, while I was officially the slowest student in level zero.

The grim realization sank in during the short ride home that, not only would I have no chance at Raynee, but I was likely to spend the rest of my life in kindergarten. Annie told me through her teary eyes that she knew I was in pain. Mastering resonance was nothing. Even a chimpanzee could walk, but would never have a chance as an adult in human society.

When we arrived home, I spent a few minutes staring at the bare walls in my room, then at the never-ending forest outside. But it wasn't endless, was it? During the flight, I'd seen houses in its midst. Annie's house enjoyed a great deal of land, but it was still part of civilization. Others lived here. Perhaps Raynee was one of them.

This universe was nothing without her. Resonance or gravity, neither mattered without those deep brown eyes and the twitch by her mouth. There had to be a way to see her, and it didn't need to involve school. It was time to explore.

"Where are you going?" Annie asked after I'd resonated outside.

I hesitated, since here I was still practically a toddler. "I thought I'd take a walk."

Her all-knowing eyes went straight into me, then she nodded ever slightly. "That forest goes quite a ways. How exactly do you intend to find your way back?"

"I'm not going too far." I lied, though from her narrowed eyes I doubted she bought it.

"Just be careful. If you go too far, you can't control the suns. The animals might turn them off."

Well, that was a sobering thought. Even the friendly furries were smarter here. I nodded and set off. Yet before I'd gone three feet, she gently grabbed my arm.

"You probably want to go that way." She pointed in the opposite direction I was going. I smiled and obliged.

Upon reaching the edge of the forest, I paused to contemplate my stupid idea. The land sloped down at least a few hundred feet before it disappeared into the tangles. I'd grown used to the concept that trees grew from the ground, but here there was a grand entanglement of every kind of greenery protruding from every other direction. In fact, what I'd been calling the ground in the first place was more like a cliff, leading to a precipice of unending limbs in every direction. How would I find my way in this three-dimensional mess?

With Annie watching me, I stepped onto a wide spiraling trunk and went twenty feet in. There had to be no visible hesitation here. Everywhere on my body shook with the things all trying to resonate with me. My legs began to wobble when I looked down to witness the endless patchwork at least a thousand feet below. If I fell, not only would I die, but I'd have plenty of time to think about it.

I resonated the shit out of that trunk while I inched my way to a tuft of brush that hung onto a trunk at least thirty feet in diameter. When I jumped onto it, my feet sank straight into mush. The entire tree was like quicksand! In an instant, I was covered to my waist.

I grabbed onto a nearby vine with all of my strength and attempted to pull myself out. Yet its smooth surface provided no traction, and my hands were slipping when three eyes appeared from its end and the whole vine coiled over to me. It was, in fact, more of a snake.

Then I heard a slurping sound and the tree spit me out on the opposite side. There was now nothing below me for several hundred feet. I had no chance to scream.

Only I didn't fall. My body hung motionless in midair. I slapped myself awake. Of course. There was no gravity here. I was in no danger of falling. A tingling came from my right hand and I reached out to resonate to the nearest tree, then plopped my feet on its side. I stood to peer at the pit below me, then walked into it.

In this cacophony of limbs, the trunks *were* the paths. My senses cleared to reveal twisting pathways through the woods. Most reached and spiraled to no end, but in a world with no ups and downs, that didn't mean much. It was like walking the track of a looping roller coaster without the fear of falling.

Earth forests had nothing on this. With a shout, I headed full speed down the nearest trunk, doing loops and corkscrews while ducking under giant yellow flowers and serpent vines. A huge bud rested on one branch and when I jumped over it, the thing burst into a million fragrant white petals. Instantly, the area around me turned into a snow kingdom of blossoms. I twirled under it, then leaped onto an adjoining trunk and raced over another one.

A hundred bright yellow birds fluttered around me, picking off as many petals as they could. They weren't avian at all, of course, since they lacked wings, had black eyes with circles that looked drawn by a kid, and possessed tiny arms to grab the petals. Still, they fluttered and were cute.

This was like having my own gigantic theme park in my back-yard. It possessed no lines and more rides than I could fit in in a lifetime. I leaped into an opening and resonated to a tree fifty feet away, then sat to admire the view. There was only one problem. I'd gone so deep into the jungle that I had no idea how to get home. Which way was it? Up, down, or to one of the sides?

I buried my head in my arms. How far did I go? It was impossible to know. While I'd been gone barely a half an hour, I'd changed directions so many times I could be a few feet away, or a mile. I reached into my pocket and pulled out a few beans I'd grabbed before leaving. Maybe a fuller stomach would clear my mind.

"Pardon me," a deep voice called from behind.

I was saved!

Instead, I now faced a medium-sized rodent. He walked on two paws, while the other two were short and useless like a T-Rex. His fur was light brown with white spots, while his stomach was fully white.

"Are you going to eat those? I'd be so grateful if you'd give them to me."

There was only a handful, and most were already in my mouth. I took a bean from my palm and placed it just in front of him. To my surprise, his short paws elongated so he could gingerly pick it up and plop it in his mouth. I swallowed the remainder, then smiled.

"May I have another, kind sir?" he asked with wide eyes.

"I'm sorry. I ate the rest."

"Well, go fuck yourself then." He turned his back. Just before he left, he let out a low growl and the light disappeared. I was now lost and completely in the dark.

I sat and cried. Raynee was furious at me, and I easily qualified as the dumbest student in this dimension's school system. I still had the Oreca badge with its key, but that was pointless. There was absolutely no hope of locating whatever it unlocked, because even the way back home was beyond me.

10

WITH NO MOON to go by, I couldn't even make out my hand in front of me. I tried to clap the suns back on, but they were on a different program here. I must've gone far enough to leave Annie's property.

I sat there on my tree for a good thirty minutes. My only hope was for Annie to find me. I could barely navigate this jungle in the day, let alone at night. The thought occurred that there may be critters here who could eat me.

"You know, you're not very smart for your age," a young girl's voice called from behind me.

Just when I whirled around, the suns appeared and a light beam nearly blinded me. The tree shot me off, but I remained floating.

"Sorry about that." It was dark again. "This is Sareya."

I'd never been so happy in my life.

"You know you're not human, right?"

I couldn't say anything.

"You don't need the light," she said.

"Umm, kind of."

"Nope. Do you think because you can't see, that things aren't there?"

"No."

"Good. Then *feel* them."

Again, I had no reply.

"Everything resonates just like you. Use that to know where they are."

She wasn't returning the suns on purpose. I closed my eyes and reached my hand over the wood underneath me. Not only did it resonate, but each bump and knot did so differently. There was a minute change where it reached slightly toward me, or bucked away.

When I held my hand farther away, I detected not just what was next to me, but traces of things distant. I let my entire body take it in. There was a branch just to the left. I felt its three spirals that ended in an explosion of leaves. I could count them. Thirty feet from me was a much thicker trunk. I turned, and there was Sareya, her curls winding like the forest around us. She had an embroidered dress on, and she was smiling.

"How did you find me?"

"Annie asked me to keep an eye on you. Thought you might get lost."

I couldn't argue with that logic.

She turned the lights back on and no longer did I just see the winding limbs encircling me, I felt them. Sareya was now crossing her arms.

"You got lost, didn't you?"

"Yeah. Then some crazy rodent cursed at me and turned off the suns."

She laughed. "I think someone had fun with your translator."

My head bumped back.

"You know we don't speak the same language, right? Our translators make us think so."

"Translator?" I was dumbfounded. I didn't recall anyone handing me one.

"It's in your brain, silly. They put one in you when you moved here."

That was the least surprising thing I'd heard that day.

"How was your first day at school?"

I sighed. That was the last thing I wanted to think of at the moment. "I'm the dumbest one in level zero."

"Don't be so hard on yourself," replied my six-year-old shrink.

"Well." I tried to not act so down to this cheerful little girl. "It was just my first day, and Rome wasn't built in a day."

"What's Rome?"

"It's a city."

She blinked several times. "Do you mean, where you lived it took an entire day for someone to build a city?"

"Actually, it took a lot of someones many years."

"Wow." She was aghast. "That's horrible."

She sat next to me and barely reached my shoulder. "You still think you're one of them, don't you?"

"Well, yeah. I mean, we look the same."

"But you aren't. I'll show you."

My Lilliputian mentor hadn't failed me yet, so I said not a word while she stood, faced her palms forward, then seemed to scan her immediate surroundings.

"Did your teacher tell you about essonance, yet?" She stepped forward and back.

I shook my head.

"It's another of our forces, like resonance. It's what keeps things together."

"You mean like different atoms?"

"No. Completely different. We don't have those."

She was now concentrating on a specific area. "The cool thing about essonance is, it's very strong, but if you pull it apart just right, you can do some things. Did you learn how to make a worm-hole yet?"

I shook my head again, remembering that here I was, in fact, a moron. "Other kids made them, but I don't know how yet."

"That's essonance. But I'll use it a different way right now. This is first-level stuff. There're two types of matter, you know. Matter and dark matter."

I felt happy to have had actually heard of this.

"Matter's in our dimension set, and dark matter isn't. But if dark matter is in a lower dimension set, our forces can affect it. If it's in a higher dimension set, then it affects our forces."

She'd lost me already. The first grade evidently involved some complicated stuff.

"Look." She had evidently noticed my vacant expression. "Imagine you're in a box with medium-sized holes in it. You have a small ball and a guy outside has a big ball. If you have the small ball, you can hit him, but he can't hit you with his ball, because the holes are too small. But if you have the big ball, then he can hit you."

"But what if I catch his ball and throw it back?"

She shook her head. "That's against the rules. But do you understand? He's dark matter and you're matter?"

I kind of did, so I signaled her to continue.

"So, what do you get if you essonate our matter and dark matter at the same time?"

"A duck?"

She gave me a quirky frown. "A what? No. You get a dimensional portal."

She slid her hand into something and her fingers disappeared.

"Come here. But when you get inside, don't freak out."

I walked cautiously over to where she'd now formed a dark crack in midair. While everything looked normal where I stood, my skin turned cold where I placed a finger on the edge.

She took my hand, smiled, then led me inside.

The instant I entered, billions of stars surrounded me. I was in the midst of space. Everything was cold, and I couldn't breathe.

My hand reached for the portal, but it was already gone. Sareya was floating next to me, but was completely fine.

"You need to relax."

How I could even hear her in space?

My lungs were empty and I was freezing to death. Every muscle was completely incapacitated.

Sareya was laughing. "Come on, silly. You can still breathe."

I shook my head while gasping. Sareya leaned her head back, sighed, then tossed me back through the portal.

Air rushed down my throat and I spread my body across the trunk. Everything felt so warm again. I was safe.

"You could breathe the whole time."

"We were in the middle of space! How?"

"You were in another dimension. One similar to where you lived. But you were still here."

I gave her a quizzical look.

"You were witnessing another dimension, but you were still in ours. Your mind was playing tricks on you. Nothing in that place can hurt you." She put her hand on my shoulder while I coughed. "Now we're going back. And I want you to remember that you're still here. It's like looking through a window."

Sareya was right. After only twenty-six attempts where she had to yank me back, slap some sense into me, then toss me again into the void, my body finally understood that there was nothing wrong. Once I forced myself to realize that air was still available through my dimension, I was able to float to my heart's content in the darkness.

She stood gloating while I performed somersaults. Yet after only a few, I stopped. There was no resonance here. The rich sounds that permeated Sareya and Annie's world were gone. Next to where I'd come from, this place, despite its myriad stars peeking around me, was boring.

"We can go now." I was a little surprised that I wanted to leave.

"One more lesson," she said.

Briefly I felt like a pancake, then Sareya pulled us into another section of space. Though the star patterns appeared slightly different, this place was basically the same as the previous one. She pointed below me.

There were no stars.

"This is a black hole. I want you to touch it."

I vaguely recalled from between my naps in physics class, this was a bad thing.

"A black hole is a collapsed star that exerts so much gravity that it consumes light particles. But gravity doesn't affect us."

I looked down. Other than the lack of stars, I couldn't make out where its surface was. I was also still concerned that most physics texts and Hollywood movies advised against this.

"Your first challenge is to see it."

"But how? It doesn't resonate."

"You don't need resonance. We have more senses. Listen for them. See them."

If all level one kids were this smart, I was in deep trouble.

I closed my eyes, but as predicted there was no resonance. Then I heard and felt them, slight waves that flowed across my hands and face. It was almost like the black hole was singing to me.

"You can feel the gravitational waves, can't you?"

"But I thought you said gravity doesn't affect us?" This was still thoroughly confusing to me. Though I wasn't about to admit it, I also had no clue what gravitational waves were.

"It won't. But that doesn't mean we can't notice it. Our bodies sense every force, but only our five can affect us. Now try to see it."

I squinted, but still saw black, then slowly my eyes adjusted. Something was different about that empty space. There was a red light emanating from all around it.

"You can see the radiation? Can't you?"

I nodded.

"Humans can only see a narrow band of light, but we can make out a lot more."

A gigantic whirling disk was now below me. From its surface

emanated red rays, which stretched in every direction across the universe. The gravitational waves hit me like heartbeats, and my head wandered across the horizon to witness this living thing in the midst of nothingness. Its rays were like blood flowing life into the universe, while its dark interior hinted at the death that awaited when one came too close.

"Do you want to touch it?"

I smiled, and she grabbed my arm and flew me to its surface. Around me, the gravity intensified, but it no longer controlled me. Instead, it felt like gently fluttering feathers, letting me feel their fibers without ever tickling.

Its surface shimmered red, and I carefully reached out my hand and petted it. The black hole felt like a slow porous current that was softly caressing my hand. With each stroke, a tuft of red rays flew outward and its song changed slightly.

Sareya smiled, then in a flash we were home. Yet, it was all too soon. Just when I thought the roller coaster of limbs in the forest couldn't be beat, she'd introduced me to two new worlds. There were billions of stars in those universes. What lay there, unexplored? What other universes were out there? I had to return.

"How do I do that?" I was desperate. "Make a portal?"

"I can't teach you that yet. You got lost in your backyard. Raynee would kill me if I let you wander in a trillion universes."

My heart stopped. "You know Raynee?"

"Of course. She's my neighbor. Now your meadow is thirty feet that way." She pointed at a break through the jungle, then she was gone.

11

THE THOUGHT THAT Raynee was only a short walk away pre-occupied me so much that I got lost again, which is much easier to do when there are six possible directions instead of four. Yet just when I was about to panic, I noticed a familiar spiraling tree just above me, and followed it to reach an opening to the meadow.

I stood there, gazing at the handful of clouds that barely obscured each sun, and knew then that Raynee might be sharing the same view. I was so deep in thought about her I didn't notice Annie.

"It was kind of bright," she said, "so I put those clouds up."

That popped my bubble quickly.

"Could you teach me how to essonate?" I asked.

With Raynee so close, it was even more important now not to be a turnip. Despite having no clue on my first day of level zero, I had to learn these things. I was desperate to accomplish whatever would impress her.

"Essonance isn't like resonance, dear. Your body won't pick it up automatically. You need to work at it, and there's a little bit of math involved."

Something told me that "a little bit" meant a postdoctorate in physics.

"I'll do it. Do you have any books on the math?"

"Books?"

"Is there anything I can read?"

She tried to teach me how to create a screen like they did in class, but that involved math, too, so we eventually settled for a credit card that created one for me. Annie showed me the page on creating basic wormholes with essonance, which were easier than dimensional portals. Of course, the math was completely alien to me, so we kept simplifying it until we got to differential equations, then I moved it back to calculus.

It was shocking to see lessons on calculus accompanied by drawings of various animals. Since this was the very first level of preschool, they obviously felt the need for visual aids. In truth, they helped a lot.

The first lesson was on Mr. Potter the Snowman, who wished to calculate the rate of change of his volume as he produced snow-balls from himself at various speeds. Not having reached calculus in high school, it took me the entire night to comprehend the subject. Annie, for her part, tried to explain. I sympathized for her plight. It was kind of like me teaching addition to someone who had no concept of numbers.

The next day, my teacher was nice enough to arrive early to help me. Her face turned to a slight frown when I revealed that I hadn't learned everything in the calculus text the previous night. She had hoped to finish differential equations by the evening.

"I know you're trying," she said while I was struggling with the integrals of trigonometric equations. "You have a bright mind, but even your classmates here in level zero have been studying this for several years now. I know you have a goal of going soon to the upper levels, but I just don't think it's possible."

That evening I wanted to slam the door, run into my room, and smash something. However, there was no door, and everything I tried to resonate to the floor just stayed there. I couldn't even throw a tantrum in this place.

Annie calmly resonated into my room and sat next to me. "I can't imagine how hard this is for you. And it's not your fault."

I couldn't hold back the tears now. This new world was wonderful, but I couldn't stand being such an idiot.

"You'll figure out everything eventually. It'll just take you several years, and there's nothing wrong with that."

"But then I won't be with her!" I was a bit shocked to say it aloud.

"With Raynee? If you think she's going to be impressed that you know how to essonate, then you clearly don't understand her."

"You know her?" I wiped away some tears.

"Of course. Since she was a baby. She's had a difficult life, too, and won't care what you know. She's looking for all the intangible things."

In a conversation concerning how stupid I was, I didn't want to admit that I had no idea what intangible meant.

"There's something else you should know." Her face was down. "Raynee, is an exceptional girl. Even by our standards she's smart. She's in a special school for the gifted, called Oreca, so you're not going to impress her on that level."

The word "Oreca" stunned me. Could Raynee have slipped it in my pocket? Yet why would she do that? Still, I now knew where that key worked. I only needed to get there.

Of course, that was a school for the gifted, and I was an idiot. So, as far as Raynee was concerned, I was still a turnip.

The next morning, all my little classmates were more excited than usual. Their mouths were chatting a mile a second and there wasn't even an attempt at order in the classroom.

"We're going to play essoball!" one screamed when I asked about the commotion.

I asked another for more details and got "It's this game to teach essonance, but we get to shoot people!"

I finally gave up and asked the teacher, who summarized the rules. The game was a bit like super-dimensional dodgeball. Players ride a flying motorcycle through different worlds, reached using dimensional portals. Players shoot essoballs at each other and teams score one point for each hit. Any single player is out after seven hits.

Immediately, I knew this would be fun for everyone but me. Without the ability to essonate, I stood no chance. My teacher smiled, then began handing out black-and-yellow gloves to the entire class. Of course, she had to specially make mine.

"What are these for?" I asked a little girl.

"They help us. They help us essonate. The bigger kids don't have them."

Well, that was cool. This game wasn't sounding so bad.

"I think yours need to be turned up all the way," she said, then fiddled with my gloves for a few seconds before handing them back to me. My confidence did not improve.

Pandemonium ensued when our teacher announced that it was time to play. They ran so fast I barely kept up with them, even though my legs were twice as long. Game central was the three-hundred-foot tall enclosed roller coaster thing in what I originally thought was a playground. It consisted of a steep ramp that ended in a near vertical plummet after which an enclosed loop dropped the rider in midair.

Other students explained that its job was simply to accelerate us in a way that made essonance easier. My mind blanked when they explained the math behind it, so I just took their word.

Our opponents showed up a moment later. They were the fifth level class, and though I was easily the tallest of the group, they towered over my teammates. Each of our opponents was staring directly at me, with a big smile.

"Wait!" one of the boys in my class said. "Is *he* on our team?" He was pointing at me when our teacher nodded.

"That's no fair!" a little girl yelled. "We're going to lose!"

Evidently their confidence in me was only slightly higher than my own. I began removing the gloves, knowing that they were right.

"Put those back on!" Alina ordered. "Jason is your teammate, so it's your job to teach him the game."

"But last time we only won by two points!" a blond boy yelled. "He'll give them an easy seven."

"Well, then, Robby," our teacher said, "you'll just have to watch from the sidelines."

Now the entire class was fuming at me. Robby was our best player, and the fifth levelers were already high-fiving each other. I forced myself to remain calm. This looked like an advanced video game, and I wasn't so bad in that department.

While we were queuing for entry, Robby approached me. He was nearly two feet shorter, but carried himself with the confidence of the finest investment banker.

"Look in the sand," he said. "Lots of balls get stuck there."

"Thanks for the tip." I looked up to the device that was shooting riders at bullet speeds. "Has anyone ever died playing this?"

"Of course not. But you may throw up. Try not to look with your eyes backward. Use your resonance to see."

I was glad that Sareya taught me to do that when I was directed to lie down inside a gray metal tube, which when shut, sealed off every bit of light. I grasped two bars, and my legs were suddenly curled around a metal body. I used resonance in the darkness to reveal I was on a sleek motorcycle-like craft with two jet engines. I smiled. This was exactly like a video game.

A few minutes later, I was no longer in a good mood. First, I threw up on the launch. That damned thing didn't just shoot players forward. It spun me around, flipped me, then sent me backward at some thousand miles an hour until I spewed. Did those fifth-graders have any pity? No, I lost a life before I'd even wiped my mouth.

Determined to take my revenge, I soon found those little bastards were quick, and every time I thought I had one, they'd enter a wormhole and wind up behind me. Before I even managed to find a ball to fire, they'd shot me four times.

Some buzzer went off and jettisoned me into a portal: I'd been hit too many times in a row, so it sent me elsewhere. For the first time I checked out the background scenery. The previous one was just tons of green fields and blue sky, but this one was some form of desert world complete with canyon. I remembered Robbie's advice about finding balls, and managed to grab a few before a fifth-grader blew me to oblivion.

This time I created my own portal, thanks to my new gloves, and headed out of there before they could finish me off. Now a bit panicked that I might truly cost our class the game, I devised a new plan: Get away from everyone. With their strategic wormholes, I stood no chance against these kids. This was not a video game. Those had controllers and screens. This was real.

Ahead was some city, and I pushed my ride's throttle to max, since there would certainly be places to hide among the 10,000 skyscrapers. The downtown was a lot larger than Seattle, but otherwise it resembled any other city, with the exception of the flying cars. Also, the buildings were shinier and looked like pieces from a Picasso painting.

Soon I was among them, and the smells of street food and exotic restaurants filled my nose, and my eyes couldn't help but admire the minute details. Every single person looked different, just like the real world. Some moved slowly, their faces indicating remorse, while others barged through the day. There were schools, pick-up hoops games, workers swarming about office buildings, and even a courthouse. And then it dawned on me.

The entire world I had known was completely fabricated! Every kid at my school, Flemence, and even my parents were no more authentic than this city around me, which existed solely for a game. Hidden within these buildings were romances and affairs, triumphs and breakdowns, and politics and theatrics. Yet none had any notion that everything they held true was made up. They were nothing more than scenery.

I glimpsed a fifth-grader in a gap between two buildings.

I'd had enough sight-seeing. Did he know I was there? Because I still hadn't mastered wormholes even with the gloves, I stood no chance of taking him straight on, so I chose a different approach. It was time to become a sniper.

My first idea was to park my cycle somewhere, then pull out the shooter and carry it to a high window. Yet, when my feet touched the cement, I annihilated a lightpost. Since this was a lower dimensional world, everything I touched was like that man Raynee disintegrated in the alley. Before I took off, I nearly obliterated a kindergarten class on a field trip. Unwilling to commit mass murder to win a video game, I found a parking garage and carefully maneouvered to an opening, where I awaited my prey.

To my luck, the fifth-grader passed by moments later, his eyes scanning up and down for signs of me, completely unsuspecting of my trick. I gave him no chance. When he was but yards from me, I fired and immediately had my first point. I shouted, and then the world reacted.

The boy stared at me from his cycle with wide eyes as the parking garage disintegrated, followed by every other building. People ran screaming from everywhere but there was no escape. Everything was turning to dust. Had I cheated? Who was doing this?

We both headed out, yet there was something erratic about his flying. He was sputtering, then flailing, and finally headed his cycle's nose straight toward what now was an endless desert. And then it occurred to me. He wasn't escaping the disappearing city. He was fleeing from me.

He crashed onto the sand and his cycle quickly burst into flames, though he was unharmed. Two other fifth-graders landed next to him, while I hovered another fifty feet away.

"Get away from me!" he screamed, glaring at me with bloodshot eyes. "He's going to kill me!"

Perhaps the largest kid in the fifth level reached him, but was tossed into the next dune. His friend suffered the same fate, being jettisoned a hundred feet away in a burst of resonance.

His mouth was agast and he clawed frantically, helplessly against the sand as I dismounted and approached. I smiled, held my hands wide in friendship, then tried to walk forward. He was desperately resonating me away now, and I used every bit I had to resist.

"It's okay," I said calmly. "There's nothing to be scared of."

"He killed them all!" he screamed.

I was only ten feet away now, but he doubled his efforts. My teeth were chattering and my legs felt ready to break in half, but I trudged on against the shaking boy while his two friends looked on in amazement.

"Get away from me! All of you!"

I was five feet away and my lungs were compressing. He was resonating against me with everything he had, but I was bigger and stronger. My mouth felt ready to fly open and eat my head, but I had almost reached him.

Every bit of him was shaking and his eyes looked on in stunned hatred while I struggled forward. At last I seized him with both arms and pulled him tight even though it felt like force hugging a grizzly.

"Everything's going to be fine. There's no reason to be scared."

The hug seemed to help. My teeth stopped shaking and he reduced his resonance, then calmed somewhat.

"You don't understand," he whispered.

"What don't I understand?"

"He's coming for us. He's going to kill everyone."

"Who is?" I already knew the answer.

"Mordriss. He's back."

12

MY LITTLE CLASSMATES were busy devouring a near bushel of lamma fruits when the celebration stopped. Stretched across my arms was the stricken fifth-leveler, barely able to move. Our class had won on my last shot, but that didn't matter anymore. Though I'd been talking softly and trying to discuss more lighthearted things the entire way, nothing had stopped his shaking.

Several teachers rushed to me and pulled him from my arms. A medic was summoned and the class grew deathly silent save the young boy who kept screaming in a now hoarse voice, "I saw him!"

Upon seeing his wasted face and blank eyes, a few of my classmates, being all of five years old, commenced sobbing. Immediately, we were ordered back inside, just as a pair of medics reached him. Our teacher did her best to discuss what we learned about essonance that day, but no one was thinking of that.

"Was he bad?" a little girl asked.

They were all born after the events.

"I never met my older brother," Robby said through the silence. "He was staying with my aunt and uncle. They all died."

Our teacher, Alina, tried to say something, but couldn't hold back the tears herself.

"Everyone lost someone," she said to her horrified class, none of whom had ever witnessed a teacher cry. "We were supposed to be married."

The rest of the school day was useless.

When Annie picked me up that day, her face, too, was red from dried tears. She said nothing until we were in the vehicle.

"He's not back," she said somberly while facing forward.

"But, he said—"

"They should never teach orasance in the fifth level. Not anymore, after what happened."

"What's orasance?"

She shook her head, perhaps debating whether to tell me. Then she continued with solemn eyes. "The only force we can't control. It's what controls time. Makes some things happen before others. We can't change it but . . . ." She paused to look away. "It affects certain particles in a predictable way. We can use it to see what happened in the past."

"With anything?"

"Anything we can understand. But the problem is when they teach it, everyone wants to try it on the dead."

"You mean they go to cemeteries and . . . ?"

"Our cemeteries are a lot different, I think, from yours. A small part of the body is exposed, so we can visit and reminisce. Relatives who passed away long ago can be a part of us. But, when not careful, there's nothing preventing us from seeing darker things."

"So, he saw Mordriss kill someone?"

"Yes." She looked away. "If he was back, there would be far worse signs, and no survivors."

"Who is *he*? Mordriss?"

"No one knows where he came from." She wiped her face with her sleeve. "We've always been peaceful here. No wars. Nothing to die from but old age. Even accidents didn't kill. You know it's impossible to hurt yourself from your own resonance? I was a nurse, and the worst we ever dealt with were panic attacks. We weren't prepared."

I didn't want to bring it up, but the question had already been waiting so long. It was better to ask it then, than wait for it to ruin a happier time. "I'm sorry about your son. His name was Arven, right?"

"Yes." Her head stayed down. "He and my husband were my everything. I was working that day when he showed up. I didn't know what to do—" She was falling over and in complete sobs now.

I rushed over, then after a brief hesitation, held her.

"People were cut in half. He didn't just kill. He tortured them. Pulled spines out with them still alive. Split them wide open in parts. We'd never seen such things. We didn't know what to do, and when I finally came home, he'd gotten them. My son! He, he . . . ."

"You don't have to say it." I hugged her. "I'm sorry for bringing it up."

After that discussion, my room freaked me out a bit. It had been Arven's room, and now that I knew about orasance, I found myself jumping at every little thing. Some part of him was still in there.

To get my mind on other subjects, I went wandering in the meadow. The straw-like grass was blowing slightly. It felt so peaceful compared to the violence we'd just discussed. Annie had placed two huge clouds over the suns, like smudges over a fine day. Just when I decided it was a useful waste of time to figure out how to move them, something in the grass stirred.

There were a few snorts, then two black noses appeared from the short reeds, followed by fur and spots. They were the same type of rodent I'd seen earlier.

"Do you have any food, kind sir?" one asked.

"I'm not falling for that. And no, I don't have any."

"But we're so very hungry, and we'd be so grateful if you gave us anything."

I thought for a moment. They had those irresistible puppy dog eyes and the house was only a few feet away. All the food was materialized anyway. It wasn't like Annie had to go to the store. Also, perhaps a tiny good turn was what the world needed right now.

They were jumping like a pack of kangaroos when I returned with a pile of beans and spread them across the dirt. The gobbled up everything in seconds. They even licked the ground to make sure they missed nothing.

"Let's go next door," the other one said. "This piece of shit keeps giving us these cheap-ass beans."

"Yeah," the first said. "Go fuck yourself, asshole."

Perhaps on a different day I would've been offended, but at that moment of pain it was a desperately needed laugh. After watching them scamper away, cussing with each step, I moved to sit, then noticed a bulge in my pockets.

I'd forgotten to return the essonation gloves, and with all the confusion no one had asked for them back. Though technically they weren't allowed outside of school, those gloves were now my keys to essonance. While being able to float and walk upside down was cool, traveling to other dimensions and universes was far more interesting. I glanced toward the forest. Perhaps I could explore just a little bit, only a few feet inside the trees where Annie couldn't see me.

After looking both ways, I darted into the woods and slid the gloves on. Remembering how Sareya had held her palms out to midair, I did the same. Though I couldn't see anything, my hands felt jagged edges, as if the air was composed of thousands of tiny boxes. My fingers slipped into a crack, and I pulled it open until a bright light appeared. After another tug there was a door. Before entering, I looked around me. There was no one, so I pulled myself inside. Immediately after I slipped through, the portal automatically shut behind me.

The sky here was zaffre blue and full of swirling clouds of the tornado kind. A lone, dark-green hill towered over everything else. Beyond, there was a glimmer of light that barely covered the horizon.

I paused for a moment to consider that movie where aliens popped out of people's stomachs. For some reason, this seemed like the ideal place for them to live. Yet this was a lower dimension set. Nothing here could hurt me, or so Sareya had said. I followed my curiosity.

Beyond the hill was a sea of small mounds. I stopped. At first glance, they looked exactly like the alien pods. I held my stomach. But no, they were something far more familiar. Each one was round, about twice the size of my fist, and mostly purple. There were millions of them, maybe more. The hills rolled on endlessly in front of me, each completely covered with these vegetable-like things.

"They're turnips," a familiar voice said from behind.

It was Sareya. Her blond curls were newly braided.

"Next time you check if the coast is clear. Remember to look up."

Great. She had been watching me the entire time. Regardless, I was more curious about the scene before me.

"What are they?"

"You don't remember, do you? Look closer."

We walked over to the nearest patch. I half expected them to jump up and down or run away, but they remained motionless while we stood over them. They were just like turnips, with one major difference: each had engraved faces within their peels with traces of a mouth, nose, and eyes. I stooped to stare directly at one, but it didn't blink or move at all.

"They can't see us. They're from a lower dimension."

I wanted to touch one, but then held back upon realizing that each was a living being.

"So, people in a lower dimension look like this?"

"Sort of. It's a lot of math."

That figured. It seemed impossible to even fart in this world without computing an integral.

"This is what I looked like when Raynee found me?"

"Yup. Only you moved. They're not supposed to do that."

I stared at them for several seconds, but as she said, not a single one budged or even blinked an eye.

"Do you like her?"

From her broad smile, I knew who she meant. "Yes. I do. A lot."

"So," she asked a bit sheepishly, and pulling her braids, "are you going to marry her?"

It would be a lie to say I hadn't fantasized about that, but at that moment I had no answer. Sareya just stood there with her broad smile.

"From what I hear, she hates me."

"Maybe she does." She grinned. "But if you could marry her, would you?"

I turned away, unable to look her in the eye. "I don't know. I mean, that's a tough question to answer."

"Fine. Do you dream about kissing her under the blankets at night?"

I paused on that one, unsure exactly how much a six-year-old knew about some things. Then when her eyes grew wide at my hesitation, I knew I was making things worse.

"Umm, I'd probably kiss her, but . . . ."

"Raynee told me some things are really disgusting."

This was a barely six-year-old girl I was talking to. I needed to change the subject. "What happens when they die?"

"They rot. It kind of smells bad."

After taking one more look at the ocean of turnips before me, I stared down at my gloves. The turnip patch was interesting, but there had to be far more amazing places out there. A little exploration was irresistible.

"Essonation gloves. You're not supposed to have them." Her arms were crossed and her face was completely serious.

"It was by accident. A kid got scared during essoball."

"So, you opened a portal to here by accident? I was standing above you, remember? You looked around to make sure no one saw you."

"Fine." She had me. "I couldn't resist. There's so much math involved. I needed some help."

"Hand them over." She held her palms out.

I stood there, motionless. Now that I could essonate, it was painful to give them up. Entire universes were literally at my fingertips now.

"I'm asking nicely. Raynee would've hurt you."

Somehow, I didn't doubt that. Yet here I was in another dimension. So far, I'd touched a black hole and finally found turnips. What else was there to explore? Could I find the way back to my old world? My hands felt an edge in the air. There was a portal in front of me.

"Whatever you do, don't use them. I might not be able to follow you. You'll get lost."

"So, it's kind of like hide and go seek?" I smiled.

Her eyes popped and she moved to yell. Before she had the chance, I'd sprung open the portal and was gone. Since this was probably my only chance with the gloves, I had to make it count. Once I was confident the portal was gone, I looked at the new universe around me.

It was nothing but dull brown fog. This wouldn't do. I felt around for another portal and jumped inside.

Water flooded into my mouth and eyeballs, but I held myself calm. Remembering Sareya's lesson, I breathed deeply. Despite being underwater, I was perfectly fine. Nothing could hurt me here.

"Pardon me," a small green fish with a bright yellow underside said, "but you don't appear to be a fish."

Being used to both talking animals and the ability to speak underwater, I smiled. "I'm just a visitor."

"Well, then, do you mind if I live in your mouth and use your tongue as a blanket? I promise not to bite too much."

I wasn't expecting that question, so I began to politely refuse, and when it darted at me, I quickly found another portal and jumped through.

The bright reflection of the beach in the full sun nearly blinded me. After a few minutes of squinting, I looked down the strand. Huge palm trees stood out from the forest just next to me. They were inexplicably turned upside down. There were people strolling down the sands, too, each one with arms for legs and legs for arms. One waved to me. I waved back, then slipped through the next portal.

There was a faint wind and a dark forest of eerie trees. At first, I swore I heard Sareya, but it was just the creaking of limbs, followed by some sort of howling. I walked a distance through the shriveled trees, each with fingered limbs that seemed ready to grab me. Then it attacked.

A gigantic wolf full of snarling teeth jumped from a mound just above. Had I not been several dimensions superior, I would have been wolf food. Instead, I was now left with the disintegrated remains of two bloody paws, half a tail, and a near heart attack.

I sighed. The fun was over. It was time to go home and face Sareya. The truth was, only she knew how to find the interesting places. She'd shown me the intricacies of a black hole, while all I'd managed on my own was an uncomfortable fish and a couple of wolf parts. Maybe I'd been playing this wrong anyway. I nearly strangled myself when I considered that she could have taken me to Raynee. Either way, it was time to leave.

The list of universes passed through my head: wolf and scary trees, weird people and palms, strange fish, and brown fog. I only needed to reverse the order and I'd be home and ready to apologize. After looking every way for more wolves, I turned and felt for the crack back to the previous world. A few anxious moments later, I'd found it. With a sigh, I pulled it open and disappeared inside.

Only this wasn't the beach world. It was something else. There was a grand forest, complete with trees hundreds of feet tall. A cacophony of strange creatures called out from within. I didn't wait to encounter them. Clearly, I'd made a wrong turn. Putting my hands exactly where I'd entered, I returned to the wolf land, but again was somewhere else.

The darkness of empty space hovered everywhere. My breathing became heavier as I searched the nothingness around me. This was a lesson I hadn't learned: Portals only go one direction. I had no idea how to get home.

13

THE COLD, EMPTY space provided the opportunity to clear my thoughts. There were no stars, black holes, or anything else I could discern. There was just infinite black. Every way I tried to put things, I was royally screwed.

One could go a million lifetimes wandering aimlessly among universes, but of course I didn't have that amount of time. In fact, all I really had were a day or two, since I was bound to starve. Raynee never ate when she was with me, because it was impossible to digest anything from a lower dimension. I thought back to the decombulator. That would've come in handy now.

After attempting to jumble the impossible math in my head, I resolved to at least find an improvement in the scenery. A new portal led to a strange world with giant cubes and toads hopping all over them. The next one was a forbidding swamp. After a dozen more attempts, I arrived at a sweeping desert and paused.

It seemed normal, though it wasn't a desert in the typical sense. There were neither sweeping dunes nor camels walking around. There were distant canyons, small patches of grasses, and a skeleton twenty feet away.

On a closer look, the skeleton looked a lot like a cow's. This world didn't seem much different from my own, so I went farther. Far away, I heard voices. I was initially surprised that I could hear them, since they were a good half mile away, but they were clearly human. I understood them.

"They're coming! We should run to the mountains. Get out of here."

"No," an older man replied.

There was something in his tone that prevented the younger one from arguing with him.

After continuing through the scrub for a while, a small town materialized from the sands. The word "town" was probably generous, since it was nothing more than fifteen to twenty scattered domes surrounding a much larger one. Each was carefully constructed of animal skins, while a handful of camels wandered the camp. It felt exciting to see animals again that wouldn't curse at me.

When the first villager caught sight of me, several screams arose, then silence. At first, they seemed completely terrified, running everywhere and stuffing their women and children into the domes. Then the mood changed to curiosity. Three men, one brandishing a curved sword, another too old to carry, and the third too young, stayed by the camp's edge and stared.

When we were only a few dozen feet apart, I halted and held up my palm with the best smile I could muster. "Hello!"

"Who is your father?" the elder one asked.

"I don't know my father."

"What is your purpose here?" The armed one had a wide stance, though I feared more for him. I was still in a lower dimension set, and these seemed like nice people.

"I'm trying to find my way home."

"And where is that?"

"Very far from here." In truth, it was just a few portals away, if I could find them. "Somewhere that's different."

Now I knew how Raynee had felt. A truthful answer would

have blown their minds. We stood there staring at each other for a few uncomfortable minutes. Finally, I raised my hand as if asking a question. The old man nodded.

"I come as a friend. I mean no harm."

"A guest is always a friend," the old man said, and the armed one relaxed.

That was a welcome sight. I'm not sure which I was looking forward to least: seeing a guy split in half when he attacked me, or explaining what had happened to the rest of them.

They led me into the largest dome. It was considerably cooler inside. The floor was strewn with handwoven blankets, and several women with perhaps ten children no older than nine were huddled to one side. The old man poured a hot liquid into a saucer cup. It looked like tea.

Well, this would be awkward. "I apologize. But I cannot accept your drink or food."

"It is offensive here to refuse such an offer," the burly man behind me said. He still had a firm grasp on his sword.

"You traverse our hot lands with no supplies, and you refuse even a cup of tea?" the old man commented.

The temptation to call them turnips was great, but instead I decided to change the subject. "Who's coming?"

Immediately the sword's edge was by my ear and the women and children crowded together in tears.

"Are you one of them? A scout perhaps?" the armed one asked.

I shook my head, and was sweating, but not for my safety. If that sword even grazed me, I'd have a lot of explaining to do.

"Relax, Jamol," the old one said. "The Khan needs no scouts. He'll ride over us like a flower on the desert steppe. This one has strange customs, but he's not one of them."

"As you say, Ilyos."

"Why do they attack you?" I asked once the sword was lowered. "You don't seem to be harming anyone."

"We are not. But one of our brethren has been foolish."

Several children started to cry, and he motioned me to follow him outside of the tent.

"Maybe a day's ride from here, there was a poor villager named Zafar. His parents died early, and he grew up with the cattle. One day, an evil man from far away offered him riches in exchange for a favor. For young Zafar, it was an easy choice to make.

"The man trained Zafar in the ways of assassins, then inserted him into the Khan's most trusted slaves. But when Zafar made his move, he was caught. They tied rope to him and sent horses in two directions. They poured scorpions over his body. In exchange for a quick death, they asked only from where he came. Of course, for poor Zafar, this was an easy choice to make."

"So, what does he have to do with you?"

"We are the lesson." He sighed. "Our people are to be wiped from the Earth as punishment for our tribesman."

The word "Earth" rang in my head. Somehow, of the billions of places I could've landed, I'd wound up here. Yet this was almost certainly a different time. I'd never heard mention of a Khan in the news.

"You should continue your journey," Ilyos said with his head down. "You will receive only death here."

A distant thunder removed both hope and escape. They were still too distant for them to hear, but I knew he was right. Thousands of horses were heading our way. Riders were uttering blood-curdling roars. They weren't trying to be stealthy.

"They're here," I said.

Jamol reached for his blade and ran to the edge of the camp, while Ilyos calmly followed him.

"Put down your arms," Ilyos said when the horde appeared in the distance. The desert turned into dust on their approach. "A strike against the Khan's men is an attack on the Khan himself, even in self-defense."

"They won't spare us," Jamol said.

"No, they won't. But they may offer less painful deaths."

Jamol dropped his sword, as did the handful of other men who were now behind us. They had proud but sad looks as they watched the stampeding mass that dominated the horizon. I considered opening a portal and just leaving, but being on my original planet, even in a different time, made me want to stay. Were Raynee here, she would've sent them fleeing under an army of pink leopards. Once again, I felt the limitations of my own stupidity.

Moments later, they surrounded us. Each horse warrior wore a thin layer of chainmail and brandished a short saber. Bows and arrows weren't drawn. We probably weren't worth the cost. A bear-sized commander with a rolling mustache strode forth. He looked annoyed.

"I was expecting a little fun for my men," he bellowed.

"We are nothing but servants under our Khan," Ilyos said calmly. The commander man snorted, and five horses rushed forth. Ilyos grasped the boy, but the horse lords severed Jamol's head, along with the other men's.

"That's for failing to defend your weak!" the commander howled, and the entire army, covering the whole valley and easily ten thousand strong, roared their approval.

In an instant, the huge man was off his horse and lumbering toward Ilyos. He stopped when he saw me, then turned to look me over. I spread my stance as I'd witnessed Raynee do. While I was incapable of releasing a holy terror, one-on-one none could touch me.

"Don't touch this one. Summon the Khan."

He turned away from me and was now facing Ilyos. The boy was trembling.

The commander signaled and the boy was pulled away, kicking and screaming, into the dome with the other children.

"Your actions indicate an honorable man," the commander said.

"Mercy for our women and children is my only plea," replied Ilyos meekly.

"You will receive a bloodless death. Your friend here will decide the others' fate."

He gestured to me, and the man's eyes grew wide. Then his face filled with terror. He had no chance for words.

Like a giant playing with a doll, the commander yanked the old man's head back, then jammed it forward. Ilyos's body fell, lifeless, to the dusty steppe.

I widened my stance and remembered Raynee. Yet how did she do it? She created out of nothing, but the commander only laughed while I grunted and snorted, but nothing happened.

"Looks like he's still learning," a voice said behind me.

I whirled around to see a middle-aged woman with roughly cut straight black hair. She had a piercing glare and possessed form-fitting clothes, similar to someone from my time. When she walked, her army fled from her path and averted their eyes. She grinned at me, then turned to her commander.

"Burn them all."

"Stop!" I shouted. "Why?"

Screams echoed across the plains when the flares were tossed onto the thatch. I considered running straight through the soldiers. Though I couldn't summon my own demons, I could still cause damage. There were only women and children inside. How could someone do this?

"I'll kill you," I said to her, and meant it.

"I don't doubt you can, but that won't save them."

The screams were growing louder. Every dome was now fully ablaze. There were only moments left now. But what force had Raynee used? How had she controlled everything so effortlessly? It was neither resonance, nor essonance.

Then the cries stopped. Fire had nearly consumed the main

dome, and there was more smoke than flames now. My body felt dead and utterly defeated. They were all dead.

"That's a pity," she said. "I was hoping to see more from you."

I seriously considered shoving my hand down her throat.

"I think you'll want to join us."

"Why would I join you! You killed them! They did nothing to you!"

"No. You killed them. You had the opportunity to save them, but did nothing."

"You're one messed-up bitch to think that." I walked toward her.

Two guards moved forward to protect her, but she waved them off. "Things have never seemed normal to you, have they Jason Bezna?"

I stopped. How did she know my name?

"You knew this growing up in a dimension where you never belonged. The air felt wrong. Every bite of food felt wrong. You never made any friends, because you weren't the same. You never could relate with anyone."

"Maybe. What's it to you?"

"Now you think you've uncovered all the doors. You think you know what's real, but you're still so blind. I'm here to tell you that when you truly wake, trillions of universes will quake at your feet. You are special, Jason Bezna."

14

"HOW DO YOU know who I am?"

"That will become clear in due time."

Well, that sucked. Seriously, why did everyone have to be so cryptic?

She pointed to the domes around us, now completely burned to the ground. Then she took one look at my gloves and laughed.

"Essonance gloves! So that's why you couldn't save them. I take it no one's taught you avalance yet?"

I think someone might have mentioned once what avalance was, but it escaped me. Now I was in a completely different dimension, and still an idiot.

"That's taught in a higher level."

"My dear." She looked me over. "In which level do they have you?"

"Um, level zero."

Ten thousand soldiers had a raucous laugh. That was just great. She moved closer.

"But you don't want to be with those little kids, do you?" She smiled, wide. "You want to be with students your own age, and what better way to prove that you belong than showing you learned avalance all by yourself?"

"I can't stay here." I had no idea why I was even entertaining this. She'd just burned a dozen innocent families alive. Her end goal could not be good.

"You think you'll starve." She gave a haughty laugh and again ten thousand joined in. She hushed them. "Our time moves far differently from yours. A month in our land is but fifteen minutes in yours. I've yet to see someone starve in such a short time."

"And what's in it for you? Why are you so eager to teach me?"

"You'll open that door soon enough, Jason Bezna. My poor child. You're so smart that you don't yet realize where you're completely ignorant."

I didn't know whether to take that as a compliment or an insult. But what could she gain from this? I could leave at any moment, and the fact that even when she approached, she kept her distance told me she ultimately wasn't from my dimension. I had no idea how she knew these things, but she seemed incapable of utilizing them herself.

"If I sense wrong intentions, then I'm gone."

"Well, you have the gloves. However, those essoball gloves are made for a simple game. They're designed to go from one dimension to another. If you want to actually navigate, you still need to do that yourself. So, I'm afraid you're stuck with us. But you have my word that once I feel you've mastered some avalance, I'll teach you how to get home."

"But you're not one of us. How do you know these things?"

She gave a wicked laugh. "It's not time for that door yet. In the meantime, follow us."

This entire thing didn't sound right, but she had a point about the gloves. I couldn't find my way anywhere. Like it or not, she was my only ticket home.

To my surprise, the entire army of ten thousand horsed soldiers intentionally rode at a slow pace so I could follow. Since I hadn't mastered avalance, any attempt to sit on a horse would split it in half.

The Khan rode behind me, and whenever I stopped she raised one hand and ten thousand horses creaked to a standstill. It was more than a little embarrassing, so I quickened my pace and didn't pause. The heat of this place radiated onto my skin, but I didn't feel any effects. Neither were my legs tired, so I just kept going until two hours later we arrived at a town nearly identical to the last one.

Her henchman quickly pulled roughly a hundred villagers, kicking and screaming, from their huts and lined them up in front of me.

Then the Khan spoke. "Avalance for you is actually a native trait. Everyone else in your dimension has to learn it the hard way, but your body's known how to use it since birth."

"They said I had a decombulator."

In truth, I was just curious how much this bitch knew.

"Sort of. I severely doubt your average medic is going to know the intricacies of avalance. They're trained for panic attacks, so a high school education suffices. They haven't spent their lifetimes mastering it."

She leaped off her horse and motioned for one of her henchmen to grab a small boy. His parents broke out in shouts and tears, and in a bit of weirdness, she didn't kill them. Instead, she motioned the boy to the end of the line, and placed the parents at the front.

"It's impossible to make a decombulator that lasts for seventeen years. Now I won't bother you with the math because you don't need it. You're special, Jason, and it's time you learned. Avalance is what keeps things separate. It's why your dimension doesn't completely obliterate mine. To control it requires manipulating every particle individually, then combining them. In its simplest form, it allows you to shake my hand. It gets more complex from there, but today we'll just shake hands."

There was a shriek next to me, and I turned to see the boy's mother flying toward me. Before I had a chance, she reached for my hand and instantly her entire arm disappeared into my torso and a wave of blood spurted out. With one last shriek, she plunged into me and only two dangling bloody legs remained. The father collapsed in tears while the boy sobbed.

"What the—!" I screamed, and moved my gloves to make a portal. A sudden flash destroyed it and threw me to the ground. "How the hell—"

"That was not my power. As I'm sure you guessed, I'm incapable of doing what I ask of you, because I'm of a lower dimension set. Of course, the creators of this universe had to put in a few safeguards, to protect you from your own stupidity. Now, next!"

The huge guard lifted the father to his feet. When he refused to move forward, the Khan pointed at the son and the father nodded. I tried to keep my hand away, but he kept walking until his body was cut in half and the steppe was covered in a warm coat of blood.

"Why are you doing this!"

"Why are *you* doing this? Shake their hands. You've done this a thousand times before. Learn to use your avalance, and we'll spare the rest."

"But I don't know how!" Another villager ran into me and exploded.

"Then remember, or every single one will die."

There was no way out of this. I turned toward the villagers just as another burst into pieces at contact.

"Give me a warning, will you!" I yelled.

"What? Do you not expect there to be bumps and accidents?"

Another one exploded into me, and I sighed and faced them. I held out my hand, which was shaking. The villagers noticed and continued to scream in terror.

I thought back to my parents while another burst apart. I'd touched them plenty of times. They'd probably held me as a baby, or maybe not. After all, I wasn't a tablet. Another damn villager exploded while I was deep in thought. How did I do this?

For the next one, I grabbed her before she reached me, but only succeeded in disintegrating her arm and lungs. I took care of the rest since her eyes were bulging. There had to be some trick to this.

I remembered back to what Raynee had said. Everything was simply bits. They were just turnips. I wasn't seeing these people correctly. That's what my problem was. Every person here was just collections of particles. If I could visualize them as that, then I could keep them away from me.

I closed my eyes and heard another one go splat. No. That didn't work. This wasn't resonance. I opened them again to witness another villager dying. And then I saw it.

All around me were trillions, maybe quadrillions or more, of particles. Though there were so many, I could count them. When the next victim burst, I saw every particle disappear. Each ceased to exist when it ran into me. I had to figure out a way to keep us separate.

Another died while I moved his particles back and forth. That one threw up on me just before he went. Of course, the barf disintegrated too, but I'd caused that. It was progress.

One-by-one, each villager was marched to his or her death while I desperately tried to control the right particles, and enough of them to create a barrier. After an endless stream of agony and cries, only the original little boy was left. He was trembling.

Yet, he was also smaller. There weren't so many particles to correct. While he screamed, I raised my hand to request the guard not to toss him, then walked forward on my own accord. I knelt next to him, and reached out my hand.

The little boy gave me a fierce stare, then held out his hand. With every bit of my concentration, I latched onto every particle on his skin and created a thin coat around them. We shook hands.

When the Khan nodded her approval, the boy pulled his hand back. The guard approached and held out his saber. The Khan shook her head, then approached.

"You're a feisty one, aren't you?" she said with soft words.

He said nothing while his stomach heaved up and down.

"Well, we can't leave you here now, so you'll travel with us. What's your name?"

"Temujin." His eyes were still trained on me.

"Well, little Temujin, I think we'll see great things from you. Don't ever lose that anger."

I wanted so desperately to forget avalance and plunge my fist into her. I was close enough. But I also didn't know my way home.

"And now you know your way back. I'll let you figure out yourself how to get between lower dimensions, but to reach your paramount dimension, just avalate yourself. You'll be right where you started."

I didn't thank her. The methods weren't worth the lesson. After turning away, I looked down and witnessed the narrow band that already separated the dimensions. She was right. My body knew the entire time how to avalate. I just wasn't paying attention. When I pulled those particles away, I was back in the forest. Sareya was gone.

A strange guilt came over me. For some reason I felt far worse about leaving Sareya alone than murdering ninety-odd people. Yet, since I had no idea where she lived, an apology would have to wait for another day.

After walking the short distance to the house, I resonated into the living room to chat with Annie. Annie wasn't home, but she had a visitor.

The piercing brown eyes and wavy brown hair were unmistakable. The tightened fist and clenched teeth were new. It was Raynee, and she was beyond pissed.

15

"YOU ABANDONED A little girl in the woods!" Raynee shouted.

She looked much the same as at the hospital, though for some unquantifiable reason, she was even more beautiful. Maybe it was because back then I was strapped onto a bed, and now I saw her straight on.

"Well! Why the hell did Sareya come back to my house crying?"

I shook myself out of the stupor. "Sareya? She was teaching *me*. How could she get lost?"

"She didn't get lost. She freaked because you essonated away when she explicitly told you not to."

"I wanted to explore. Here, take the gloves back."

I handed her the essoball gloves. Raynee took a moment to cradle them in her hands, then promptly slapped me on the side of the cheek with one. "What were you thinking! And how did you even get these?"

"There was an accident at school. A kid had an attack, and in all the panic I forgot to return them."

"So instead of helping him, you stole the gloves?"

"Actually, I—"

"You're such a liar. I was *nice* to you. Here I was, thinking that maybe I'd been too tough on you earlier, but you played me the entire time."

"I thought I was a turnip. I still don't know why this happened to me!"

"Bullshit. You knew the entire time. It was just some twisted plan of yours to screw me."

I paused for a moment to actually think how that could have possibly worked. She stood there with her arms crossed, and I then realized that my hesitation wasn't helping my cause.

"I traveled to another dimension today," I said. "Someone there knew my name."

"So what? If you alter their minds, they do things like that."

"I didn't mess with her mind. I don't even know how to do that. She taught me how to avalate. I even shook hands with one."

She shook her head. "And how many did you murder before that happened?"

"Well, um—"

"You're one sick asshole. And you're all proud thinking you learned something of a higher level. I knew how to do that in the first level and I didn't kill anyone learning it, you sick jerk."

"I didn't mean to hurt them." I was in near tears. "They threw them at me. I had no choice!"

"You know, I cried myself to sleep that day I accidentally killed that man. Sure, he was a prick, but I never meant to kill him. Had I the chance, I would've just messed with his mind and make him screw a car exhaust. You, on the other hand, just slaughtered I-don't-even-want-to-know-how-many people, and you're completely calm!"

With each villager who had burst apart in front of me, I'd wanted to scream. Being a former turnip myself, I empathized with them more than she could know. However, ever since I reached this place, my only goal had been to be with Raynee. Now she was right in front of me, but farther away than ever. I had to move this to friendlier terms.

"Listen, I'm sorry about everything, but I need your help. There was a desert and some weird woman who knew my name. I need you to help me essonate back to her."

"Help! Is this your latest game to screw me?"

I shook my head, but probably not convincingly. The reality was, though I truly did need her help, another part of me perked up at the idea.

"I did help you, asshole. Who do you think sent Sareya?"

"I thought Annie—"

"No. I sent her!" Her voice went up. "I felt bad for you. Figured you had no clue in this world, so I sent her. Then you ditched her in the middle of the woods."

"I'm sorry I did that. I should've listened to her—"

"Lucky for you she taught you how to avalate back. Otherwise, you would've essonated to random dimensions until you starved."

"Actually, she didn't—"

"You know." Her tears were now streaming. "I thought you were special. When you took Boongarry to the vet, I was very impressed. And then I find out you were playing me."

"I wasn't. I swear. Maybe, maybe if I could go to your school instead of one with little kids . . . ."

She began to laugh. "You're so ridiculous. First, you should be groveling on the floor and begging given the shit you pulled. But no, you ask for a favor. Then you think that a moron like yourself, probably the worst student in level zero, can handle my school? This is making me sick. I'm out of here."

She moved to resonate outside, and I immediately collapsed to the floor and pleaded. "Please! Please, don't go! You have no idea what I've been through. What I lost!"

Her tears stopped, and she wiped the rest away. Raynee's face was stone cold now. "You insensitive piece of shit." Then she was gone.

That did not go nearly as well as I wanted. There had to be some way to fix this. Something about seeing her this way made me feel like the worst piece of excrement in existence. Yet even with an apology, there was no way she'd speak to me ever again. I would also almost certainly not see Sareya again. There was only one place to go for help.

I took out the credit card screen Annie had given me, and began reading the books on essonation for the first time in depth. There was no more of those "it's too complicated" thoughts. After having just rearranged the particles on a boy's hand, dimensional portals couldn't be that bad. I had to figure out how to navigate. There was one woman who could help me. She was an evil sadistic bitch, but she was my only chance now. I had to get back there.

I studied nearly to when school began the next day. Three times the rodents tried to turn off the suns, and each time after I turned them back on, I heard a chorus of insults. Finally, when one threatened to bite my dick off if I didn't turn out the lights, I relented and went to bed.

The next day, I paid every bit of attention while each student produced a wormhole. They weren't the same as dimensional portals, but it was still essonation. Of course, I failed miserably when I attempted to create my own. It was as big as a finger and collapsed immediately. Still, Alina proclaimed that it was a marked improvement.

Several days later, I was beginning to understand the layout of the universes. One individual portal from ours could lead to a billion others from a single spot. Just like with avalance, where I had to deconstruct the individual particles, with essonance I needed to understand and enumerate the possible universes before me, then pick one. That's why Sareya paused before creating a portal, and why the essoball gloves were useless. They had no idea which universe I wanted, so they just picked one.

I practiced creating a dimensional portal to the first universe I found, then avalating back. There was nothing wrong with entering the incorrect universe, but knowing how to reach home was crucial.

Finally, I returned to exactly where I'd left Sareya, and searched for the turnip patch. It was from there that I'd reached the desert world. It took me nearly a half hour of examining every inch of that place before I found it. Then it took another full hour among the turnips until I once again uncovered that hot, bleak world.

I'd never felt so glad to see a cow's skull. I could've hugged the thing. Instead, I wandered toward the ruins of the first village. The Khan and her army wouldn't be there, of course, but I had to start somewhere. The desert was a huge place, and even with my strong hearing it would be difficult to track an army of ten thousand. The village, to my complete surprise, had been completely rebuilt.

Ilyos, Jamol, and the boy stood by its edge when I arrived. I rubbed my eyes. Perhaps this was an evil mirage of the desert?

"Who is your father?" Ilyos asked.

"I have no idea. But, are you Ilyos?"

"Scout!" Jamol shouted, and instantly he was on me. I focused on his hands, carefully pulling each particle out, when his spear flew into my head.

Instantly, the metal and wood burst apart, followed by the rest of Jamol's attached arm. Blood spewed from the stub of the limb, and he gasped for the last time and collapsed into me.

"Damn it all!" I said out loud.

The boy had taken off, yelling and screaming for help, while Ilyos backed away. Only a severed hand and two feet remained of Jamol.

"I'm not a scout. I honestly thought you guys were dead, or I wouldn't have bothered you."

"The Khan sends his demons!" Ilyos shouted, and backed away farther.

"Actually, the Khan is a she."

"Go back to your hell!" He then muttered a variety of spells and incantations while he twirled a blunt staff in front of me.

"Honestly, this whole thing is a huge misunderstanding."

"Now, leave our village and return among the demons!" Then he unexpectedly collided into me with his staff.

I now knew how that man had caught Raynee by surprise. Half of Ilyos's head lay by my feet.

"Double damn!" The remaining villagers huddled into the largest dome.

In my frustration, I hadn't noticed that there were ten thousand horse warriors behind me now.

"Don't touch this one," the same burly man said. "Summon the Khan."

Twenty horses roamed through the camp, but I'd sufficiently scared those inside.

"I expected more from you," a familiar voice said.

I turned to face the Khan. She had the same piercing glare and evil grin.

"Burn them all," she said.

"Seriously! Why do you keep doing this?"

While she exclaimed, again, that it was my fault that they would die, I returned my gaze to the huts and focused on the fire. Yet every time I obtained a bit of concentration on the blazing surface, their tortured cries distracted me.

"Stop screaming!" I yelled a bit insensitively. "I can't concentrate."

Moments later, their cries stopped and two minutes later I learned to control the fire on the main dome and had completely extinguished it. Every other one was now only cinders. Relieved, I approached with a smile, only to find a pile of charred bodies.

"Things have never seemed normal to you, have they, Jason Bezna?"

I rolled my eyes and faced her again.

"You knew this growing up in a dimension where you never belonged."

"Yeah, yeah. We've been through all that already."

"We have?" She seemed slightly confused.

"Yes. You already went through all that crap with the doors and how I haven't opened them all."

"Very well. But you still haven't mastered avalance, so we need to go to the other village."

I groaned, then followed them and patiently waited for the warriors to round up every villager. In the meantime, I breathed deeply and concentrated on their skin. When they were finished, I calmly walked up to the little boy and held out my hand.

"Pleased to meet you." I grasped his hand.

The boy spit at me. Paying no attention, I walked down the line and shook each of their hands. When I reached the parents, I hugged them.

"Watch out for little Temujin. He has a bit of an angry side. Could cause some damage when he grows up."

"He kills seventeen million people," the Khan said.

I double turned.

"The people are real, but this isn't. He grows up to be my most trusted general. Eventually, I convince everyone that he *is* the Khan."

"And he then slaughters seventeen million people?"

"More or less. I never bothered counting them."

"What the hell is with you sick bastards?" I paused. "Did you say none of this is real?"

"What were you expecting when you returned? Let me guess: You pissed everyone off who can help you in the paramount dimension, so you came here."

"Yeah, more or less. But why did everything repeat?"

"This entire universe exists just for you. I already said that you're special."

This was making no sense. It was like a movie that restarted every time I watched. And why would someone create a universe where I murdered villagers? Why couldn't it be something more expendable like leeches or those cursing rodents?

"So, what's today's lesson? Are you going to boil villagers alive and I'll have to piece back their bodies using avalance?"

"Not a bad idea, but no. You still have much work ahead on your avalance, but you may ask any questions you wish."

Well, I sure did have plenty of questions. This was finally the opportunity to answer them all. "Who are my mother and father?"

"I'm sorry. I don't know that."

"Who and where is Mordriss?"

"I don't know that, either."

"I thought you were all knowing?"

"No. I never said I knew the answers. I only gave you permission to ask the questions."

I sighed. Maybe something more personal would work.

"How do I receive forgiveness from a woman?"

Her head drew back and she snorted slightly. "The Khan of a Thousand Armies provides you the opportunity to pose any question, and you ask that?"

"I care for her."

"Well, the answer is . . . you don't."

I squeezed my face with both hands. This wasn't happening.

"A proper woman will never forgive you. She'll bring up your mistakes every opportunity that works for her, until death pulls you apart. However, that won't prevent her from loving you. Whether she loves you or not, depends on what you do after your failures, not on how you attempt to receive forgiveness for them."

I opened my eyes again to the bright sun and gentle breeze of the desert that swirled sand to our sides.

"Who are you?"

"I am nothing," she replied.

Raynee's school returned to my thoughts, along with the badge and the key. Perhaps there was still hope, but I had to face her again, probably several times. There had to be a way in.

"There's a school. It's for the gifted, but there's some secret inside, something I think only I can find. I want to get in. Can you teach me what I need to know? I can keep coming back here."

Her eyes grew narrow and she stroked her chin with her hand. "I know this school. But you would need to spend years here, and even then there's much that I can't teach you. Only avalance and orasance can be practiced in this world. The other forces, and a great many other things, can only be learned in yours."

"Then it's hopeless?"

"You disappoint me. There are *other* ways."

She put particular emphasis on the word "other," and I was beginning to not like this. After all, how many had died so I could learn avalance? The Khan motioned for me to join her, and the mass of horse warriors spread to create a straight path before us.

"Oreca gifted has very formidable defenses. Because they change constantly, I cannot help you there."

Well, this was starting to sound useless.

"But, if you do happen to defeat them, the final challenge is so insurmountable that you will only pass it if Algard himself wishes. He is the headmaster of Oreca Gifted, and even though you won't see him, he'll hear anything you say."

"So, do I tell him a joke, then?"

She gave me a look that would've been accompanied by a slap had that been dimensionally possible.

"There's something Algard desperately wants. He lost it long ago, and that may be enough for admission."

"What is it?" I leaned forward.

"I have no idea. But if you do happen to find it, show it when all hope is lost."

I nodded. Well, that was a wasted effort. All I had to do was pass defenses that even a smart person from here couldn't manage, then find something without a description or place. She'd answered none of my questions. All the time reaching here was wasted. I'd learned nothing, and it was time to go.

"One last question," I asked just before I avalated home. "Who built this place?"

She smiled. "The same person who placed you on Earth."

16

IT HAD BEEN obvious since I arrived in the paramount dimension that someone was responsible for placing me on Earth, the validation of that fact still gave me the chills. Who was this person? Was he or she my mother or father? Why? The Khan had none of the answers.

I considered staying there longer to learn more about avalance, but too many thoughts were racing across my head. There was a reason why I was placed on Earth. That was for sure. I had to discover the truth, and that would require help.

"So, who taught you to avalate?" a squeaky voice said when I returned.

Sareya, with her blue eyes brighter than ever, was standing directly above me. My neck ached when I looked directly up at her.

"I figured you wouldn't be allowed to talk to me."

Raynee was already pissed beyond relief at me. Turnip or not, she was still capable of killing me.

"My question first." She folded her arms.

"It's a bit of a strange story. I wound up in this desert. A woman there taught me."

"A turnip?" She continued with the folded arms.

"Now my question."

"Fine," she said with a whine. "Yeah, Raynee forbade me from talking to you. When you disappeared, I was scared you would die."

It was becoming difficult chatting to someone directly over me. I was cracking my neck, so she gave a disgruntled sigh and resonated in front of me. Her arms were still crossed, and I knew it was my turn.

"Listen, I'm sorry about leaving you. I shouldn't have done that. You were only trying to help me."

"Agreed. But that wasn't my question."

I laughed. "Yes. She was a turnip. No. I have no idea how a turnip would know that, but it was really strange. She knew my name."

We stood there staring at each other uneasily for a few moments.

"So, if Raynee forbade you . . .?"

"She's not my mother. And I was curious. Now, how much avalation do you know?"

"Well, I know how to avalate back from a portal."

"Yes." She groaned. "Everyone knows how to do that."

Again, I had to remember that this six-year-old was likely more brilliant than the best of Earth's physicists.

"I didn't learn too much. All I did was shake hands and hug a turnip . . . And I put out a fire."

Her face lit up. "That's more than I know. Could you teach me?"

In a world where people could walk upside down, go through walls, create wormholes, and travel to other dimensions, the idea that this little girl would actually ask *me* to teach her something was almost ridiculous. There was no way I knew something she didn't.

"We could trade," she added, noticing my hesitation. "I could teach you orasance."

I jumped back. "I thought they only teach that in the fifth level."

"Yeah. But not because it's complicated. You just need to be mature. That's why they wait, but I kept waking Raynee up at night until she taught me."

"I'm not much of a teacher." I paused. "Why doesn't Raynee teach you?"

"Well"—she kicked up some dirt—"she's kind of worried. With avalance, if you're not careful, turnips can die."

That was just great. I didn't have the heart to admit that I'd already killed about a hundred of them. Then again, since they kept reappearing, did they ever actually die? But there was the real possibility that Raynee would murder me herself when she discovered I'd taught Sareya avalation.

"But I won't kill any! I promise! I only want to meet some turnips, like she met you."

Visions popped into my head of entire civilizations wiped out due to her mistakes, their leaders ruing this very day, when I taught her incomplete avalance. If I was going to do this, I'd have to raise the stakes.

"How about I teach you what I know about avalance, and you help me with Raynee?"

She shook her head. "You're beyond hope with her. Stick to the possible."

The reality that it was simpler to teach me to communicate with the dead than to put a few nice words in to Raynee crushed my soul. "Very well." I bowed. "You have a deal."

Since I was doubtful that she'd enjoy ripping apart villagers, I made no offer to visit the Khan. Instead, she chose a simple universe that consisted of nothing but fruit trees. There were vast forests of them, billions of planets covered with every kind of fruit, none of which anyone would ever eat.

With the pressure on, I felt a bit nervous while she watched me pick what appeared to be a blue banana. Yet, dealing with an object that wasn't human proved a much easier task. Its particles were simpler to control, and within a minute I was juggling it.

"So how do I do it?" she asked.

A good question. Only then did I realize why it took a little girl to teach me resonance. It was like telling someone how to walk. Several times I started to explain, only to stop because nothing was making sense. Soon, she was tapping her foot impatiently.

"So, you know how things are made of particles?"

She just gave me a "you've got to be serious" look. I might as well have been teaching playwriting to Shakespeare.

"You've got to visualize each particle. It's kind of like seeing things with resonance, only once you see them that way, you can change them."

For several minutes she held her hand out and stared at a fruit. When she finally grasped it, half went missing. Immediately, she shrieked, threw her hands up, and took out several more branches. Out of sympathy, I lifted the entire trunk from the ground with my mind and planted it elsewhere. Sareya's eyes grew wide, and she stood mesmerized before me.

"How did you do that!"

"I just visualized down to the roots." Yet the truth was I had no idea. For some reason, avalance just clicked with me. Essonance was still troubling, yet the Khan was right. My body just knew how to avalate.

"What do you mean by visualize? What's the math?"

I had to think for a bit on that one, and again I sensed her frustration. Yet, somehow, I did know the math. I only didn't know the terms. After some vague explanations, she started to understand, and even named the concepts. Somehow, my mind had accumulated a better mathematical acumen than I'd ever dreamed.

After she destroyed another dozen fruits, Sareya was again on the verge of a tantrum.

"It's like the fruit wants to die!"

"I needed a hundred." I left out that they were people.

She wiped away a tear and tried again. Within minutes, the tree was bare. I grabbed her hand.

"Don't rush things. Concentrate on each one."

I was a bad student, and a far worse teacher. We went through nearly an orchard that day, but the best she managed was to convince a fruit to wobble before exploding. Had we been in the desert, there would have been no more villages.

"I know you're saying the right stuff." We were both exhausted. "But I don't know how you make it so easy."

"Like Raynee?" I grinned.

"No." She gave me a serious look. "Don't get too confident. She's still way better."

Sareya was certainly right about that. While I had moved a tree, she'd created entire armies from scratch. I still had no idea how to make things. I could only keep them from disintegrating.

We retired with the agreement for an orasance lesson the next day.

Annie joined me for dinner. She'd been a bit of a recluse since we'd discussed her son, but now for the first time her face wasn't red with tears. Our table hung from the ceiling, which still gave me enough vertigo that, after a sigh, she moved it to the floor.

"I've learned a lot. Resonation is easy now. I can essonate portals. I can even avalate a tree out of the ground, and I'm going to learn to orasate soon."

"Yes." She nodded. "You're moving along. If you learn to create a wormhole, maybe we can move you up a level."

Not long ago, I would have jumped and danced at that prospect. Now I wanted far more, and there was still one force missing.

"What's the last force?"

She looked away. "Cenosance."

"When will I learn that?"

"Hard to say." She continued to look elsewhere. "If you go to university, maybe there. I've heard the gifted students learn it in the last year. You have to be careful with that one. It can cause some real damage."

"What does it do?" The thought of carnage interested me only more.

"To be honest, I never progressed far enough to learn it. The problem is, if you're not careful it can consume you." She turned her focus back to me. "But right now, you should worry more about wormholes. Without them, you can't travel."

I shook my head. It hadn't dawned on me that there were other interesting places in this universe. Since the neighborhood had already blown my mind, I couldn't imagine what lay in store beyond it.

"You know this entire universe is one big planet, right?"

My euphoria about not being an idiot was gone. Not only did I not know this, but I hadn't even noticed that there were no stars in the sky.

"So, you can travel light years in any direction. But, of course, you know with the speed of light, what seems like a few minutes in a ship can turn into several years."

This sounded like something simple enough to learn on Earth, but again I had no clue.

"The wormhole . . . It allows me to go back?"

"Yes." She had a content look because I finally understood. "Back to your time." She looked toward a nonexistent window. "Raynee has to create one every day. Her school is two light years away."

The thought of her school brought back my plight. Given how intelligent Raynee was, her professors were probably the top geniuses of the universe. Perhaps one of them could help me find my parents? I only needed to locate it.

"Can anyone visit Oreca Gifted?"

She grinned and shook her head. "No. If you're planning to surprise Raynee, it won't work. The location is well known. Any craft can find it. But you'll find it quite difficult to get inside. That school has . . . protections. Ordinary people like you or me would never get in."

"What do you mean?" I was hoping for any hints. "Is there some resonation field around it?"

She laughed. "I really have no idea, honey. When I was little, the smartest boy in our school traveled there. Like you, I think, he wanted to enroll there. He'd heard a legend that one only has to walk through the door. When he came back, he said there was just a field. He couldn't even see the school."

This was a setback, but maybe not a permanent one. The Khan had said there would be obstacles. First, though, I had to learn wormholes.

"About wormholes, if you can go into the future, how . . .?"

"How do you not run into yourself? Sometimes you do. It happened to me once, and was a bit awkward. You never learn anything, though. That you is in an alternate timeline. What you learn from that you, won't necessarily happen in your own life. In fact, it can be a lot worse. Sometimes people find out the future them died. So, most of us just try hard not to do it."

The next day, I found myself the proud creator of a wormhole. The entire class clapped while I entered my side and came out the other. Even Alina was impressed, and after class she mentioned the possibility of moving up to level one after a few weeks. Only, I intended to move much quicker.

"Do you know what cenosance is?" I asked Sareya when we met. It was at a cemetery, so any small talk was worth it. The thought of entering the realm of the dead was unsettling enough.

"I asked Raynee that once. She didn't know back then, but I think she's going to learn soon."

She resonated open a gate and we entered a vast yard of tombs. Other than being a bit more compact, it didn't seem too different from those on Earth. The graves had almost identically-sized tombstones, about three feet high of polished stone. Each rectangular-shaped grave contained the name of the deceased, without a surname, and a list of loved ones below. The graves were close to each other, but each contained a small stepping stone before it. There was only one fundamental difference. On top of each gravestone was a bone.

Most were small, probably from the hand or a piece of the spine. According to Sareya, the size of the fragment didn't matter. Orasance was always the same.

"So, who will it be?" she asked.

The question freaked me out a bit. Surrounded by their bones, I now fully realized that these were actual people. In a few moments, I would enter their most private moments. It didn't seem right.

"Is any of your family in here?"

She stopped for a moment at the question, and I suddenly realized it was a bad one.

"My great-grandmother isn't far from here. My parents and grandparents are in the restricted section now. After your friend in the essoball game . . . they resonated them closed. So, I just visit her now."

"Mordriss?" I asked, though I didn't want to.

"Yeah. I was a baby then. I was sleeping and my mother threw a blanket over me, so I guess he didn't see me."

"I'm sorry."

She shrugged her shoulders. "It's not like you did it. I just hope he's gone now. Anyway, it's time to freak you out."

We picked someone she'd visited before, but didn't know. She said his life had been relatively boring, which made orasation a bit easier.

Sareya had to explain the math to me five times before I grasped the basics. The trick was understanding the patterns of particle behavior, and then deconstructing them step-by-step. Once I had calculated where they should be at a particular time, it only required closing my eyes and visualizing where they must have been earlier. It was in truth less complex than the other forces, since there was no way to control orasance. One could only use it for a ride.

We both placed a hand on top of the bone, and I instantly latched onto each particle. It took some moments to calculate where each had been the moment before, but after a minute or two the math came more naturally, and not long after we were immersed in a world embedded in our imagination filled with places I'd never seen and people I would never meet. The effect was a bit like seeing someone with resonation, only from a different part of the brain.

Our subject, whose name was Turgen, had been so boring during his old age that Sareya cautioned me against going there. His childhood had been more interesting, and in moments we were in a bright field with twenty screaming kids. As we walked through the playground, various kids disappeared into dust and reappeared.

"We can only see what he saw. Orasance is weird that way."

Sure enough, the entire landscape disintegrated and reanimated with each glance from Turgen. Suddenly, every kid fell from the view but one, a tiny girl with short, braided hair.

"Do you want to join me on the resoslide?" she asked.

Turgen remained still, but shaking. Finally, he returned a nervous nod and stepped forward.

"He eventually marries her," Sareya said.

In a flash we were in a bright green field. There, a clean-shaven man with a broad smile was tossing a baby into the air. His wife lay next to them, with her long blond hair spread across the grass and her bright blue eyes admiring the pair.

"This isn't right," Sareya said with a stammer. "This is my head now."

"How do I stop it?" I asked. We could speak to each other, but it was like talking through an intercom.

"That's fine. I like this part. It's how I remember them."

The baby Sareya giggled each time she reached the air, but the longer we watched the more peculiar the scene became. I couldn't narrow it down, but there was something odd about her eyes. I walked slowly over to her father, then stooped to see her face better. The scene changed to indoors.

We were in what seemed like a house. Sareya lay in a wide bed, while her mother frantically moved about the room. Her long blond hair was frazzled, and she started throwing clothes into a large suitcase she'd avalated, then she shook her head and in a snap everything in the room was gone.

"It's too late," her father said through quick breaths after resonating into the room. "He's here."

"This isn't right!" the Sareya I knew yelled. "We shouldn't be watching this. But I can't make it stop!"

I knew instantly who "he" was. Rapid calculations flew through my head to undo this, but no matter how much I tried, the scene continued. Her mother threw a blanket over the baby and everything got hazy.

Although the baby Sareya could no longer see with a blanket over her head, she could still resonate, but it was so weak there were only the dull shapes of her mother and father with their faces turned away. Then there was a third.

"We have to go now!" Sareya yelled. "I don't want to see this."

Her breathing quickened, but neither of us could stop the scene. Who was doing this?

"Tell me the math," I pleaded. "How do we get out of here?"

"Well, well, leaving, weren't we?" a cold voice said.

"I don't know!" Sareya cried. "It won't let me stop!"

"What do you want?" her mother asked through a sob.

The third shape gave a quick laugh, then said, "How kind of you to offer. As a matter of fact, I do want something."

The three stood there for a moment while Mordriss just glared at them. Other than being slightly taller, I couldn't make out any details. They were just long blobs.

"There's a certain artifact I understand to be in your possession. I understand Algard may have given it to you."

"Algard the headmaster?" Sareya's father asked. "We've never spoken, but whatever you want, it's yours."

"We need to go!" Sareya shrieked, but no matter how much I tried to reverse the particles and go back, nothing happened.

"It's a very simple badge with 'Oreca' on the front. On its back is a key. It's very special to Algard, which is why of course I must have it."

I stopped trying to go back. Had he just described my badge?

Both parents shook their heads. "Please!" her father pleaded. "I've never seen it."

His wife screamed as Mordriss tossed her across the room with resonation and pinned her against the wall.

"She will suffer." Mordriss was dead calm. "And you will watch."

Sareya's father fell to the floor. "Please! Please!" he pleaded. "If I knew this item, it would be yours. We have nothing but each other."

Mordriss gave a long laugh, then dropped Sareya's mother.

"I believe you. Of course, you don't know."

Both parents were breathing heavily now, but gave long sighs. Then their movement stopped as Mordriss cracked his knuckles.

"But I'm sure you're aware from past precedent that it doesn't matter."

Sareya's mother gave a bone curdling shriek as her form began to crumble together, and the Sareya I knew was sobbing. There had to be a way out. She couldn't witness this again.

With every bit of my energy I strove to reverse the particles, and slowly the screams fell to oblivion and Sareya and I were together in the cemetery.

Though my first priority was to comfort the crying little girl before me, I now knew what I had to do. Entering Oreca Gifted no longer worried me. Whoever gave me that key wanted me to go there, and I suspected the real terrors awaited inside.

17

I HELD SAREYA through her tears for some time. It seemed a crime that horrible events like these were preserved in this world to experience over and over again.

When I bid her farewell, it was time to strategize. Mordriss had mentioned the very same key that someone had bestowed on me. Though I still had no idea what it unlocked, it was now both my ticket into school and a liability. If Mordriss did return, I now possessed what he wanted most, and someone knew I had it.

I needed a vehicle for a trip two light years away. Annie had one, but would she let me borrow it? Most people built their own, but I had neither the know-how nor the time to do so. There was only one choice.

"Annie, may I borrow your ship?" I asked at dinner.

The poor woman nearly choked on her pasta. "My dear, I'd be happy to take you wherever you'd like, now that you can create your own wormhole."

"I kind of need to go there myself." My head was down. There was no hiding it. "I want to go to Oreca Gifted."

She shook her head and chuckled. "There's nothing to see, my dear. I already told you. It's just a field. That's all simple folk like us will ever see."

"I need to speak with a professor there. His name is Algard."

She was briefly motionless, then said, "I see."

"Do you know him?"

She slowly shook her head. "No. Not personally, but he's the school's headmaster."

Annie stood and resonated outside. I followed.

"Yes. You may borrow the ship. I've never heard of anyone getting inside without an invitation, but who knows." She looked at me and smiled. "You're already unusual."

Annie handed me the credit card.

"The ship already knows where the school is. You can leave now, dear, but have it plot a course to arrive in the middle of the school day. Good luck."

Annie watched while I constructed a wormhole, then verified that it was correct. With one half of the hole next to the house, and the other inside the ship, I had my ticket home. One side would travel with me, while the other would remain, though that wasn't my primary concern. How exactly was I going to enter a school that didn't want to be found?

When I entered the silvery flying Volkswagen, I suddenly realized that I had no idea how to fly this thing. There were no controls, nor was there a screen anywhere. Only a few chairs and a glistening white floor adorned the inside. Given that I was about to request enrollment in the most advanced school in the universe, it seemed more than a little embarrassing to ask for instructions.

"I need to fly to Oreca Gifted, arriving in the afternoon," I said out loud.

Nothing happened.

I closed my eyes and felt the entire vehicle resonating to me. There were no wires, controls, or machinery on board. The craft itself was no more complicated than a cardboard box. It only looked a bit nicer. Frustrated that I'd been defeated on such an elemental step, I exited to search for Annie. Only, she wasn't there, nor was her house.

A bright green field stretched for several miles in either direction. The sky was deep blue, and I was midway up a tremendous but gently inclining hill that dominated the view. The grass was similar to that on Earth, but every blade was straight and utterly perfect with a tiny drop on each tip. A small pillar poked out from the top of the hill.

I walked a few steps up, and noticed that my path had ruined the hill's perfect texture: Each drop had fallen and the grass was downtrodden where I'd walked. There were no other steps in sight.

Was this a test? Perhaps, but at the very least I could try not to make a mess, so I concentrated on levitating myself just above the blades, then floated to the top. The pillar was a large plaque.

DARVALDUS, FOUNDER – ORECA GIFTED

So, I was in the right place. In absolutely no time, in a manner I still didn't understand, Annie's ship had gotten me here. Yet, just as she had said, this memorial was the only thing in sight. Remembering what Sareya had taught me, I closed my eyes again and felt everything around me.

There was no wind. Each blade of grass was motionless. There were no animals for miles, and trees were only in the far distance. Underneath the ground was a body.

I jumped back, then stared at the plaque. Since I could now handily see underground with resonation, I glimpsed the corpse just below. This was the founder's grave, only there was no bone fragment outside to touch.

Of course, this was a test. Certainly, every entering student would be expected to know resonance, essonance, avalance, and orasance. There was only one way inside, and it was disgusting. I would have to visit the founder.

I'd never used resonance on anything but warding off squimmers, so it took a few minutes of concentration to grasp every piece of dirt that surrounded the decayed body. Who knew how long it had been there, but I was about to see for myself. The last thing I wanted to do was explain why I'd broken the founder's corpse on the first day, so I carefully lifted each clump of dirt as the body returned to the surface.

At last, what floated before me were the ancient bones of someone who could've incinerated me with the snap of a finger in real life. The hair and clothes were long gone, though a few pieces of flesh still hung from the browned skeleton. Being as delicate as I could, I reached up and touched it and blink! I was in a classroom, where Darvaldus was lecturing about avalance.

The room was dusky, and the stout man, so old that he needed the pulpit for support, was going into the intricacies of biologics. It sounded interesting, but the math was way above my level. Where did I need to go? Since Darvaldus was the founder, he must have hidden the school. I only needed to find the right day.

Recalling one of the few times I paid attention in class back on Earth, I utilized a binary search. Since on this day the school was already built, I went far back to when he was a third-level child. All I needed to do was keep dividing the time in half, and I'd find the day.

As a child, Darvaldus was shorter, but otherwise looked mostly the same. Then I was again back in a dank classroom. A few teachers sat in the back, while several rows of mostly bored students listened to the founder give a lecture on the avalance of biologics. Word-for-word the material was the same. This guy was even brighter than Raynee.

As I moved back and forth through his life, I found that he spent the overwhelming majority of his time teaching. It wasn't all avalance. There were advanced courses on resonance, where he discussed how to communicate with other living things by constructing sound waves. He discussed theoretical aspects of orasance, or how to control it if it were controllable. Finally, he covered some crazy uses for essonance, including nested wormholes and dimensional portals that allowed same-dimension-set travel—or basically moving turnips across them. The only thing he didn't touch on was cenosance.

At last, I reached a middle age Darvaldus standing in the same field as I. He stood exactly where the monument now lay, and held out his hands wide.

"Our world needs a school!" he shouted into thin air. "Where the brightest of every time can challenge their wits, and be pushed to their limits. Yet such an institution needs protection. It must remain an imperceptible entity from those not worthy of it. Only those accepted into its hallowed walls may venture here, and so on this day, I shall hide it!"

I moved forward and watched patiently while he just stood there. In just a few moments, I would know the secret. Then, I would be walking in those exact hallowed walls.

"Now! Pay attention, and I shall do it!"

That seemed an odd thing to say. There was no one for miles, or at least that he saw.

"Doop! Dee dop! Dop. Doop doop doop. Ya ka woop!"

He was now dancing with his arms in the air across the field. After completing a full loop around me, Darvaldus faced me directly.

"You didn't think it would be this easy, did you?" he asked.

I searched around me for another person, but there was no one.

"Well? I'm speaking to you."

"To me?" How this could be happening?

"You didn't seriously believe digging up a grand master was going to work, did you?" He was scratching his chin with his gaze right into me.

"How are you doing this?"

"While time can't change, it's certainly doable for those who know how to reorganize particles a bit. This prevents overzealous applicants from digging up my bones for the answers to their own deficiencies."

"So, you made all of this up?"

"Of course! Did you finish any of my lectures?"

"Um, no."

"Yeah. Pretty boring shit, wasn't it?" He winked. "Almost as much a waste of time as disinterring my bones."

"You won't give me even a little hint?"

The old man approached me, then peered into my eyes and lifted my palms. "You're a pretty stupid one, aren't you? Just learned wormholes yesterday, right?"

I stepped back.

"Well, off you go. Back to where you came. Just don't mess up my field when you leave. And put my body back where you found it!"

The orasance session ended. I was standing at the top of the hill, alone. His bones still hovered above me, though not by his doing. His mouth was crooked as if sneering, but in this world he was long dead. With no one watching, I gingerly placed the skeleton back in the hole and covered it. Even the blades of grass were returned, along with their dew drops.

I groaned out loud. How else could I get in? There was nothing in sight. The school did a perfect job of not being found. Darvaldus had thought of everything, or had he?

Certainly, there was a way for actual students to enter. I thought back to his lectures. How many people spent hours, maybe even lifetimes, trying to listen to them all? Yet Darvaldus himself had dismissed them. He wasn't looking for memorization maniacs. He wanted those who saw what others couldn't.

I wasn't going to leave this field until I figured it out.

I noticed it. The path I had earlier traversed was gone. Every blade of grass was straightened. Every dew drop was replaced. For someone as brilliant as Darvaldus, that must have been intentional. I then realized, he *had* given me a hint! I wasn't to mess up his field.

While still hovering, I lay down and examined one of the blades in detail. Other than being completely straight, there was little difference from standard grass on Earth. The dew drop, though, did look a little strange. The blade ended in a tiny point, as thin as a needle. How did it manage to balance?

What if the school were in an alternate dimension? After holding my palms out for a few moments, I felt the edges of a portal and popped through. Again, I found myself in a classroom hosted by none other than Darvaldus.

"Today, our lesson is on the avalation of squimmer shit." Recalling that they were a cross between a squirrel and a mermaid I'd encountered my first day, I resolved there was nothing to see here.

I exited to another world, which covered the metaphysics of squimmer shit in a wormhole. Yet another was populated entirely by squimmers, which each shit every three seconds. A final world contained laughing squimmers and excrement flying in every direction. I got the point. Darvaldus had thought of that angle, too. Every single dimension reachable from this place involved squimmer shit.

Yet I knew the school was here. Could it be invisible? I considered wandering the field, but it couldn't have been that easy. I was more likely to run into invisible squimmer shit than any building. No. It was here, in this dimension, and wasn't invisible.

I stooped back to the dew drops. They were the most unusual thing here, but why was I so concerned about balance? There was no gravity, so if the drop wanted to resonate on the grass tip, nothing prevented that. But why would every blade have a drop? And then I knew.

Somehow, Darvaldus had placed the school inside one of the drops. There was no other place. I remember a science teacher once telling me "When all the possibilities are exhausted, consider the impossibilities." The only question was, which one?

I did a few calculations in my head. If the field stretched for five miles in each direction, though it seemed more, then there were approximately one hundred and thirty-trillion dew drops. A simple investigation wouldn't work. There had to be another way.

Could resonation work? I closed my eyes, and tried to sense which drop was different. There was no wind. Every blade was the same. I was onto something. The drop I was seeking would have a nearly imperceptible difference in vibrations. This wouldn't be easy.

For some reason, I felt myself thinking of Raynee. Her face was before me, urging me to be calm. I could do this. I felt the blades nearest to me, the trees miles away, and everything in between. Complete peace was required. Which blade was wobbling, not even a micron more, because its dew drop contained something different? I reached out my arms and became part of the field. Every grass blade became my intimate friend. I felt it.

Less than a half mile away was a drew drop a billionth of a gram heavier than the others. The school must be there. I resonated to it. Then it was gone.

Of course, they had to cover for someone walking over it. The entire institution couldn't be toppled by a rampaging two-year-old. The drop changed its location upon approach. How could I enter it, then?

I had to make myself smaller. Actually, it was even worse. Once that small, the distance across the field would be tremendous. Both myself and Annie's ship needed to shrink. We hadn't covered that in school, and I was fairly certain it was a more advanced subject. I was screwed.

Or was I? This was a simple scaling operation. Just like I could resonate objects from one place to another, I could reduce the empty space within them. The mathematics were accessible. The only thing was, I would have to do this to myself. One miscalculation, and all that would remain of me would be a microscopic blood stain on a blade of grass.

There was so much at stake: my real parents, Raynee, my future. It was worth it.

With a last gulp, I returned to the ship and concentrated on scaling down. After a few tense moments, I was hurtling along in a sea of green.

Again, I felt for the different drop, then imagined a path toward it. I figured that must be how the ship worked. No speech recognition was necessary. It just knew. At this size, the drop loomed as a behemoth, but again it disappeared.

I had to be smaller. Shrinking myself so miniscule that I felt myself passing out, I again located the drop and navigated forward. Now there was a tiny opening on the front, a trillionth of a human hair wide. My heart pumped rapidly as I slid through.

There was nothing. I was in the depths of space. Ahead were the stars of a billion galaxies. The school had its own universe. I was such a fool. There was no possible way I'd find it, even in a billion years.

I sat there for some time, just pondering the stars and hoping to find some pattern. The last time I'd been in space had been with Sareya. She'd given me everything I needed to know. Nearby was a black hole, so massive that it was swallowing an entire galaxy.

I exited the ship and felt the gravitational waves vibrating into me. It was the song of the end of entire planets and civilizations. Yet just like anything in this universe, it could be manipulated. If I changed it just right, I could use it to send a message.

"Algard," I said through twisting the black hole, "I have your badge with key."

No more than a few seconds passed before one star of the many brightened. Just as the Khan had said, Algard was listening. Here was my beacon.

A few moments later, I was parked in front of what appeared to be your standard high school built on its own artificial moon, with the purple hue of a nearby nebula dominating the sky, in a universe built explicitly for it.

A disheveled man with a wide mustache and gray suit stood outside the school. Another professor, heavyset and dark in complexion, was next to him. Without a word, they ushered me into a bright room.

He gave me his hand. "Algard," he said, then allowed an uncomfortable pause. Then: "We know who you are, Jason. Your story has been most interesting, but this place is not for you."

"So, you know who my parents are?"

"No," the other said. "We know as much as you, but like you are curious for more." He reached out his hand. "I'm Darstan, by the way."

I happily shook it, then remembered why I was there. "I'd like to enroll at your school."

They both laughed, with Darstan slapping me on the shoulder. "You've barely learned wormholes. Go through the levels, and maybe we'll see you in a few years."

"But I found your school."

"True," Algard replied. "You have promise, I'll give you that. But there's simply too much you don't know. You're better off where you are."

They both stood.

"Now, we don't need to be rude," Algard said, "but you can imagine we're quite busy here. It was a pleasure meeting you, Jason. I'm sure our paths will meet again."

This wasn't going as I planned. There was only one hope now. "I have this for you." I flung the badge with key onto the table.

They both sat and stared at me with an eerie silence.

"Am I supposed to be impressed?" Algard asked.

Darstan laughed and tossed an identical badge on the table. "I have one of those, too."

"But, I thought Mordriss took yours?"

I did not expect to suddenly be a pancake on the wall behind me. In one blast of resonance, I was thrown there, while Algard approached with a frown.

"That's a very strong accusation. And who led you to believe this? Tell the truth, now. I'll know if you're lying."

"I accidentally orasated Sareya. It wasn't on purpose but . . . I saw Mordriss kill her parents after mentioning this. He said you lost it."

The resonance blast ended, and I fell toward the floor, then predictably wound up on the ceiling. Algard lifted my badge.

"This artifact has no purpose." He pulled out the key. "Have you seen any doors here? There's nothing to unlock, and were there a need anyone could easily avalate the key. As a prospective student, you should know that."

"None of this makes any sense!" I buried my head into my hands. "I don't know anything. Who put me on Earth? Why didn't I grow up here? Where are my actual parents? It's not just that I'm desperate to go to school here. I need help. I need answers."

Algard motioned to Darstan, and the two resonated outside. They must have placed some resonation shield up, because I had no chance of overhearing them. After five minutes that felt like eons, they returned. Algard had a smug look, while Darstan appeared most displeased.

"Very well, Jason," Algard said with his hands at his sides. "You've shown some aptitude in finding us, but I warn you that this school is of a level for which you're completely unprepared. Most likely, your determination is about to destroy you. Yet, I feel there's a tiny probability you'll prove truly special. We'll just have to see."

I stayed seated, still unsure what he was saying.

"Welcome to Oreca Gifted, Jason. You will receive no mercy here."

18

ALGARD HANDED ME a homing signal that enabled my ship to find the school easier the next time, and I floated out of the school and into my wormhole as if in a dream. Had I finally managed it? I'd enrolled in the most prestigious school in the universe!

Instead of Annie, a quintet of the spotted rodents greeted me on the other side.

"Hey asshole, do you have any more of those fucking beans?"

I was still in so much of a stupor, that I failed to notice their language.

"Uh, yeah." I lumbered inside, still in a trance.

When I handed them a healthy pile of beans along with a few other fruits and vegetables, the largest one approached me, his mouth nearly full.

"So, what the fuck is wrong with you?"

"I just got into the best school in the world!" My eyes were toward the sky.

"Oh, fuck!"

"Yeah, I know. Amazing, isn't it?"

"Fuck, no." He finished the last bean. "You're a fucking moron.

They're going to kill you, and then we won't have any more fucking food."

My stupor ended. "Why do you swear so much?"

"We don't swear, you rotting dingleberry. You're just too much of a shit fucked idiot to fix your translator."

They disappeared, so I resonated inside to find Annie.

"I got in!"

She nodded, but didn't seem overly excited. When I said we'd discuss it over dinner, she replied that we'd just eaten only minutes ago. In all my excitement, I hadn't kept track of the time change. Due to the wormhole, barely a few minutes had actually passed. In some ways, this made school even more exciting. Little of the day would be wasted. Then I remembered her ship. I'd left it at school.

"Don't worry about that, dear. You'll see it tomorrow."

It felt completely alien to be so enthusiastic for a school day, but that was my state. I promised to tell her something about cenosance when I learned it, but she advised me to spend less time celebrating and more reading up on things like avalance.

The next day, I clapped the suns on, wolfed down two lammas, and found the credit card ship awaiting me in the living room. I paused for a moment to consider how it came back, but for all I knew she created a new one. Maybe there was some planet by the school, full of discarded ships. Regardless, I was too excited to dwell on needless details like those. I applied my homing signal, and in an instant I was cruising next to that familiar purple nebula.

A crowd of students was already walking in, so I quickly joined them. When I smiled at everyone, I received frowns in return. There were a few whispers out of my reach, and none bothered to look my way. I didn't see Raynee, but she was probably already inside. Algard stood in the hallway with a grim look.

"Advanced resonance," he said when I passed. "Resonate below us. Take a right."

My day was already starting well. Of all the forces, resonance was the easiest. In fact, I'd already demonstrated it quite well in finding the school. I was ready.

I mistook my first professor for a Halloween decoration. With her long gray hair and gaunt face, I foolishly looked for what held it up when her mouth opened.

"Sit down, Jason," she creaked without once blinking or moving her eyes.

True to form, the room's seats existed on both walls, the floor, and the ceiling. Still not comfortable hanging like a bat, I grabbed a spot near the front on the floor, and when the class was seated, I looked around again for Raynee. She wasn't there, and though almost everyone was chatting among themselves, no one acknowledged me.

"Resonance," she began with her hoarse voice. "Is our only innate force. That, of course, makes it the most difficult to master."

She threw a slew of equations across the board, but it could have been ancient Armenian for all I knew. Other students were nodding or furiously annotating things across their screens, which operated off neither keyboards nor voice but were instead directed from the mind. I had nothing, not even a clue of what she was discussing.

"Jason!" The entire class stopped. "Do you already know this?"

"No, ma'am."

There was a chorus of giggles.

"My name is not 'ma'am'! It is Fantasa!" Her emphasis was on the second syllable. "Now, explain the Heborean Principle of the Quantum Median, so I may gauge your level."

I slowly shook my head. "I'm sorry . . . Fantasa. I don't know that."

A force suddenly constricted me on all sides, and my seat was rapidly thrown to the back of the class. Another student hurriedly moved forward to the empty place.

"I will waste no more time on you this session. You will receive zero points today. Understand that I expect a certain pace from my students, and if you cannot keep up then I have no use for you."

"Stupid turnip," a boy just in front of me muttered.

I sighed, then remembered my first day of level zero. Then too I'd felt out of place. This was all temporary. Considering that, I did my best to concentrate on the lesson, but the math was unlike any I'd ever seen. Maybe she was just enumerating something I already knew? Wouldn't that show her! Ignoring the ancient Armenian, I anxiously awaited the demo.

Just when I was nearly asleep, the entire front wall disintegrated and the room around us moved forward. The nebula roared over us as our classroom-now-spaceship sped toward it. Around me, everything grew cold and my lungs were straining. Desperately, I tried to relax and recall Sareya's lesson, but this wasn't an alternate dimension. We were still in the paramount dimension, and there was no air here.

While I wobbled and shook, Fantasa pointed at a thin blond girl, who promptly stood at attention. With her hand held straight out, she stared directly toward the heavens and . . . a star began to move. I wasn't quite sure of things, since my hands were at my throat and my body was tumbling off the side of our class-ship. Visions of my future as a lifeless frozen popsicle drifting through space flew through my head.

Fantasa groaned.

"Minus ten points, Jason!" After a snap of her fingers I was back in the school. The chairs were gone and the wall was still open, but I was breathing and alive again. I was also the only student there. This wasn't a good start. Algard stood behind me.

"Back so soon?"

I didn't say anything.

"Avalance of Biologics. Top floor. In the corner. And don't resonate through the other classes in session."

The latter proved difficult. When I closed my eyes and sensed around me, every single room had a class and there were no hallways. Then I figured it out. Since the class was in the corner, I only needed to walk through the open wall and resonate up to the next level. However, the outside wall was resonated closed.

Those jerks! How was I supposed to get anywhere? Maybe they just wanted my life to be difficult? Resigned that there was no easier way, I found a route that only traversed two classes and began my journey. Raynee was in the first class.

Upon seeing me inch across the front of the classroom, though I had thought for sure it was the back, she shook her head and then covered it with her arms. Realizing that I'd stopped to look, I bypassed the evil glares and ran through the next class, where the professor shouted at me to stop.

Knowing any discussion would cost me points, I bolted through the wall, which promptly resonated closed with my foot still stuck in the other room. Raucous laughter rang out while my mouth kissed the floor. I struggled to bring my foot in, but there was no use.

Algard stood before me, the cuffs of his pants meeting my eyes.

"And why exactly is your foot in one room, and you're in this one?"

"You resonated the outside closed! I tried not to disturb anyone, and the teacher told me to stop and I didn't."

"And what did I order you to do?"

"Not disturb any other classes, but—"

"No. I told you not to disturb any classes *in session*! The exercise was simple. You only needed to wait for them to end."

"Oh." That had been an easy one.

"Minus ten points for each class you disturbed, and minus fifty points for disregarding the explicit orders of a professor to stop!"

"So, how many points do I have?" I was near crying.

"You received no points for your lesson today, because you were not prepared. You are therefore at negative eighty points. At negative one hundred points, you are expelled."

This was the worst day of my life. There was zero possibility of receiving any more credits today from knowledge, so I just had to concentrate on not screwing up. Unfortunately, that seemed nearly impossible.

"I'm sorry, Algard," was all I could muster.

He opened his palm and the wall released my foot. I was still sprawled across the floor. He kneeled down to me.

"Don't do this. Once you're expelled, it's forever. Take this lesson to heart, and return to your school. Then come see us again when you've completed level ten, like the rest of the students."

The offer was enticing. One more mistake, and I could never enter these hallowed walls again. My teacher had already said I would soon move to level one. Perhaps I could traverse the other levels just as quickly. I stood, and Algard smiled at me.

"Your offer makes a lot of sense, but I just don't think it's right."

"You're a bright boy. You just need more time."

He was almost certainly right, but something told me I didn't have that amount of time. Mysteries awaited me: my parents, Mordriss. They weren't likely to wait long.

"I'm very sorry, but I need to do this."

"Such a disappointment," he muttered, then walked off.

Raynee was in the next class. Seeing me at the back, she turned and found the geometrically farthest place away, at the top of the classroom in the opposite corner. Her eyes caught mine once, and they were filled with hatred. I gulped, but then remembered that the tiniest of errors now met expulsion.

Our teacher entered. Aviana, much younger than Fantasa the funeral caretaker, was barely in her thirties with long braided brown hair. She had glowering eyes, however, and the mean look of someone not to trifle with.

The lesson began and again there were strange mathematics. This time I swore they were Sumerian, but rather than stare, I opened my screen and frantically searched for the meaning of each symbol. I had little chance to actually understand what she was teaching, but that didn't mean I couldn't learn anything.

Each symbol was agonizingly complex, requiring many nested searches just to begin comprehension. She moved so quickly that I failed to look up nine out of ten of them, but at the very least she wasn't calling on me.

After forty-five minutes of Sumerian, she instructed us to create a portal to a specific dimension. That, at least, I could do. The universe was plain, with a flat brown surface that extended out of vision in every direction. Everything else was black.

"Let's start simple," she proclaimed. "Each of you shall avalate a dimorphed viasile."

I considered raising my hand and asking what the hell that was, but instead I bit my tongue and waited for the first student to succeed. It was a six-inch plain brown slug. The problem was, I had no idea how to create anything with avalation.

My sole goal had been to avoid destroying things. Though I'd witnessed Raynee create everything from pink leopards to spaceships to an amazing car, I was incapable of creating anything. I breathed deeply. This couldn't be so hard.

Avalation was simply the rearrangement of particles into something else. So instead of avalating things away from me, I had to put particles together. But where would I find the right ones?

I'd read texts on avalation. I remembered them for a basic cube. The correct particles were all around me. Slowly, over the next few minutes, I pieced them together and glowed when a tiny brown cube appeared on my palm.

"That's not a dimorphed viasile," Aviana proclaimed while I proudly cradled my cube.

"No, it isn't. I paid attention during your lesson, but I don't know how to make one. I did avalate this for the first time I avalated anything."

She looked down at my pitiful cube, and I grimaced in anticipation of losing points. As long as she didn't dock twenty or more, I was still alive.

"Every other student was capable of far more before matriculating here."

"Yes. I understand that."

"You have not demonstrated any understanding of the material I presented today, so you will not receive the ten points due."

"Yes, Aviana." I was at full attention.

"But you did not disturb our class with your failure. You paid attention, and attempted to understand. I will therefore give you one point for this lame cube. Make sure to review tonight everything I covered today. I will not be as generous tomorrow."

I searched for Raynee's approval, but she kept her head turned away. Aviana looked to follow my gaze, but I quickly turned back to her and smiled. One point was a start.

Next up was lunch. I prayed that there was no way to lose points here. All I had to do was get my food and eat it.

"So, what's the deal, Turnip?" asked a tall, redheaded kid with a voracious strain of freckles.

My eyes scanned side to side in the vain hope he didn't mean me. There was no one else at my table.

"I'm not a turnip," I replied with my eyes down.

My food splattered and a force lifted me from the table and held me in midair. It was some form of resonation, but I was now pinned there, unable to move. From all around and above me I heard every student roar in laughter.

"I give you the turnip!" The kid glared at me. "Now get out of here, and stop wasting our time."

Lunch ended, and one-by-one the students filed by and pointed at me, helpless. My arms and feet were sprawled and my tongue was sticking out as if I'd just been run over by a steamroller. Raynee was last. She looked up at me, and I was hoping for at least a tear. There were none.

"You don't belong here, Jason. Go home."

Then she was gone. They had all gone to their next class, but I couldn't move.

After a few minutes, Darstan found me. "You're late for class." He failed to withhold a bit of laughter.

I couldn't even move my lips and tongue to respond.

"You know this is fourth level resonation, right? He put you in a case. Just resonate it open."

I closed my eyes and, sure enough, sensed a thin shell around me. Remembering how I had to push the squimmers away, I did the same for the case and in a few moments I was gliding back down to the floor.

"Minus ten points for not knowing basic resonation."

"You didn't see what he did to me?"

"It doesn't matter. If it was something serious, then he would've lost hundreds of points. But this should never have affected you. There's a lot for you to learn, Jason."

I nodded, and made for my next class.

"Oh, and that's another ten points for being late."

Double shit. I was now officially the first kid in history to fail lunch. I was also down to one measly point to my name, thanks to my lame cube. Next up was variable essonance.

Raynee was in this class too. The strawberry bastard was also there, and what pissed me off more, he was happily chatting away with Raynee. I bit my lip and tried to concentrate. There was no way I could give in so easily. Even though I had no clue about variable essonance, this was my last stand. A single mess up here meant the thought of that redheaded prick would torment me for the rest of my life.

Darstan was the professor, and it caught me as strange that he'd started class late on my account. I kept my mouth shut and avoided looking at Raynee and that bastard for fear of screaming. All I needed was to not lose any points. There could be no distractions.

"How are we able to essonate?" he shouted over the chatting.

Everyone went quiet. There were no volunteers.

"We've covered many aspects of it. But how are we able to manipulate it? Why are we the only ones who can move between dimensions? For example, why can't someone from a lower dimension set essonate to an even lower one?"

I thought back to the desert world. The Khan knew perhaps everything about essonation, resonation, and avalation, but could exercise none of them herself. On Earth, though, my parents had proved themselves extremely strong, as had the creatures who killed them. Yet they weren't of the paramount dimension. If they could resonate, why couldn't they essonate? It suddenly occurred to me that there was only one answer.

This was my moment. I raised my hand, then lowered it upon realizing they didn't do that here. If I answered this stupidly, I was gone.

"It's because we made those dimensions." I stuttered a bit. "We made everything, and we didn't want them visiting each other."

"You are absolutely correct. And how did we do that?"

"Cenosance?" It was a complete guess.

He smiled. "Very good, Jason. Very good."

19

BASED ON DARSTAN'S broad smile, I thought for sure a few points were heading my way. But instead, we just lumbered into theoretics on essonance. Given the miniscule thread on which I was now operating, I did my best to pay attention. Again, I looked up everything on my screen, but he moved too quickly. Lucky for me, this was a pure lecture. There was to be a test to fail in a few days, but I had survived.

That was also the last class of the day. Red shithole deliberately ran into me while shouting something about turnips, but I was just grateful to have made it through my first day. The celebration would have to wait, though. After all, I had failed lunch. It was still possible to lose points until I left.

Without hesitating, I jumped through my wormhole and arrived home. It was still morning, but there was no time for play. Virtually nothing in any of the lessons was familiar. If I was to turn this day into many, I'd have to get studying.

It took everything not to scream out loud at my lack of knowledge. Actually, I did scream a thousand times. The amount of material was daunting, and after three hours I think I understood just one of the symbols used that day. There was a knock on the wall, which felt odd.

"What the hell, asshole!" one of the spotted rodents said. "Why aren't you taking a fucking walk? We're hungry, you poor excuse for a shit turd."

I tossed some random fruits at them, then resumed studying. Two hours later, there was another knock. It was Sareya.

"How was your first day?" she asked with bright eyes.

"Well, I'm at negative ninety-nine points. One more and I'm expelled."

She laughed. "How did you lose so many?"

"I disturbed two classrooms because I forgot to wait, disregarded a teacher, failed to crack a resonation shell, was late to class, and . . . I couldn't breathe in space."

"Ah. For that last one, you just need to avalate air particles."

Even though I had no idea how to do that, I nodded in understanding. I made a note to figure it out after dinner.

"Did you see Raynee?" She was swaying and grinning.

"Yeah. She told me to go home."

Sareya ignored my response and resonated inside to see the multiple screens I now had set up. Several chairs and couches were clustered around them.

"So, what are you learning tomorrow?"

"Cenosance."

"You shouldn't be telling me that." She was examining my screens. "It's supposed to be a secret. Also, you're not reading this right."

"I'm not reading Raynee right?" My thoughts were now entranced by those few glances I stole that day.

"No, silly! You're researching the tarvazal properties of matter. The right sided tarvazal consists of myratile and moratile substases, but this screen has the miaratile substase. That's a different thing."

"Oh." I realized I'd spent the last three hours studying the wrong subject. "How do you know all this?"

"Learned it a few weeks ago," she replied without thinking. "Well, I'll let you get back to studying."

After she left, I cried for a few minutes and then turned to studying what I now knew was first-level material. When I'd given up on that, I returned to avalating air particles. However, to learn that I needed to study up on paramount dimensional avalation, and there were several branches of mathematics to comprehend that.

Way after the rodents turned off the suns, I'd nearly asphyxiated myself while trying to avalate air particles. Maybe if I just fainted instead of falling off the platform, I wouldn't lose any points? The day ahead of me looked hopeless.

When the credit card ship appeared on the table, I made a note to figure out how it got back. After all, I had technically left it two years in the future without a wormhole. In the meantime, I had a school day to survive. To my surprise, Raynee was on her way inside the school. To my horror, the strawberry turd walked next to her.

"What are you doing back, Turnip?" he said.

"I just had to see your face again. Together with your hair, it looks like a lobster died giving birth to you."

Raynee snorted, which interrupted any concentration for the bastard, who had already raised his palms to do something. Before I could say anything to her, she shoved past both of us to get inside.

To my relief, we didn't have the same classes every day. That meant another day or two before I would suffocate in space. Up first was Principles of Entanglement, taught by the rather thin and almost bald Farlan.

"Good morning, Jennifer," he said to Raynee when she entered. I was still confused why she answered to a different name when he grabbed my shoulder and proceeded to look me over.

"Have we met?"

"No. I'm new. Name is Jason."

"Ah, yes! I heard of a boy, stuck in another dimension on a planet called Pluto. Had the most amazing decombulator we've ever heard of. His name was Argyle. Is that you?"

While I stood stunned, another kid behind me whispered "Just say yes."

"Yes."

"Well, glad to meet you Argyle! Have a seat. Now," Farlan said after tidying his beige suit, "we're going to cover the principles of teleportation."

"We did that already," a student muttered.

"We did?"

The student replied with a short lecture that rehashed the subject well enough that Farlan halted him.

"Very well." Farlan hesitated. "Have we covered full duplex communication across light years with entanglement?"

"Yes," answered a chorus.

"The miaratile substase?"

There was silence.

"That's nice. So, can anyone offer something about the miaratile substase?"

Again, there was absolute silence. With some trepidation, I spoke up.

"The miaratile substase is the counterweight to the heveral stage of ariatosis, most commonly found in dark matter." I then recounted nearly everything I'd learned until Sareya made me realize it had nothing to do with resonance. Farlan had a broad smile.

Raynee, from a quick glance, had her hand over her mouth to restrain her laughter. When her eyes met mine, she frowned.

"Well, someone here is proactive!" Farlan said. "Ten points for your outstanding fortitude."

Those points were the most precious gift I'd received since arriving in that dimension. I only wished they were physical things, so I could've kissed them. Now I just had to get through the day without losing them.

I'd like to say that I finally understood an entire lesson, in truth, I could only follow the first few minutes. He then moved into symbols I didn't know, and again I spent the class furiously attempting to follow on my screen.

Because Darstan had a special extended class prepared for us, lunch was next. To my amazement, two other kids sat opposite me.

"Name is Sarlat," said a thin one with chestnut hair that burst almost from a tesla coil. "That's Henry."

Henry was a head shorter, with thin brown hair and a furtive smile of someone constantly on the verge of a joke. I cautiously introduced myself, aware that it could be a setup for a prank.

"So, how'd you know all that about the miaratile substase?" Henry asked.

I laughed a little. "I read the wrong thing last night. Thought I was studying the myratile substase."

They both had a long laugh.

"How the hell did you get in here?" Sarlat asked at last. "I'm sorry. I don't want to offend you, but the myratile substase . . . isn't that like level-two stuff?"

"Yeah, level one, actually." My eyes started to scan for Raynee. "I know—"

My sentence was interrupted when I saw her. She was chatting with several girlfriends, and looked more beautiful than ever. I pulled my stare away before she noticed.

"Oh, I see why you're here!" Henry said with a laugh. "I like this guy. He's got high standards."

"Yeah," Sarlat said. "But dangerous ones. Seriously, don't mess with Raynee."

"You know Revis, right?" Henry said.

I shook my head.

"Redheaded creep. Keeps calling you a turnip. Well, anyway, he had the balls to spread a rumor that he was going with her. She got so pissed that she resonated a toilet bowl that kept flushing on top of his head. Her resonation's so good that the poor bastard spent the entire day getting it off."

My day was getting better by the minute. I decided it was worth trusting these two.

"So, what's with Farlan? Why does he get all the names wrong?"

"Haven't you noticed?" Henry asked, then remembered that I was an idiot. "He's big into teleportation. Uses it all the time to get places."

"So—" I said, completely aware how ignorant I was.

"It's entanglement," Sarlat added. "Two particles are connected across space. What you do to one affects the other, so you send particles through a special type of wormhole we can't go through. Then you change the particles over here to be you, and now there's a copy over there."

"Sounds cool."

"Hell, no," Henry replied. "The original you goes bye-bye. The copy's the same, but loses some short-term memory. That's why anyone sane doesn't do it."

While chatting with them, I realized that I'd never had such a discussion before. Everyone decent on Earth always ignored me, even my parents. It felt nice to talk about nothing at all for a change.

Just before Darstan's lesson, the entire class was fidgeting. No one had any idea what cenosance was. I gathered that it wasn't top secret, but the reality was few students ever reached this level of learning.

There was a near applause when Darstan appeared. His dark skin was gleaming and he wore a broad grin. His face turned serious.

"Before I begin this lesson, I have some words of warning. Cenosance is the most complicated and demanding of our forces. You will not master it quickly, nor will you find it intuitive. Instead, it contains so many intricacies that a lifetime of study isn't sufficient. Many have been driven to madness attempting to understand everything."

"Let us essonate," he said loudly, and each of us created a portal to an empty, black world.

"To cenosate is to play in an unparalleled arena, where every other force takes a back seat to the creations possible through cenosance. Now, let us begin."

Darstan motioned for all of us to form a sphere around him, then asked that we step several dozen feet back. There was absolutely nothing in this world, just darkness. Each of us was instructed to avalate in a way to allow lower dimension objects to pass through us. I quietly began to hyperventilate, since I had no idea how to do that, until Sarlat slapped me. He whispered several equations in my ear, and I confidently followed suit.

"Cenosance is a force that exists between two particles, or between multiple sets of particles. We'll get into the details of that later. It's ordinarily a weak and unnoticed force, but when manipulated in a certain way, the results can be spectacular."

While we all stooped to catch a glimpse, he carefully cupped his hands and blew softly through the opening. "It'll just take a second," he said, then added, "you might want to move back."

A momentary spark appeared in the darkness and then suddenly we were engulfed in a sea of fire and light. The blast was so deafening that all I felt was a roar of blinding flashes, turning into a storm of plasma. Entire planets seemed to explode from tiny specks and hurtle straight through me. Across the burst I tried to look around, but so powerful was it that I was now virtually alone in a sea of burning mist and galaxies.

"The power of cenosance," Darstan boomed over the onslaught, "is to create the unknown. It is the beginning of all life and essence. To master cenosance is to become an artist of universes."

We stood in awe as entire galaxies and nebulae formed around us. It felt weird to think that multitudes of species would grow up in this universe, having no idea that everything they knew was just a class demonstration.

A gigantic quasar flew past us, then Darstan and the others came back into view.

"The key is to place the two particles in a way that their combined cenosance causes an explosion, then mold and bend the result. The math is the most complex we have. The effort to create a properly functioning universe is extreme, but when successful, it is beyond satisfying."

Darstan snapped his fingers and we avalated back to school.

"Now, it's your turn. We'll focus on what we call bead universes these first weeks. Those are the simplest kind. The idea is to create a world encapsulated in a single marble. You can then visit it whenever you like."

While I expected to not begin to comprehend the mathematics he was about to present, it wasn't so bad. Because he had to explain even the basics, since none of us were familiar with this force, for the first time I was on a level field with the others.

When it came time to produce my own universe, however, I failed. A few students burst their marbles, but the rest of us accomplished absolutely nothing. Darstan didn't seem to mind. We were just starting our adventures with this new force, and failures were to be expected. Of course, I didn't receive any points.

After several more failures, the school day ended and I felt exhilarated. I'd still earned ten points and two friends this day, so it easily counted as the best day in my life. Finally, I had something cool to share, and I couldn't wait to pop through my wormhole and tell Annie and Sareya all about it.

The day was so wonderful I was whistling when I jumped into Annie's ship. Then my tune stopped and my feet halted. In seconds my life went from an all-time high to complete destruction.

Written in black across the wall of my ship were the words, "Go back to your field, Turnip! You've just lost two years."

It wasn't the lame insult from lobster face that bothered me most, but the absence of something far more important.

My wormhole was gone.

20

A SERIES OF emotions from complete breakdown to the desire to resonate every shit I'd take for the next two years on Revis's head occurred to me, but nothing could ease the reality that my life was over. There was no way to get home unless I made another two-year journey. That would mean missing a full four years.

I considered just flying somewhere, maybe to lobster face's home to beat the crap out of the future him, but that solved nothing. Resigned to the inevitable, I left the ship and wandered back into the school.

Algard, with his mustache in full twitch mode, was just inside. "Well, this is unexpected. Did you compute the next day incorrectly?"

"No." I was aware that a positive response would've docked my remaining points. "My wormhole is gone. I think Revis did it."

"I see." His slow movements seemed like he was resonating everything around him, making sure no one else was coming. "And why are you telling me this?"

Unsure which answer wouldn't lose me points, I paused.

"You wish us to punish him?" he said.

"Well, if he did it . . . then, yes."

"Very well." He escorted me to a room at the far corner of

the building. "Darstan will see to your request. I need to be off to Heskera."

Darstan was reading something on his screen when I entered. His mouth went wide and he jumped on noticing me. "A surprise visitor! To what do I owe the pleasure?"

"Revis destroyed my wormhole." I was desperately holding back tears. "I'm ruined."

He approached, peered directly into my eyeballs, then straightened himself. "Very well, then. Let's take a look."

I escorted him to Annie's ship, where he placed a hand over the words written behind the empty void that should have been my wormhole. Though I'd thought that only people's remains could be orasated, Darstan was a professor who knew a bit more than the average person.

"Yup. That was Revis. We'll dock him one hundred and ninety points."

"A hundred and ninety?"

"Well, two hundred for the prank, but ten for figuring out how to collapse someone else's wormhole. That's some complicated essonance."

"But what about me! How am I going to get home?"

"Relax, relax." He motioned me to leave the ship. The moment we exited, the ship disappeared in a single pop, and presumably began its long journey back. That must have been how they reused them.

"Now, for your predicament—" he said out loud. "Ah! Raynee lives right next to you. So, you can both just take her wormhole tomorrow."

Though my day had brightened immensely, I feared what Raynee would think of that.

"In the meantime, we can have a little chat, and then I believe you have some studying to do."

He led me back to his office, which consisted of a single chair and twenty screens across all six walls, each full of crazy symbols.

"Sorry, don't receive many guests." He sat in the only chair. "Feel free to avalate yourself something comfortable."

"I'm fine." I really didn't want to lose more points for not knowing how to do that. "I can stand."

Darstan smirked, then avalated a bean bag chair and, with a blast of resonance, pushed me onto it. He seemed more at ease than in class, with his feet on a futon and his hands holding a milkshake he'd just created.

"Where's everyone else?"

He shook his head. "They have places to go. Don't live here like poor old me."

"You live here?" I noticed a small, worn bed on the ceiling. "Why?"

Darstan looked down. "Mordriss killed my wife and daughter. I came home that day, and—" He looked down and wiped his eyes. "I closed the door and never went back. Some things should never be seen."

Though I didn't want to press it, I had to ask someone. Every person here had their Mordriss story, so no matter what, I was bound to upset someone with the question.

"Is Mordriss still around?"

He sighed. "You don't do small talk, do you? The truth is, we don't know. I believe he is, but several years ago the killings just stopped."

"Do we know what he looked like?"

"You'd think so. We orasated every victim, of course, but he wore a black mask and prevented any resonation inside. Weird, isn't it?"

"I'm sorry about your wife and daughter—"

"Yeah." He looked up. "You kind of missed out on everything, being stuck on Earth. Tell me about that. How was it?"

I wasn't expecting that question. It took me a few seconds to tell myself how it was. "It seems so long ago now. I mean, in retrospect everything was flat and boring, but it all was so real back then. It's weird. I feel like I'm living for the first time now, but it's not like I was dead back then. I'm just something different now."

"That's all cute." He smiled. "But what we scientists would really love to know . . . is about that decombulator. Any idea who made it?"

"I was going to ask you the same question." I grinned. "That's why I came here, to ask Algard."

"Good luck getting anything out of him. He runs the school well, but if it doesn't have to do with class, then forget it." He leaned forward. "But speaking of Algard, what's the deal with that badge?"

I moved lower in the bean bag.

"Well, there was this other world. It was a desert. A woman there told me about him. She said he wanted something badly. She taught me to avalate, too."

"A turnip?" he asked incredulously. "How would a turnip know about avalation? Are you playing with me?"

"No, no. I swear it was some world built for me. She said the same person put me on Earth, but I don't know who."

"Well, that's some serious use of both avalance and cenosance. I don't know if even Algard has those skills. Entire universes programmed around you. That's unheard of."

I nodded, though in my mind I was determining how to get Algard alone. Perhaps he knew something. After all, the Khan had specifically mentioned him, not Darstan. Regardless, I had a lot of studying to do. Tomorrow was still another day to lose points.

"Thank you for your help." I moved to stand.

"Of course! Of course! Visit me anytime."

There was a ton of resonation to review, but I paused just before leaving. The poor guy had been living in this room since his family had died. Every student and other teacher had left, and this was maybe his first casual conversation in a year.

"Back, before Mordriss, what did you used to do?"

Darstan frowned, thought for a moment, then grinned. "I used to be the biggest gamer. That's why I learned cenosance, actually.

I created entire game universes, then we'd play them." He looked down. "I always used to let my wife and kid win."

"Do you still have any of them? A game would be great to get the mind off of things."

The biggest smile I'd ever seen spread across his face. "What kind would you like?"

Though I'd been thrilled by essoball in my primary school, that had nothing on full gaming universes created by a master of cenosance. My favorite was one where we tried to shoot each other from fighters as we flew through countless galaxies, avoided supernovas, and skirted across black holes. Another involved being the general of real-world armies made up of any type of creature we wished. I borrowed Raynee's pink leopards for my only win of the night.

We clashed until late, though it was difficult to know for sure since there was only that huge nebula outside. By the time we finished, we were both sweating in the real world from the exhilaration.

"Thank you for that," he said. "It's been way too long."

When I left his office, I realized that there were neither showers nor beds in the rest of the school. The shower proved the easier part. After a few attempts, I finally figured out how to avalate water particles, and created just enough to wash up. The bed was an insurmountable obstacle. I couldn't avalate something that large, so I gathered several chairs together, instead, and had an uncomfortable few hours of sleep. As my mind drifted off, I wondered about Mordriss. I'd heard his name back on Earth. If my world was pre-programmed, why was he included?

Just before school started for the day, Darstan gathered me and Raynee in his office.

"It's not my fault he's an idiot," said the seething Raynee when Darstan explained the situation. "He can just stay here until he figures it out."

"Please! I'm sorry about everything. I didn't know I wasn't a turnip. I'm sorry for ditching Sareya. I'm sorry for being an asshole. I won't bug you anymore. I just want to go home."

"When were you an asshole?" She crossed her arms. "If you tell me something specific, I'll take you back home."

I thought for an uncomfortable few seconds, while Darstan looked on and Raynee fumed.

"When I said you didn't know what it was like to lose someone . . . because you probably lost someone, too?"

"Fine!" She threw her arms up. "I was hoping to leave you here, but a deal's a deal. Just don't talk to me."

Her hair flew back and she ran to her first class. I thanked Darstan, then prepared to face Fantasa for advanced resonance. She immediately shoved us back into space, her grim stare directly on me. It was obvious: If she wanted me to die, it had to be at the beginning of the lesson.

Yet something about being extremely tired made it easier to avalate. After some uneasiness, I had enough air to breathe. Fantasa, with an air of disgust, continued.

The lesson covered moving actual stars through resonance. With her eyes continuously on me, I stayed near the back of the class, but paid attention and attempted to follow on my screen. Perhaps satisfied that I was no longer collapsing, she didn't call on me to demonstrate, which would have surely cost me precious points.

Sarlat and Henry joined me again for lunch. I didn't mention that Raynee was taking me home, out of a very real fear that she'd refuse, but we did scheme on how to get back at Revis. For his part, the lobster just ate his lunch with his mouth open straight at us. He had a look of contentment that made me want to smash his teeth in, but I still had to be careful. I only had eleven points keeping me from expulsion.

The rest of the day was spent in cenosance again. Being an entirely new subject, they were giving us a lot of time to practice, but it was of little use. No one could create even the simplest universe yet, nor generate any kind of spark. It felt strange that such a calm and complacent force could be so violent when forced in a certain way, kind of like a quiet kid in the back who just goes berserk one day.

At long last, the lesson ended and my dream ever since arriving here was about to be realized. Raynee would have to talk to me, even if it was only for the brief time it took to get home.

My eyes found hers just after school, and she gave me a fierce glance that would've frightened a polar bear. After waiting patiently for her to finish chatting with several girlfriends, she waved me to the correct ship, then shoved me inside. My heart rose at the sight of an intact wormhole.

"You're a real piece of work, do you know that?" she shouted once we were inside.

"I'm sorry—"

"No, you're not, you piece of shit. You don't even know what you did!"

She didn't make that up. I kept my mouth shut for fear of never getting home.

"Why didn't you take your ship back!"

"My ship, but—"

"It has a wormhole, too."

My mouth stood agape.

"Are you serious! You didn't know that? How the hell do you think it gets home? We just make new ones each time?"

"Well, kinda—"

Raynee groaned. "You're such a—"

"A turnip?"

She shook her head. "Whatever . . . Now, we're going to have to hold hands for this to work."

I jerked my eyes up to meet hers.

"One hand. And if you start massaging my fingers or touching me anywhere but my palm, I swear I'll tear the thing down with you in it."

I didn't want to admit that I had no idea what would happen, but her clenched teeth were enough to ensure it would be horrible.

She grabbed my hand, and every vein rushed while my heart beat faster than a hamster in a centrifuge. For just a moment, her eyes weren't full of scorn, then they changed back when I stared for too long.

In an instant, we were through the wormhole and back to a small cluster of houses by the forest. Her house was roughly similar to Annie's, though unlike hers, there were others near it.

"Well, we're back," she announced.

Though the woods looked similar, I still had no idea which direction was home. She turned her back and started moving away, and immediately I knew her plan. Sareya was to escort me home.

"Would you like to take a walk?" I blurted.

"A walk?" She halted. "Why?"

I wanted to say because I adored her, and couldn't stand being so long without chatting with her. She'd opened some door in me back on Earth, and after just a few seconds with her it was wide open again. Even a few minutes' walk was a lifetime to me.

"Because, I'd like to walk with you?" I said with a cautious voice.

Sareya was next to me now. Raynee took a long look at me, then at her.

"Very well, then. A walk it is. Sareya, you can go home."

Sareya jumped and skipped to the next house, and I followed Raynee into the forest. However, as we ventured inside, without a peep between us, I was without words. There were so many questions I had for her, but now that she was beside me, I feared asking them. It wasn't that I was afraid of her response, though I was a little, but that I was enjoying my brief time next to her and didn't want to ruin it.

"Thank you," I said after some time, and a few false starts.

"For what?" She didn't turn around.

"For bringing me here. For finding me in the first place."

"Do you know the odds of that?" She walked up a tree and signaled me to follow.

"The odds of what?"

"Me finding you."

I shrugged. "One in a million?"

"You really do suck at math. Imagine that an old man asks you to play a game. He picks one grain of sand somewhere on Earth. You have to guess which one. If you guess right, then he'll give you one dollar. You use that dollar to buy a lottery ticket, and if you win the one-billion-dollar reward, it's paid out in pennies and you then have to pick one special penny at random."

"Wow, that's—"

"Then imagine, that you do that once and the old man tells you to play the same game one million times in a row, and you have to win every time. Even then, your odds are better at winning the game than me finding you."

"So, you're saying . . . we're very lucky?"

"No." She turned to me. "Those odds don't happen. That's why I blew up at you in the hospital."

I was confused. "So, you never really found me and this is some crazy dream where I get to spend time with the most wonderful girl in the world who hates me because I'm an idiot?"

There was that hooked smile again. "I don't hate you. You just piss me off . . . But, I was just saying that me finding you wasn't an accident."

"Then, you were meant to find me?"

"I don't know. But I can say this. Those ships and robots back on Earth. They weren't Mordriss'."

"But one of them said Mordriss by name."

"I know. I still haven't figured that part out. Think about it, though. If Mordriss wanted you, he'd just kill you himself. He doesn't need minions."

Even though I had no experience with Mordriss, it made sense.

"But I do think that something wanted to flush you out. Something wanted you to come here. You probably were always destined to, but why? And why now?"

She'd obviously been giving it more thought than I had. While my efforts were focused on my parents, she was still dwelling on the events on Earth. Regardless, she was no longer seething at me when discussing it.

"There was another world," I said. "It was all desert. There was a woman. She taught me avalance and how to get into Oreca Gifted."

"You mean, she taught you to dig up the founder, cause our school to emergency relocate twice, then pawn some avalated metal with the school's name on it?"

I paused, unsure how she knew about that.

"Seriously, Turnip." She gave her crooked smile that nearly melted me. "I'm still way ahead of you."

We stopped for a moment facing each other, and for a second I seriously considered pulling her close and attempting a kiss. Yet, she still scared me. I looked down.

"But it's still strange, isn't it? She was a turnip, but knew about avalance and our world. Even Darstan thought it was cool."

She shrugged. "Not really. I mean, it's interesting that someone created that whole world for you, but this woman— she wasn't a turnip."

That idea had never occurred to me.

"Whoever made that universe obviously knew about avalance. She must have lived in our world and modeled that universe on real things. I've been reading up on cenosance, of course. It's possible to create programmed universes like that, but difficult. Whoever did it must've been like Algard."

"Yeah, I suppose you're right."

We walked in silence for some time. Yet with each step, I feared that Annie's house was around the corner, and I'd have to let her go. There were questions to ask, and she was walking too fast. There was no easy way to start.

"What did you lose . . . when Mordriss came?"

That made her pause. She hunched over as if out of breath, but I knew my question had hit too close. She didn't want me to see her crying.

"Everything."

"I'm sorry about what I said. I had it easy. Just hanging out on boring Earth while everything happened here."

Raynee sat on a log and let the tears flow. I hesitated for a moment to consider whether she'd let me, then sat next to her and put my arm gently around her. Before she had the chance to push me away, two spotted rodents arrived.

"Fuck!" one of them said. "She's crying, so we're not getting any fucking food!"

She dried her tears and avalated a few fruits.

"Told you these fuckers are sure bets!" the other shouted, then pointed to me. "That piece of shit and this bitch give us something every time. Morons."

"I think I need to get my translator fixed," I said out loud.

Her arm had been halfway to shoving me away, but she then relaxed it and put her head on my shoulder. "Doesn't matter. I tried it and they still cuss. I think they like to screw with us."

Raynee was hurting, and I probably should've kept my mouth shut, but I still had so many questions. "Val . . . he didn't make it, did he?"

She lifted her head and straightened herself. At first, she had a look of disgust, but then turned away.

"He was my brother."

"Mordriss?"

"Yes. Val thought he could beat him . . . stupid asshole." Tears flowed down her cheek.

I slowly pulled my arm from her shoulder, while softly caressing her back on the way. "They say Mordriss is gone now. He disappeared. Maybe he's dead."

"No." She shook her head violently. "He's not dead. I've never told anyone this, but I know something no one else does. He didn't die. I know that for sure. He's coming back, because there're still more to kill."

21

"WHEN I WAS little, Val and I used to portal to the turnip fields and play a game. We'd each avalate our own armies and have a war. He always let me win."

Raynee brushed her hair back, then stared into a narrow opening through the trees.

"When we started I didn't know how to avalate, of course, so he taught me. He's the reason I'm in Oreca Gifted right now. He was eight years older than me, and the best student they ever had. The teachers thought he'd be a professor there one day, or a top scientist. I was his best student. He taught me the coolest stuff. But then Mordriss came.

"No one knows where he came from; he never bothered to introduce himself. Whole towns were wiped out. While Val and I were away playing, he murdered our parents. Val didn't let me see their bodies, but a year later I orasated them to see what happened."

"You saw Mordriss?" I asked.

"No." Her mouth was trembling. "He wore some mask. No one ever saw him. He killed each person differently. The perverted monster just wanted to make it a sport. After that, Val and I never played again. The professors always praised him, so Val felt only he could stop that freak."

She grabbed my hands. "Before he left, he learned something about Mordriss's power. He never told me what, but he thought for sure he could get him. All I know is it had something to do with portals. I tried to stop him that day, tried to lure him into another game, but he just resonated me home."

"What happened to him?"

"Officially, he's one of the missing. There were others whose bodies they never found, but that's because I never told them. I—"

I put my arm around her and held tight.

"You don't have to say it. I understand."

"No," she said, but didn't move away. "It's important." She stood and began to pace. "I found his finger." Her eyes were filled with tears. "Back in those days, we found a lot of parts. There were people we called who tried to put them all together, notify anyone who knew them who survived, but I knew it was his. There was a ring he always wore."

Raynee leaned down and pulled up a thin strand from between her breasts. I tried to look only at the ring, which was plain silver, with a burst of rays across its face.

"It's for avalation. You trade particles between it and other things. Makes it easier."

She frowned upon noticing that my eyes were no longer focused on the dangling piece of metal, then stood back up.

"So, I orasated it." She grabbed a branch. "Mordriss toyed with him. He ripped off his leg, and while Val was dying, he started saying stuff about *me*. That creep knows who I am. But my brother was just preparing the whole time. Val then hits him with a resonation blast . . . complicated stuff that pushed both of them several light years apart. Then, he whispered 'I bought you time, Raynee. Find Avarus.' Mordriss killed him then, but Val's finger was outside his portal, so when it closed, that part was cut off."

"He did it on purpose?"

"Yes. And that's how I know he's coming back. Only I haven't managed to find an Avarus at all. Whoever the guy is, he's a ghost."

While I probably should have been completely freaked about the prospect that Mordriss, an undefeatable being whose sole goal was to murder people in sadistic ways, was destined to return, I was far more entranced with my company. There was so much to tell her, but now wasn't the time.

"No one has heard of him?" I asked at last.

"I even orasated half the cemetery. I know pretty much every family secret, but nothing about an Avarus."

"Maybe he orasated himself out? That's what the school founder did. He changed his own orasance."

"Yeah, but that was his own. Changing anyone else's is a lot more difficult."

Not ten feet away, several bushes twitched and we both froze. There was something hidden within the jungle, and it wasn't a swearing rodent. Raynee laughed a little when I instinctively rose and cautioned her back with one arm. Slowly, I crept to the shaking bushes, and before I could jump a dark shape darted away.

Whatever it was, it moved low and fast. A row of bushes blew off their leaves, but even at full speed I was no match for this culprit. It was nearly out of sight, until one shout of Raynee erected a force field, and a tiny "Ow!" echoed from the thicket.

Panting and heaving, I ran over to the spot, while Raynee calmly resonated herself over. Two blond braids were caught in the twigs. It was Sareya.

"Congratulations!" Raynee said to me. "You caught her."

Sareya pulled the leaves off her, then defiantly faced Raynee. "I just wanted to see if you were kissing."

Raynee grimaced a little too much. "What?" she said, and took one look at me. "That's disgusting." She turned to Sareya and knelt. "But how much did you hear?"

"Nothing, nothing." She twirled one of her braids. "I didn't hear anything about Mordriss or Val or—"

Raynee shushed her. "You can't say anything about that to anyone. You shouldn't know any of this."

Sareya jumped back, then her eyes grew more devious. While darting glances between the two of us, she held down her braids and walked forward. "Agreed, but on one condition."

Raynee waved her hand and every tree in the forest creaked. Yet this was no contest. Sareya knew that Raynee would never hurt her.

"We all play that game you talked about."

"What?" Raynee shrieked. "Absolutely not! I've told you a hundred times: Avalance can kill turnips."

"Is that what Val told you when you first asked?" I added.

She glared at me, and an unseen force tightened around my hands and legs. My breathing grew more rapid. I shared no such guarantee from harm.

"Jason taught me avalance," Sareya said. "Why won't you?"

I could barely breathe now as Raynee's resonance grew tighter.

"You taught her avalance! Don't you know how foolish that is?"

"She taught me orasance." I gasped. "It was a trade. Besides, it's not like she's irresponsible."

Sareya had a mischievous grin now.

"I didn't want to do this." Sareya aimed her hand at Raynee, who was stunned at the act but cautiously lifted her own arms in preparation for whatever meek assault was coming.

"If you don't teach me, then I'll tell Jason that you said—"

"Fine," Raynee shouted. "You win."

She left no time for questions. In an instant, we were all in the turnip fields. Thousands of blank-faced vegetables awaited our epic battle, though every single one would go through its life without knowing it.

Anxious for an upbeat change to our recent sad discussion, I smiled, then avalated a cup of water and splashed Raynee's face. "I win."

She shook her head while Sareya laughed, and returned with a broken frown.

"That's against the rules," Raynee shouted. "You can't touch the other player. Only the things you avalate can fight what the other avalates."

"But I can only avalate water," I said.

Sareya avalated a small sponge ball and tossed it at Raynee. Though I was proud to have helped her learn that, I was a little discouraged in knowing that she now was more proficient than I was.

"That's all I can do," she said while it innocently bounced off Raynee's face.

Raynee groaned. "It's all in the math. Just imagine what you need in mathematical form, and bond the particles that way."

So, I did just that, only my math capabilities weren't quite the level of hers. After considerable stress and some grunting, I managed to create a sort of walking gummi bear. Sareya conjured a bouncing marshmallow. Both sat there, awaiting our orders.

"So . . . how do we make them move?"

Raynee had already prepared a platoon of dagger-wielding soldier monkeys. Evidently the pink leopards were too good for us.

She groaned. "You program them, of course!"

Now, I'd taken some beginner programming courses in high school, but I couldn't recall anything that covered automating life-sized gummi bears. This was made more difficult by the fact that they lacked processors, memory, and brains.

Since giving them any intelligence wasn't working for me, I just resonated it forward until it collapsed onto one of Raynee's monkeys, consuming it in the process. Sareya took another out with her marshmallow.

"That isn't fair!" Raynee complained, but Sareya and I were already in the process of creating more candy troops.

As a wave of gummis and marshmallows devoured Raynee's proud monkeys, she waved her hand and instantly her finest warriors took the stage. Their soft roars and pink fur belied the vicious creatures underneath. In our celebration, she had unleashed her pink leopards.

The legion of pink demons poured forth and met our newly formed gelatin mass. The first group met head on, and quickly the leopards proceeded to devour the stomachs of my gummis, only there had been one gross miscalculation. Neither marshmallows nor gummis had brains to control. Every single cat was promptly overcome.

Sareya and I shouted and gave each other high fives while the last of Raynee's legion collapsed. When her wrath turned into a wry grin and that entrancing smile returned, I regretted in hindsight not making a kiss the game's prize. Then again, it hadn't been that long ago that she was furious at me.

We avalated back to our own dimension, then sent Sareya skipping home. "We beat you! We beat you!" she cried with each jump, and for an awkward moment Raynee and I faced each other.

Just before I mustered the courage, she turned away.

"Annie's house isn't far," she said quickly.

We walked in silence those few precious minutes. My hand was only inches from hers, and once, our fingertips even touched. Would it be too bold to reach for her hand? That was far more innocent than a kiss. And maybe if she didn't resist that, I could draw her in, put my arm around her, and lose myself in her trance.

The simple white box that was Annie's house appeared through the foliage, and I knew my chance was up. Raynee halted, and again my hand brushed her fingertips. She avoided looking me in the eye.

"So, are we good?" I asked. "Are we friends again?"

This time her brown eyes met mine. They were wide with longing, and she moved an inch toward me, then backed away. "We were never friends." She gave her trademark grin. "But I like you, Turnip. You're a quality vegetable."

That night, I found it easier to comprehend the foundation

of universe creation with cenosance than to come to any form of conclusion on her answer. When the rodents turned off the suns, I found myself collapsing into a deep sleep, an artifact of my previous late night.

❧

Given an important question I needed answered, I arrived early to school and barreled into Darstan's cluttered office. So sudden was my entrance that he peered up at me like a deer in headlights.

"Why didn't you tell me my ship had a wormhole the entire time. Raynee wanted to strangle me."

Darstan straightened himself and did not smile. "Excuse me? You should be thanking me."

I just glared.

"You've been pining after that girl this entire time. And she wasn't giving you the time of day. That is, until I helped."

My mouth opened and air went in, but no sounds came out. Darstan stood, and the reality occurred to me that bursting into a professor's office earned a hefty fine.

"Thank you," I said earnestly, then bolted before he could respond.

When I reached my first class, to my amazement there was an empty seat next to Raynee. Revis stood not six feet from it. When he noticed my eyes focused on the prize, the bastard just grinned. I moved forward, desperate to get there first. Farlan was in my way.

"Well, hello." He had a friendly tone. "Have we met before?"

"Yes." I tried unsuccessfully to budge through.

"Ah! Now I remember! Take a seat, Smith."

I was too slow. Revis already had one hand on the chair, and the other on Raynee's shoulder. That proved to be a big mistake.

He had no time to even give me that pathetic smile before his own fist left Raynee's shoulder and pounded him straight in the face. Desperately, he held it back with his other hand, but he was no match for himself. Blow-by-blow his arm knocked him back until he was edged against the wall. I snagged the chair in the meantime, but didn't dare touch Raynee.

"Clarice!" Farlan yelled. "That will be a hundred points for assaulting a student!"

Raynee dipped her head and released the strawberry asshole.

"The nice thing about punishments from Farlan, is he always forgets them. Besides, I have tens of thousands of points. That was so worth it."

Raynee wore an embroidered sweater that appeared conservative, but exactly outlined her curves. Her brown hair was radiant, and her skin was perfect. To avoid staring at her for the entire lesson, I constructed a screen to block the view and proceeded to look up the symbols I didn't know. Farlan continued to explain teleportation, though thankfully with marbles instead of people. When one became lost, Farlan paused the lesson, and Raynee angrily tore down my screen.

"What are you doing? If I wanted something blank to look at, I would've let lobster face take that spot."

"Well, uh—" Her brown eyes devoured me. "The thing is, you're amazing, but—"

"But, what?" she said with more than a little anger.

"You're so beautiful that I can't stop staring at you, so I put the screen up," I blurted.

Unknown to me, Farlan had already found the marble and the entire class was silent enough to swallow every word. Surrounding us were muted giggles, toned down for fear of Raynee's wrath. Her hand reached for me, though not in a hostile way, then she pulled it back. Though I had said it, from her sheepish look, she was perhaps more embarrassed than I.

Farlan shook his head and resumed the lesson. This time, I paid no attention at all. All I could think of was her. Suddenly, the thin Algard resonated into the room, and called Farlan outside. This was my chance.

"Go out with me tonight."

Her head shrank back. "Why?" Her eyes betrayed her.

"Because I'm crazy about you. You're the best thing that ever happened to me, and a seat in class is no longer enough."

"So, like a date?" Her finger caressed her mouth.

"Yes."

Raynee rested her chin on her elbow and leaned forward. "Where are you taking me?"

"To the best place that occurs to me in the next five hours."

"That will be interesting to see." She grabbed my hand and examined my palm. "Very well. I accept."

Farlan did not return to class, but Darstan took over after a few minutes and switched the subject to cenosance, which I found more interesting anyway.

My stunning success made it difficult to pay attention. When it came time for demonstrations, I moved in a trance, threw this, that, and whatever together and in the day's second surprise, after a sharp pop, I held a small, rotating marble.

"Did you just do it?" Raynee shrieked and grabbed it away from me.

Darstan rushed forward, and all three of us essonated inside. My universe consisted of nothing but two dark planets revolving around a gigantic lightbulb. One was populated by life-sized gummi bears, each moving mechanically forward, while the other was inhabited by similarly mobile marshmallows. I looked down while Darstan took notes. It wasn't much to look at. With no one else in this world, Raynee brushed my hand, then I gently reached for and held hers.

"Very well done," Darstan proclaimed. "As you practice, the complexity will of course improve. That's one hundred points for a successful cenosation, and another hundred for being the first in the class. The rest I'll explain to everyone."

We returned to the class with all eyes on me. It felt gratifying to not be the idiot for once, even though I truthfully had no idea how I'd managed it. Every conscious thought had been about Raynee.

"Congratulations, Jason, for creating our first universe." Everyone except Revis give a hesitant applause. "But there is something even more remarkable about it. His world has a fifty percent time correlation."

Raynee gave me a stunned look, but I wasn't quite sure what that meant.

"You'll find that most creations will flow quickly. So quickly, in fact, that you'll barely have any opportunity to investigate them before they expand into nothingness. This one, however, has a time correlation not far from our own. Such a feat is usually reserved to the domain of master creators, so I'm awarding you three hundred points for either your expert ingenuity or pure dumb luck."

My muscles tensed and I felt barely able to breathe. Had I really just earned five hundred points? Those were far more than a step toward graduation. Now, I truly belonged. The next missed avalation or accident would no longer mean my expulsion. I was here at Oreca Gifted to stay.

During the applause, Raynee reached over and hugged me, then backed away just slightly for the very real fear that I would pull her in for a kiss with everyone watching. Still, her face was mere inches from mine, and for a brief, few moments that was the best time in my life.

"I have some grave news to report," Algard announced amid our celebration.

The class went quiet while he moved to the center of the room.

"We debated the timing of this, but given that your discussions at home will revolve around it, we felt it best that you learn of this here."

Algard reached into his pockets and fidgeted a few moments before saying anything. He was sweating. Before his mouth opened again, Raynee gasped.

"Mordriss has returned," he shouted solemnly.

Tears and screams broke out. Even Raynee couldn't avoid crying.

"The town of Heskera is no more. Mordriss has murdered every single inhabitant."

Where had I heard that name so recently? In some ways I felt cold to the news. Everything I'd heard about Mordriss had been just stories. It wasn't entirely sinking in how this would affect anything. I struggled to recollect while Algard resumed.

"Our thoughts and prayers go to the nearly three thousand casualties of this heinous act. We are weighing our options at this very moment. We will discuss the future of Oreca Gifted with all of you in a few minutes. Please discuss this among yourselves. I unfortunately have an important matter to attend to, and will return in a few minutes to hear your thoughts."

He had murdered three thousand people? How did someone even manage that? Before I could even speak to Raynee, Algard was between us.

"Jason, we need to discuss something." His eyes glared down at me. He turned to Raynee. "You should be there, too."

We awkwardly left with him while everyone else was hugging and consoling each other. I noticed streams even from Revis, who, I later learned, had grandparents in Heskera. Algard escorted us to his voluminous and extremely well-organized office, where sat a shaking Farlan. His hair was frazzled, and he was covered in blotches of blood. He held a cube in his trembling hands, which he now held out to us.

"I'm afraid there's something you need to see," Algard said. "It will not be easy for you."

"What happened to him?" Raynee asked, pointing to Farlan.

"As you know, Farlan has a proclivity toward teleportation. Due to its rather severe side effects, it's a science that not many of us appreciate. But for this occasion, it proved useful."

He removed the cube from Farlan's hand and resonated it into the air.

"We sent him to Heskera with a video device to show us what happened."

"So, what does that have to do with us?" Raynee replied. Something inside of me didn't want the answer.

Algard snapped his fingers and instantly we were in the remains of Heskera. I'd never visited an actual town in this world. Maybe at one point with its bright signs and quaint multicolor buildings this city had been beautiful, but now it was adorned with human heads, severed limbs, and a sea of blood.

Raynee moved to throw up and I held her against my chest. It took every bit of my strength to not join her.

"Follow me," Algard said.

Although we were only in a video, Algard was still careful to not step onto the bodies. Instead, he led us carefully over and around. We went through wide arches, walked through walls, and followed streets cluttered with the dead. I wondered what the point of all this was. Then it hit me. The corpses were arranged in a line.

Most were without heads, with the few remaining, returning a vacant stare and each of their arms was aimed forward, as if in an ultimate salute. Every arm grasped the foot before it.

Raynee and I said nothing while we followed this obscene line of death. Mordriss wanted us to go somewhere, and I dreaded whatever that meant. Then at the very end, we saw it. There was nothing but a plain wall. Beneath it were several crushed corpses. Mordriss had written the message in blood.

"I KNOW WHO YOU ARE JASON BEZNA."

22

"SO, I ASSUME I'm the only Jason Bezna?" I asked the line of professors and Raynee who were eyeing me curiously from the other side of the room.

This had become ridiculous.

"You're the only one with a last name," Algard replied. "And you're also the only ex-turnip."

At that moment, I wished desperately to be nothing more than a turnip again. This maniac had just murdered three thousand people, then thrust me into the middle of it. What did any of this have to do with me? Why couldn't they have just left me alone in complete ignorance, with robotic parents, on a planet where no one cared?

"So, who are you?" Farlan asked to break the silence.

"I came here a few days ago to ask you the same question." I backed away subtly, then briefly considered running away, but that would only look worse.

Raynee slowly left Algard's side and approached. There was a look of caution and hesitation on her face I'd never seen. This had completely freaked her. She carefully reached her hand up to my forehead and I instinctively drew back.

"Please," she pleaded softly. "Don't fight me. I have to do this."

I didn't resist while she gently caressed my hair, then she pressed her palm onto my forehead and went stone quiet. We were back on Earth.

We were on the mountain. Her focus was on New York City, while mine was on her. Then everything faded and we were in an ordinary classroom. Flemence was about to destroy me, until a sharp-tongued brunette interrupted the show.

I was back on the school bus, my head sliding down the window while no one noticed me. Then I was alone at home. The woman who'd I'd grown up calling Mother was sitting on the couch, entranced by the television, while my so-called father was on his tablet. I sat by myself, and was just watching the heavens outside.

Then I was a little child, jumping and sprinting around the room, while my parents' locations were unchanged. "Mommy! Daddy! Play with me!" I screamed, but they didn't budge. I ran outside at the voice of some children. They were playing soccer.

"Go home, Bezna!" an orange-headed kid shouted. "We don't want you here."

I was five years old and beginning my first day of kindergarten. My mother was driving me across the bridge, and I asked why my school was so far away.

"You're special," she said. "You won't understand this now, but you're different from all of us. You're better. This world is but a tiny part of all there is. One day, you'll need to save it."

"How will I save it, Mommy?"

She looked at me through the mirror. "Through things like avalance, essonance, orasance, resonance, and of course cenosance."

"What are those?"

"Forces."

"Will I learn them in school?"

"No. But one day someone will orasate this, and then you'll understand."

Raynee attempted to go back farther, but the rest was just a white blur. She lifted her hand from my forehead, then lightly brushed away a tuft of hair.

"He's connected to this somehow," she stated out loud. "But not in a bad way."

Algard stepped forward and looked between me and Raynee. His eyes seemed to penetrate me, like a cat watching a mouse that had come too close.

"There's something about you, Jason, that Mordriss finds frightening."

I just stood there in stunned silence. Sure, as an ex-turnip I stood out, but with the resonance powers of a five-year-old and the wimpiest avalance ever known in this school, I doubted Mordriss would consider me much of a threat. Yet Algard kept looking at me from different angles while I waited for an explanation.

"He chose Heskera for a reason. It forms a triangle between Jason's current residence and this school. They're all two light years apart. So, if Mordriss wanted to kill you, Jason, he's within range to do it."

Raynee eyes bulged, then clearly felt so winded she had to sit. Algard was at her side, but offered neither a hand nor a gesture of sympathy.

"If he can get here," she said in a hurried manner, "then he can reach home. Sareya. I have to protect her." Raynee looked up at me, nearly in tears. "She's my everything now."

I jostled around Algard and placed my hands gently on her shoulders.

Algard only put his hand to his chin while he thought. "You are correct that he could reach you. But that begs the same question. Why hasn't he done so already? There's something he wants from Jason. The cities nearest to Heskera will want to evacuate, but I think Mordriss' goal for now was to send a message, and he succeeded in that. We may therefore have a few days before he strikes again. That, however, is not our worst predicament."

"Having entire cities wiped out isn't the worst thing?" Raynee shoved my hands away.

"The worst thing,"—Algard gave out a long breath—"is he obviously wants something from Jason. He called him out to affect a particular outcome, the nature of which is unknown to us. So, while your natural instinct will be to search for more information, you may wind up accidentally performing what he needs."

"That's just bullshit," Raynee said. "You're just too scared to do anything, just like the last time that monster was here."

I moved my arms back to her shoulders in a quiet attempt to calm her, but she shoved them away with a glare, and said, "You're the most powerful person we know, but you just let him go on killing."

"There are some things you don't understand, young girl. I suggest you keep to your school work."

"And what school work is that? Getting murdered while you sit here, all smug?"

The old man shook his head, then knelt next to Raynee and put his hand on her cheek. There were no tears, but his eyes were a tad sorrowful. "The first problem is that I can't kill him. None of us can. The art of using our forces to end the life of another has been lost for millennia. Until he arrived, we believed it equally impossible as killing oneself using any of the forces. Mordriss is the only one who knows how. Therefore, the best we can do is delay him."

"You could've still helped." She tried to withhold her tears.

Algard stood and walked over to the silent Farlan. "You know I wouldn't ask this if it weren't the most desperate of circumstances, but would you be so kind to leave us now? I have a private matter I wish to discuss."

"Of course," Farlan said. "Scary stuff, this Mordriss. I can't imagine the poor guy who took that video." He stood. "I bid you luck, Ralph and Gloria."

When Farlan had left, I wondered why Algard had bothered sending him away. It wasn't like he'd remember the conversation.

"Very well," Algard said once he was sure we were alone. "While I doubt my skills will be of any use, perhaps my knowledge can be. I fear asking this of you, because I suspect it's the very thing Mordriss wants. Our only hope therefore is for you to find an advantage in it before he does."

"What?" I replied. "We'll do anything."

"I need you to find your father."

A combination of anger and anxiety hit me simultaneously. My father was alive and out there, but why had Algard hidden this fact? Why didn't he tell me the moment we met?

"And how are we supposed to do that?" Raynee sneered, echoing my thoughts.

"I'm afraid I can't help you there, or I would have done it myself. But anyone who can create the universes and decombulator that were prepared for Jason, has powers in the range of Mordriss. There's a chance he may be able to help us. Of course, if that's what Mordriss wants, then we may only exacerbate our situation."

"You're not giving us much to go on," Raynee said. "Do you really have no idea who he is?"

"I do." Algard sat and covered his head with his hands. "It's a name that's been forbidden for many years, and I will not utter it now. We've spent a great deal of effort removing every trace of his existence, but I knew him many years ago."

"So you know his name, and won't even tell us that?" Raynee crossed her arms.

"I only suspect someone. Besides, he's the kind to never let go of a grudge. If he even suspects I sent you, there's no chance he'll help."

"Very well." Raynee stepped in front of me. "We'll head to Earth today, this instant."

Algard nodded. "But before you go, let's see if you'll have a school to return to."

The entire student body was assembled in the cenosance room. Darstan stood silently at the head, serving more as a ceremonial figurehead among the clatter and crying. Most had wet eyes, but from the cacophony of arguments there was little semblance of an agreement on what to do.

The students went silent when Algard's rigid figure appeared. Raynee and I took places at the back. With no words, he walked among the student body, placing an arm here and there for consolation. When he reached the room's center, he took another moment to meet each student's eyes.

"What says Oreca Gifted?" he shouted.

There was no answer.

"When Mordriss arrived last time, it was by surprise. By the time we knew his capabilities, he was already gone. But now we've been warned. He can reach our school and, if he desires, destroy us."

Everyone's head was down. They knew this was the truth.

"Our school has lasted for millennia. But never before has it faced such a threat. You all have families, and I understand the desire to seek comfort with them instead of continuing your education."

"What about a third option?" Revis asked, interrupting. He didn't have that broad smirk across his face. Instead, his countenance was serious and his fists were clenched. "Between all of us here, maybe we can do something. Maybe, if Mordriss dares pay us a visit, we can make him regret it."

There was doubt in Algard's eyes, but he neither shook his head nor replied.

"It's not just Algard," Revis added. "There are the other professors, and then there's us. Mordriss has always taken his victims one-by-one. What would he do if attacked by a hundred at once?"

"But what about Heskera?" a girl asked. "Don't you think those three thousand people fought back?"

"I don't think so. They were scared. Heck, we're all scared. But maybe, if we stick this out together, we have a chance."

Raynee gave me a quizzical look when I stepped forward.

"And the longer we stay here," I added. "The more we learn.

We'll have a better chance improving here, than just waiting for him at home."

Revis gave me a nearly imperceptible nod, then turned back to the crowd. "So, what do you say?" he shouted. "We're not closing thousands of years of learning just because of one loser, no matter how powerful he is."

There were slow murmurs of agreement, but still a few vociferous opponents.

"And what do I say to my family when I return home and they're dead?" Henry yelled.

"You come back here and tell us where he is," Raynee said out loud.

The student body made a path for her as she walked forward. She then grabbed my hand and we joined Revis.

"I'm sick of being scared," she shouted. "It's time we fight back. Why are we waiting for *him*? When we know where he is, we attack—every one of us. In the meantime, let's keep learning."

There was widespread applause at that remark, and Raynee bowed slightly to Revis, then left him alone on the stage.

"What says Oreca Gifted?" he yelled.

"We fight!" every student responded.

"Aren't we getting them a bit too riled up?" I whispered to her. "Attack or not, he has resonance powers none of us know. Algard said so."

"Yeah, but they're going to tear their hair out at home. It's better here. Studying will take their mind away from it."

"And if he comes out in the open? You just ordered an attack."

"Then we need to find your father before that happens."

Her eyes, though, confirmed my own worries. How did he have anything to do with Mordriss, and what could he possibly do to help?

"Come on, let's get out of here," she said.

When we were outside the school, I headed toward my ship, until Raynee pulled me away.

"We travel together for now. Can't take any chances."

"Even at night?" I grinned, and instantly regretted it.

My head slammed against the side of her ship, then my arms and legs bound together like a sardine.

"I don't want to hear any of that crap. We have a goal here. Don't forget. If you start thinking like that," she paused to look down, "I swear I'll resonate it in half."

She let me go, and I hesitantly held my hand out to follow her through the wormhole. She sighed, then we were through.

⤙

Sareya was standing in front of us.

"They cancelled school today. Because of Heskera."

Raynee rushed toward Sareya and hugged her tight. She was bawling, while Sareya was a bit confused.

"Do you have a hiding place?" Raynee asked while wiping away her tears.

"Yes, it's—"

"Don't tell me where it is. If there's a single scream, go there. Don't worry if it's a false alarm. Go there until you know for sure it's safe. That sick monster is out there. We both know what he does."

Raynee hugged her for another minute, then walked away and motioned me to follow. I waved back at Sareya, then followed Raynee into the woods. It felt strange knowing that I was about to return to Earth. That time seemed so long ago now. How little I knew then.

We didn't talk at all while Raynee made her way mechanically through the forest. While the portal for the turnip patch wasn't far, every tree here still looked the same. It seemed a miracle that she had found it once, and spectacular that she'd managed to find it again.

At last, we reached a thicket, where Raynee promptly essonated a portal and threw me inside. The green meadow and dark sky were familiar. We were back in my turnip patch. Raynee moved toward creating the portal to Earth, but I just stood there.

"Where did I used to . . .? Where was I?"

She paused, then softened her stance and searched among a mostly empty patch. "You were somewhere here." She pointed to a handful of holes.

Many of the turnips were now rotten, while dozens of others were completely gone. Empty depressions replaced the carcasses. I perused each one, wondering where I'd stayed all those years, and how I'd never noticed.

"We have to go," she whispered.

I followed her to a portal just on the side of the field, and we were back at my school. Sadly, where there was once a relatively new building of bright red brick, there now remained but a shell that was mostly rubble. The few remaining sections were blackened by fire, their broken windows giving but a glimpse into a place that had dominated the lives of hundreds.

There was no one around. Craters adorned the street where blasts had fallen those eons ago. It was a windy day with dark swirling skies, but the only things that moved were a few rustling piles of garbage.

We walked aimlessly down the street, with neither of us willing to state the obvious. We had no clue where to start. Was my father on this planet? How would we recognize him? There were trillions of better places out there. This was a poor guess.

Raynee, her eyes showing she was just as frustrated as I, finally created a portal. On the other side was my old neighborhood, once so familiar but now a foreign memory. Far away were the crumbling ruins of Seattle. There was nothing to see here outside of half-destroyed houses and blowing debris. The lonely house I'd grown up in was the last possibility. I half expected to find the same sort of ruins there, but neither of us expected what awaited.

Where my old block used to be was now a tropical forest. Myriad twisting trees grew everywhere from the street asphalt to straight out of the houses. I gave a puzzled look to Raynee and she shook her head. This wasn't her doing and the few trees she originally avalated couldn't have just propagated. Someone else from our dimension did this.

The jungle was thick here, and we stayed glued next to each other while we made our way. Who had done this? And more importantly, was he friendly? Raynee detected something stirring in a nearby tree. Each of us grabbed a trunk and flew upward.

Not long ago I would have been completely terrified running on a limb but a few inches thick a hundred feet above the ground. Now I resonated from limb to limb while I followed Raynee. There was nothing in this dimension that could hurt us, or so I hoped.

The tree rustled again and we split up to either side. Whatever it was had nowhere to go. I readied myself to avalate this thing out of existence, assuming it actually belonged to this dimension.

Something jumped and Raynee yelled "Don't hurt it!" Remembering back to the villagers in the desert world, I created a shield just as a large object collided with me. It was furry.

"Boongarry!" Raynee shouted and grabbed him. He was crawling all over us out of excitement. Immediately, Raynee resonated some food and held it from her hand.

"You look great. But who made this forest for you?"

As if on cue, Boongarry lowered himself from the tree and crawled over to my house. Cautiously, we followed him.

My house was in better shape than the majority of flattened properties, as it was missing only the front wall. Even the tremendous bathroom Raynee had created stood intact, without a single crack in a window pane. The door creaked open, and the tree kangaroo let himself inside.

Raynee pulled on my shoulder before we entered. "There's something in there," she whispered.

She moved to go in front, but I gently pushed her away. Though she was better than me in every way, I'd at least serve as a barrier. If whatever was inside incinerated me, she'd have time to react. Boongarry hopped around the corner, and something hissed.

I jumped around, only to come within inches of the scaly plates of an eight-foot reptile. I fell back, but it made no move against me. Raynee stepped to destroy it, but it only raised its huge hand in caution.

"We haven't much time," it hissed.

Raynee lowered her hand while it only stood there.

"You and Mordriss seek the same person. So, he has been well hidden. Find him, before evil hunts again."

After that, the creature slowly disintegrated into nothing, and we were left with an empty room, a tree kangaroo, and absolutely no clues.

23

"WHAT THE HELL does that mean?" Raynee asked out loud. "We still have no clue where to find him."

I sat next to Boongarry and petted him while considering the facts. However, the more I thought the less sense all of this made. Why had neither the lizard nor Algard mentioned my mother? Why couldn't I just find her? Mordriss wanted to find my father, too, but why? And finally, how was I supposed to find any of them?

"That thing didn't provide any hints Mordriss might find out about, because Mordriss is looking, too," I said after some thought. "I mean, we don't know if he's able to spy on us, but any clue would help *him* and *us*."

"Yes," Raynee said. "Did it take you the entire time to figure that out?"

There was something I was missing. Perhaps my father had left a clue. I just wasn't seeing it. Or, maybe my father was just a ruse, and it was my mother I needed to find. The answer seemed close, but I couldn't grasp it.

"This really sucks!" Raynee screamed, and a crack instantly formed in the wall. When that turned into rubble, I grabbed Boongarry and retreated outside. After another scream, the roof collapsed.

Raynee walked to me, not bothering to avalate and creating a swathe of disintegrated wood and shingles where she walked.

I watched in vain as everything except Raynee's addition collapsed into a ruin not unlike the rest of the neighborhood. It felt strange saying goodbye to my childhood home this way, but in truth I was no longer attached to it.

"There could've been a clue in there."

"You spent your entire life there, and have no idea if there's a clue?" She gave me an evil look. "Relax. There's nothing here."

She avalated back to our dimension, and I followed.

"What about Boongarry?" I asked.

Raynee whirled around to me. "Everyone we know is about to die, and you're worried about a tree kangaroo? Listen, if you're not going to help me, then go away. I need to figure this out."

"Maybe if we just relaxed a bit—"

"There's no time! Mordriss is out there, and if he isn't coming for us it'll be for our school, or Annie, or Sareya, or anyone else we care about. Don't you get it?"

"I'm just saying—"

"No, you're not. Go away. Leave me alone for a while."

While there was no comforting her, I couldn't just leave Raynee. Quietly, I moved behind the nearest tree. Of course, she could still resonate me and I her, but with no further screams I assumed she was satisfied.

She was right, of course, but there was no way around the fact that we were stuck. It occurred to me just then how horrible a turn everything had taken. Only an hour ago I was reveling in five hundred points and a date with Raynee. Now, she wasn't speaking to me and Mordriss had returned. Everything seemed so hopeless. Perhaps I could create a new universe, a better one on my own terms, and retreat there for the rest of my life.

Only weeks ago, that would have been beyond the best daydream. Now I had the tools to attempt it. It would have to be a tiny universe, of course, but that would make it more difficult to find. Who would bother to essonate inside a marble dropped in a tremendous forest?

Remembering all of the math, I attempted to create my dream world, but wound up with nothing. There wasn't even a pop. Proper cenosance required two particles at just the right positions, but each time there wasn't even a spark. How had I succeeded so wildly earlier?

I thought about Raynee. She would never join me in the new universe, no matter how wonderful I made it. There was Sareya and her friends at school. She was also not a quitter. No, this idea would never work. How had I been so foolish? The only world I needed was the one with her.

Though she was only a few feet away, I thought about those entrancing brown eyes. From that first day I'd glimpsed her, she'd been the most beautiful thing in existence. But there was more, wasn't there? There was a reason I was drawn to her. There was a reason my only successful universe came when I was thinking of her. A sharp pop occurred between my palms, followed by the feeling of glass in my fingers, and I immediately knew what to do.

Raynee was pacing furiously in all directions. Her hair was disheveled and her eyes were sullen. This wouldn't be easy.

"It's time for our second date," I said with confidence.

She stopped and I prepared for the onslaught.

"Are you insane? Of all the times?"

"Yes. You're in no shape for this. Heck, I'm messed up, too. We just need to get our minds away from everything. Then we can be fresh."

"There's no time." She sighed. "Listen, you're a nice guy, but maybe . . . maybe we just need to take a break from each other."

"Sorry. You already agreed to a second date, and we're long past due."

"I just said yes this morning! And I'm already regretting it."

I took a step forward. "Nope. Way before that, you promised

me a second date after I came back down that mountain with you. Well, your time is up."

Raynee folded her arms, but a bit of the grimace disappeared. "And I suppose you're going to make me?"

"Listen. There's a place I just created with a one percent time correlation. So, we can stay there more than an hour, and only a minute will pass here. I'm asking for a one-minute date. Is that okay?"

She smiled for the first time since Mordriss arrived. "Well, look how far our turnip's come. First date he takes me to a lousy Italian restaurant. Second date, he cenosates his own universe."

"So, you'll go."

"Yes. But I really just want to know what you managed to create in just a few minutes."

I placed the marble on the ground, and we both essonated inside. It wasn't much to look at. We were floating in empty space. Around us were myriad stars, and the occasional black hole. Raynee had a perturbed look.

"Are we just going to float around here for an hour, or are there any interesting planets?"

"No. I still can't make biologics, but we're fine here."

I moved forward and grabbed her left hand with my right, then held it up.

"What are you doing?" she said, but I shushed her.

"Listen," I whispered.

The black holes around us were radiating. Yet, unlike the usual ones, I'd given them a particular tone. Each sounded like a smooth violin, and together they made a symphony.

She laughed as the song started. Hundreds of black holes provided an ambience, while the largest did a solo. And that was just the start.

Only a light year away from us, a star collapsed into itself and a supernova burst forth. The explosion was blinding, but not deafening. It was like the beat of a single huge drum.

Another one burst, followed by five more. The beats combined with the orchestra of violins, while cosmic explosions surrounded us and I placed my other arm around her waist. When the quasars starting blaring like trumpets, I twirled her around.

There was a glint in her eye and she briefly let go to brush her hair back. Then we danced under the music of a billion stars.

"I can't believe you did this!" she cried.

I pulled her closer while a supernova burst close by. Fragments flew past us, but there was no fear in this world. I put my hand on her back and we twirled together.

"I finally remembered the secret," I said.

She looked at me incredulously. "A secret. Really?" Her voice was sarcastic.

"It's you, Raynee." I pulled her an inch from me. "Every time I think of you, I create. Without you . . . nothing."

"No," she said soothingly. "That's not true. You know you have the hots for Darstan."

I dropped my head down and laughed, then our eyes locked together. We swirled among the blasts and the beats for what seemed like eons. Our eyes never left each other. Hers had so much longing, and that's when I knew.

Gently I pressed my arm against her, and our lips met. I closed my eyes amid our slow dance among the stars, with the sweet caress of her lips. She stopped dancing, then grabbed me with both her arms and pressed her tongue against mine.

Our arms held each other tight while we kissed, then she drew her head back and snuggled against my chest.

"Why can't it be this simple?"

I stroked her hair, feeling how it slid softly against my fingers.

"Not sure that was simple." I kissed her again. "Let's see, I had to climb a mountain, fight lizards and robots, travel to another dimension, get treated like an idiot, and finally build my own universe. All that for a kiss."

"Was it worth it?" She leaned up for another kiss, but held back slightly.

"Absolutely." I pulled her in. "Makes me a bit scared, though."

"About what?" she asked, then grew serious upon remembering our task.

"What am I going to have to do for a third date?"

Raynee gave me a gentle slap on the cheek. She was smiling, but her eyes were elsewhere. This perfect moment would not last much longer, but there was still one more thing to know.

"I'm just curious. What did you tell Sareya?"

She put her finger on my nose, then tapped it. "Wouldn't you like to know." She used her hooked smile.

"Well, you can tell me, or I'll just ask Sareya."

"She won't tell you." She looked back into my eyes.

"Oh, yes, she will. If I promise to tell her what happened just now."

"You wouldn't!" She backed away while still holding me.

I pulled her back in. "Wouldn't that make her day—"

"Fine!" She pulled me in for another kiss. "It was way back when I still thought you were a turnip. Boongarry was sick and I didn't know enough avalance to fix him. Even though your universe was ending, you took him to the vet. I'd always thought turnips were mechanical and horrible things, but I saw your heart. You were also pretty cute."

Raynee held me tight, then put her lips to my ear. "So, I told Sareya, if you weren't a turnip, I'd probably go for you."

We held each other tight for the next few minutes. Neither of us wanted to return to reality, but we both knew there was no escape. It would find us soon enough.

Not willing to return so soon, I began to wonder about Raynee's family. With so much focus on my parents, she'd revealed so little about hers.

"What were your parents like?"

She gave me a strange look. "Why do you want to know?"

"I'm just wondering what it was like . . . before . . . you know."

She brushed her hair back and smiled. "My mother was a solarnator. Don't think they have those on Earth, but they do all sorts of things, like making sure the suns are giving enough light, the universe isn't too cold. I mean, it sounds basic, but is realy complicated stuff. She loved doing it, though."

"And your father?"

Raynee tilted her head back and laughed. "My father was a master avalator. Every day I'd make up some crazy food, like chocolate brownie fudge ice cream with raspberries and cherries inside that popped when you bit into them, and he'd make it. And as delicious as I dreamed it up, his stuff was always better."

She held me tight while supernovas faded behind us.

"We had this huge house. Not like Earth. Big houses there are stupid because they're all about money. They build them for show, not for fun. Here, everyone has lots of space and we can avalate whatever we want, so we just make the house we need. But we always had so many visitors that we needed tons of bedrooms and banquet rooms."

"My father used to joke that they came to see my mother. She was so beautiful, and she used to avalate the most stunning gowns. But I think they came for my father's food. Anyone can avalate, but not like he did."

She reached for my hand, then stared for a moment at my palm.

"I miss them terribly, but Val and I had an awesome childhood. My parents were very simple. I had a girlfriend, Sandy, whose father was a master cenosator before Mordriss got him, too. He built universes in the basement. My father built slides. I loved my parents. They were so much in love that it kind of rubbed off on those around them."

She turned, and I knew our time was almost up. "What's wrong with this world?" she asked. "I mean, what did they do to hurt anyone? Nothing makes sense anymore."

She moved away and I didn't reach for her. It was better to let her vent.

"Mordriss went out of his way to kill them. Did I ever tell you that? He killed mostly in another town that day, but made a special trip over. Why? And there's weirdness, too. Take Sareya, bless her beautiful heart. How could the grand master of resonance not detect a baby under a sheet? They say that he's just some insane killer who murders randomly, but I don't think so. It's almost like he plans to murder some and not others."

"So, the three thousand in Heskera—"

"I know it sounds sick and twisted, but there's some reason he did that. It might've been just to get your attention."

Her eyes had grown fierce, and I knew that our brief but amazing moment was over.

"We have to go back," she whispered.

I nodded slightly, and we both avalated to the forest. Raynee moved away.

"One last thing." I picked up the marble and handed it to her. "Something to remember this by."

She eyed it for a moment, then asked, "Do you still have the other one?"

"Yes." I reached into my pocket and placed it in my palm. "You can have them both. They're all from you."

Raynee reached out and gently took the original one. "I'll take this one. It has more of you in it. Besides, it's not like I'm going dancing myself."

She avalated a gold necklace, then a mount for the universe, and hung it around her neck. The marble disappeared down her sweater, and when she caught my stare, she returned a devious look.

We walked for some ways in the woods while torn between the beautiful time we'd just had, and the terrors that might come. I let Raynee lead, since I still had no idea how to get anywhere because the pathways were tree trunks that looped and twisted in every direction. I started to wonder if getting lost in this labyrinth wouldn't be a bad thing. After all, there were advantages to never having to return to the real world.

"So, what now?" I asked as we walked into a bright opening at the end of a trunk.

"I need to check on Sareya first, then we'll meet your—"

Raynee's eyes grew wide and she collapsed to her knees. I was too busy looking at her to notice, but when I turned my head, the world turned real.

Her entire village had been reduced to charred embers. Mutilated bodies and blood were strewn across the field. Raynee held the ground tight, and we both in vain called out the same name.

"Sareya!"

24

RAYNEE COULDN'T MOVE, so I took on the dreaded task of searching the torn fragments of bodies for one with two blond braids. She had been absolutely correct. This world made no sense. If Mordriss were after my father, why didn't we run across him? Why didn't he take us, instead of these innocents? Why had he instead killed a six-year-old girl?

The sight of so many limbs and heads, most with their mouths agape as if asking "why," made me want to hurl, but I trudged forward. This would be far worse a task for Raynee, who knew everyone here. I'd only met one, and I was praying to not find her.

As I moved between the dozen odd houses here, the thought occurred of an even worse fate: Raynee had ordered her to hide, and Sareya was a very smart girl. She'd never make it to the forest, so there had to be a hidden chamber in one of these homes, every one of which had been incinerated. Sareya had been burned alive.

I stopped in the middle of the village and the reality hit me. Sareya was dead. Mordriss had finally gotten her. There was no blanket to miss this time. A demon like that didn't make the same mistake twice. She'd hidden in one of the houses, and Mordriss had destroyed every single one.

Why had he done this? And then everything made twisted sense. That creature still needed something from us. We hadn't found my father yet, and this was a bitter message to hurry up the job.

I was now officially from this place. Like everyone else, I'd lost someone dear. An empty hole resided inside me now, full of memories of that bright, blue-eyed girl who'd saved me so many times that first week. She'd taught me both resonance and orasance, and so many things about this horrible place I now called home.

As I looked upon the lifeless, I swallowed my tears and set to my task. These were Raynee's loved ones. She shouldn't have to bear seeing them like this. With care, I orasated to each of them only so long as to learn their names. The more times I witnessed Raynee's smiling face in their lives, the angrier I became that someone had done this to her and to them.

I avalated holes for each, then pieced together what I could of their bodies and erected tombstones with their names and history. Following the tradition, I kept a small piece of bone for the top. I only hoped they had loved ones who survived, and would one day orasate them.

When I finished burying the corpses, I resonated every bit of the embers for signs of Sareya, then disintegrated the debris to an invisible dust. Nothing now remained of Raynee's village, save twenty tombstones clustered to one side. They seemed rather lonely in this wide field, so I avalated several wisterias to give them a beautiful cover from the glare of the suns.

Raynee joined me. Her eyes were dark and she hadn't bothered to wipe her tears away.

"I couldn't find her," I said. "But I think she was inside . . . when he burned them."

"We can't even orasate her," she cried.

While I held her, an anger unknown rose within me. I would've traded my life for Sareya's, but I'd trade far more for Raynee's. She was more than my life's essence. If Mordriss ever dared to go there, I'd have to go with her.

"He wants my father. Maybe we should just stop."

"No. He's our only hope. If we give up . . . he'll just keep on killing."

I thought back to the desert world from so long ago. I'd already asked for clues there, with nothing to show, but it was our only option. Still, it was the last place I wanted to be right now, with all of its torture and murder. Yet Raynee was right. How had Mordriss even reached this place in no time? He should have been here a year from now. His powers were growing. My father was our only hope to defeat him, and we had to keep searching.

As if in a trance, I led her to that spot where I'd ditched Sareya those eons ago. It seemed like a particularly horrible thing in retrospect. I couldn't imagine that amazing girl crying now, let alone screaming.

The thought occurred that Mordriss himself might be following us. After all, why would he just torch the village and leave? But then, his task was complete. He'd sent his message, and we were acting the dutiful slaves right now. There was nothing else we could do.

"Are you sure this is it?" Raynee asked when we reached the dreaded spot.

I nodded, then hugged her and let my own tears flow. She held tight and we both bawled underneath the twisted limbs in this terrible world, until a sound startled us. Thirty spotted rodents now surrounded us on five sides, and they didn't look happy.

"Come with us, fuckers," one said.

It made no sense, but we followed as they traipsed over and under huge limbs. Soon, I'd forgotten again which way was up. They stopped at a tremendous trunk that formed under a massive swirl of vines. I tried to resonate what was inside, but couldn't. The bark was somehow too thick.

Then a blond curl appeared from inside, followed by two gleaming blue eyes, and Raynee screamed. We both ran toward the muddy but otherwise unharmed Sareya.

She was crying when Raynee seized her.

"Are they all dead?" she asked with tears streaming down.

My eyes betrayed the answer and Raynee held tighter.

"But, how—?" I started. "How are you here?"

"People started screaming, so I hid like I promised. Then these guys found me and said my spot wasn't safe. They took me here. It's resonance proof."

"You three shitheads are the only ones who give us food," the tallest rodent said. "So, we had to look out for ourselves, you know?"

Raynee smiled, then avalated piles of nuts, berries, and fruits around them. The rodents jittered and shouted as they dove in, while their leader just looked at us.

"That's all great and everything, but we're still going to want more fucking food someday, so you assholes had better stick around."

While the rodents continued to devour their prize, my heart suddenly dropped. "We have to go back."

"Nothing's there," Raynee replied. "We're safer here."

"But, Annie—" Raynee only shook her head.

"I'm sorry." Tears flowed down her face. "While you . . . cleaned up my village, I saw to Annie. She was never the same after her family died."

I sat and held my head down.

"She's at peace now," Raynee said softly.

Annie never deserved this. She took me in when I didn't have a home. She gave me her son's room, the same son that Mordriss had taken from her. And now she was gone, too, probably ripped to pieces like that creature preferred.

"Why am I here?" I cried.

Raynee sat and put her arm around me, then lowered her head below mine. "What do you mean?"

"I mean, why did I have to leave Earth? Everyone either hated me or ignored me, but at least people I cared about didn't die!"

"Would you have rather we hadn't met?"

"No, no," I looked into those stunning brown eyes. "You're . . . you're the most amazing thing in any universe. But I love you and can't protect you. I can barely avalate an apple, and he's going to come for you, too. He's trying to destroy me, and I don't know why."

"Then let's find your father and end this." Her teeth were clenched. "I know how you feel. Everyone I spent the last six years with just died."

She couldn't withhold the tears now, either. "I need you to be strong for me right now, because I'm breaking up. I don't think I could've taken losing Sareya. We can't let him destroy us."

I gently lifted her head up with the tip of a finger, raising it with mine, then brushed back her hair with my hand. She was still far more powerful than I, and in fact now that I understood some of the math and forces, reaching her level seemed more daunting than ever before. But she needed me.

"I love you, Raynee. You're a quality vegetable."

And then she kissed me. This wasn't the delicate exploratory kind like in my marble universe, but the mad-faces-pressed-against-each-other, and tongues-doing-the-tango kind. I pulled her so tight that we nearly tumbled off the log. She backed away just for a moment, and was about to go a second round when we caught those bright blue eyes staring at us.

"Cool!" Sareya said.

"Holy fucking shit," a rodent said. "Could you not do that around the food?"

Raynee straightened her sweater and I stared at the rodents eating for a bit until they were uncomfortable and I felt no need for explanations to a six-year-old.

Raynee discussed leaving Sareya at the tree trunk, but the rodents wouldn't have it. She seemed a bit perturbed when they explained that the math was complicated, and it wouldn't protect her for long, so we bid the rodents goodbye, then made our way deeper into the forest. Though we were unsure there was anywhere else to hide against such a monster, it felt the safer way to go. For food, I avalated some apples, Sareya some marshmallows, and Raynee everything else. After the emotional day, we all felt it best to get some rest. The Khan could wait a day.

When we found as level a spot as possible, I attempted to impress by avalating some blankets. Raynee only smirked, then constructed a multi-story treehouse between two snarling trunks. Inside was a warm fireplace and bedroom complete with a gigantic mattress and duvet.

We huddled by the fire, which conveniently didn't produce any smoke. It was an impressive illusion, capable of giving off heat but neither choking nor burning. We sat there for nearly an hour, each of us processing the events of the day, and no one willing to discuss the task still before us.

Finally, Raynee sighed and avalated herself a thin gown that barely clung over her breasts. I tried not to stare, as her legs and shoulders, which had always been covered, now glistened under the candles she'd conveniently added. She gave me a devilish smile, then avalated away my clothes to just a pair of black boxers.

"What?" she said. "Fair is fair."

Sareya stood halfway inside the door.

"If you two are going to have sex, could you avalate me to another room?"

"No need." Raynee laughed and motioned her to lay between us.

She gave us a strange look, then snuggled her tiny body between us, while Raynee brushed her hair. When her bright eyes looked up at me, she smiled, then fell into a deep sleep. She then drew closer to me while Raynee smiled.

"Still want to be a turnip?"

"No."

⟡

In most respects, I never truly had a family. Sure, I had beings who I grew up calling parents, but they were as caring as carrots. Now here I was with Raynee lying before me, her hair glistening in the candle light, and tiny Sareya nestled between us.

This was heaven, but there was a demon waiting at the gates. Were Mordriss to enter this cabin then and take them, there was absolutely nothing I could do. The better things got, the more fearful I became.

"If anything ever happens," she said, noticing my pause. "I love you, Jason."

She closed her eyes, and we all dreamed of our very same world, but without the monster. I had a family here, the best I ever could have wanted. As wonderful as the paramount dimension was, though, it was also cruel. Mordriss would be back.

Raynee was already dressed and pacing when I awoke. She was more radiant than I'd ever seen, and there was something new about her. I'd only dreamed of waking to her bewitching glare and hypnotizing grin, and wondered how many more I'd have.

I moved to get out of bed, but she only held me down lightly with her palm, then leaned over and kissed me.

"Don't wake her," she whispered, and I felt Sareya rustle next to my chest.

"I'll avalate you something to eat," she said. "What would you like?"

It was a simple question that no one had ever asked me before. When at last I requested a lamma fruit, she shook her head and laughed. In many ways, I was still a turnip to her.

She returned a few seconds later with something best describable as split-open lammas, with thick scrambled eggs, bacon-like meat, and a few chocolate chips in between. It was the most delicious thing I'd ever tasted.

Sareya popped on sensing the plumeria scent of breakfast, and Raynee handed her a plate of the same but with a few extra fruits she loved. While Sareya ate, I avalated myself some clothes, but wound up nearly choking myself in a way-too-small sweatshirt.

"I don't understand." Raynee dressed me in a snap of her fingers. "How could someone so clueless be so awesome at cenosance?"

While I watched Raynee turn to dote on Sareya, it occurred to me that I was the new person in this equation. Sareya and Raynee had both grown up with no one, so they'd latched on to each other. Raynee was as much Sareya's big sister as she was her adoptive mother.

When we'd lumbered outside, Raynee waved her hand and the entire treehouse disappeared. There was to be no trace of us. We were migrants now.

We said little while we made our way to the Khan's world. The essonation point was close to Annie's house, and there was no confirmation Mordriss had ever left. Of course, our silence was no barrier to him feeling us with resonance, so perhaps we just didn't want to speak of it.

When I got confused on the way, Sareya took over and led us to the spot. A short time later, I'd recalled the set of portals necessary, and the three of us stood before the harsh windswept landscape of the Khan's desert world.

Raynee avalated herself and Sareya sunhats, and I led them to the village. Jamol and Ilyos awaited us.

"Who is your father?" Ilyos said to me. "And why do your women not walk behind you, with their heads covered?"

"Pipe it, dinosaur," Raynee replied. "We're here to help."

"We come as friends," I added.

Jamol reached for his scabbard, while Ilyos rubbed his fingers under his chin.

"The Khan is coming," I said, while he decided.

"Heathen scouts!" Jamol yelled, then charged at us with his scabbard drawn.

Raynee sighed and with a flourish of her hand, he was dust.

"We're friends!" I shouted while Ilyos backed away in horror.

"And seriously, what's Jamol's problem? Every time I come here, he dies!"

Ilyos turned and fled. We took chase through the small gathering of huts, until the old man halted, then collapsed back with an arrow through his head. The Khan's army stood before us.

A dozen soldiers were already lighting the huts aflame, while inside the women and children shrieked. I'd been through this drill before. I extinguished every spark with my own powers.

Raynee gave me a glance of surprise. "Which one's the Khan?" she asked while we admired the ten thousand horsed warriors.

"I think she's the only woman."

"Easy then." Raynee waved her hand and all but a familiar face disintegrated. "We don't have time for the bullshit."

The middle-aged woman seemed unfazed by the loss of her army, and calmly approached in the same proud manner as if they were still present.

"This world is meant for you, Jason Bezna," she shouted over the blowing sand. "Why did you bring help?"

"I've been here before. I passed your tests. But Mordriss is back, and you're the only clue we have."

Her eyes gleamed. "So, it's come to that?" she asked when she'd reached us.

"Yes," I replied. "We need to find him. Can you tell us anything?"

The Khan sat on a nearby stool, paused for a few moments to stretch her aching legs and back, then stared at Sareya.

"Is this your wife and daughter?" she asked with a surprise tear.

"No," Raynee said, noticing me formulating an answer. "I'm Raynee, his girlfriend. This is Sareya, my sister."

"How interesting," the Khan said. "Most unexpected."

"In what way?" Raynee asked, but the woman only shook her head.

"Someday, I hope before the end, you'll know. Right now, I'm considering your request."

"Please help us. We're out of options. We need to find my father to stop Mordriss. We know he created this world."

"He did." She had resolute eyes. "Very well. I'm sure you understand that I'm only a creation, and that what you see here is but a copy of that place you call Earth. Where you grew up, which I'm sure felt very real to you, was another copy. I can provide some information about the original, but once I do, this universe will self-destruct and you may never return, no matter how much you'll want to."

That seemed an odd thing to say. Why would I ever want to return here? All that I'd ever witnessed was torture and bloodshed. While she waited, I nodded.

"I was unfortunately not provided with Earth's location." All three of us moaned. "But I can give you definite information on where to find it."

We perked up.

"Only two ever knew that place. The first was your father, a man named Avarus. The second was his best friend, Algard. I believe you know him."

Anger rose within me on the realization that Algard had sent us on this useless task, when he himself knew. Had he not known we would uncover him?

"The two had a disagreement years ago, before you were born. So Algard is your only hope now. Yet I must warn you. He will not part with the information willingly. There is a great secret hidden in that world, and to him Mordriss is the lesser evil."

Raynee and I both looked at each other with helplessness. How would we force someone as powerful as Algard to tell us? He'd already dismissed us once.

The mountains far away were now sinking, and all around us the sands blew, consuming every building and plant in existence.

"One last question," I shouted over the roar. "What's your name?"

The Khan beamed at me.

"Here, I am the Khan. But I was modeled after another."

The edges of the world were disappearing, and the Khan herself was barely visible.

"Her name was Sa'ira," she shouted.

Only her face was left now.

"She was your mother."

25

SO THAT WAS what my mother had looked like, and already I couldn't remember her. There was a face and a name. That's all I had. I closed my eyes and struggled to remember anything, but it had all happened too fast.

"Lean down," Sareya said.

She placed her hand on my forehead and whistled a soft tune. I was back in the desert, talking with the Khan again. She looked tired from her years. Was that how she really was? And yet, there was love in her eyes. Sareya orasated me back to our first meeting. Yes, she had been harsh, but I never noticed the excitement in her face when I finally succeeded. This copy had received the same love from my original mother.

Sareya released her hand and we were back in the forest.

"You can always visit your memories," she said quietly.

"Orasance," Raynee said out loud. "That's the only way."

"The only way to what?" I asked.

"Algard." She looked away. "We're going to have to orasate him. Your mother said he won't give it up willingly."

"But he won't like that, right?" Sareya said.

"No," Raynee replied somberly. "Not at all."

She began to pace while Sareya and I looked on.

"I could orasate him," Sareya offered after a few minutes. "If you hold him down."

I began to shake my head, but Raynee perked up. "That might work."

"Are you crazy?" I replied. "How—"

"She knows enough orasance. It's not that complicated." She looked at me. "But how's your resonance?"

Without waiting for an answer, Raynee constructed two large foam barriers in a nearby field while I nervously looked on. How was I supposed to attack someone with resonance? I had no idea.

"These are for sparring. When we hit them, it won't hurt. You just need to push me against one."

"Shove you with resonance?"

"Yes." She stood motionless.

Back in school, I'd been drilled to never hit a girl, but in this case, I felt more like a mouse trying to smack Godzilla. Even without Raynee trying, this wasn't a fair fight.

"Come on!" she said while I just stood there. "It's impossible to harm yourself with resonance, and don't worry about hurting me."

That was the least of my thoughts. The counterattack concerned me far more. Nevertheless, I closed my eyes and visualized her body, then regrettably forged a blast at her. I never even saw if it hit.

There was a whishing sound from the foam barrier that I was now embedded inside. Every joint ached from the blow, while Raynee hadn't budged. When I tried moving my arms, they were stuck. Raynee had hit me so hard that the foam had enveloped me.

She groaned, then waved her hand to push me out.

"You keep thinking like you're on Earth. Don't try to punch me. It's a battle of wills."

Again, I tried to match her, and again I was tossed deep into the foam. Raynee fumed and we set up again. This time she waited until my strongest attempt had lightly brushed her hair, then promptly sent me flying.

Raynee screamed. "I can't take down Algard myself! I need your help."

Between pummelings, an idea had formed. I crawled out of the cave she'd placed me in, then held out my palm in surrender.

"What if I find someone else? Someone even better than you."

She held back her assault. "And who would that be?"

"Darstan."

"Are you insane? He's more likely to help him."

Without warning, she pounded me back into the foam. And then it hit me. Algard had made a mistake.

"Heskera!" I shouted while struggling to get out. "Algard was there."

"What?"

"Remember that day I was stuck at school because Revis destroyed my wormhole?"

"You weren't stuck. You were just stupid."

"Regardless, I met Algard that night. He said he was going to Heskera."

I tiptoed toward her while she thought. I could be embedded in foam again at any moment.

"Darstan will help us. I spent most of the night with him. He lost his family to Mordriss. He'll be pissed that Algard was covering things up."

Raynee sighed. "*If* he joins us, then we stand a chance. If he doesn't, then we'll be expelled before class begins."

"He's our only shot."

Raynee avalated a ship, we setup our wormholes, and the three of us headed to Oreca Gifted. Every outcome here would end in expulsion. I'd spent so much effort getting in, it felt sad that this would be my last trip. Algard had said I would receive no mercy, but never did he imagine what was in store.

We arrived an hour before classes, and found Darstan reading in his office. He stood when we entered, and gave us a broad smile. "To what do I owe the honor?" He then noticed Sareya. "Come on, you know it's forbidden to bring non-students."

"We need your help," I said.

He backed away slightly from my serious stare. "Why am I not getting a warm fuzzy feeling about this?" he said, while looking at Sareya.

"We need to orasate Algard," Sareya said.

Darstan glared at us for a moment, then burst into laughter. "Holy shit!" He slapped his desk. "You had me going. That has to be the all-time funniest thing—"

"We're not joking," Raynee said. "Algard sent us to find Jason's father, and we found out that he's been hiding him this entire time. Jason's Earth was just a copy. We need the original, and only Algard knows where it is."

"My father's name is Avarus. He and Algard had a falling out. Our only hope to stop Mordriss is to find my father, but Algard will never let that happen."

"You'll be expelled immediately."

"We understand," Raynee said. "This is our last option. We can't take Algard ourselves."

"No shit," Darstan replied.

"And he was at Heskera," I added. "That night when I stayed here, he told me he was going there."

"Are you messing with me?" Darstan shouted.

"No." I walked forward and leaned my forehead over his desk. I prepared both my short discussion with Algard, and with the Khan. After some hesitation, he placed his hand over it, then collapsed onto his chair.

Darstan sat in silence while we waited, then wiped the sweat from his head. "I'm not going to attack our headmaster myself. This is my home, and I can't . . . go back. But I can give you advice."

Raynee, who was at her wit's end with hints, groaned.

"Jason here is the best cenosator I've ever seen. He's also the worst resonator. But, you can use cenosance as a weapon." He stood, waved his arms, and a spiral galaxy emerged from his hand and knocked us back. "If you concentrate, you can make one big enough. The power from the expansion is extreme. Even someone like Algard will have trouble.

"Second, it's not the location of Earth that's his best kept secret. It's whatever that universe is hiding. That's the secret he may think you want, and you may catch him by surprise by taking something else.

"The best time is right after classes begin. Any teacher will help him, but we'll all be in lessons. You'll have him alone. Jason, you blast him with cenosance. He'll need a lot of energy to resist that. So Raynee, you hold him down, and I assume you, little girl, orasate him."

We looked between each other. While we'd hoped for his help, this plan was workable.

"And finally, I do have to say this is the craziest thing I've ever heard."

After Darstan bid us farewell, Raynee and I both paced madly across the hallway. Were we really going to do this? Sareya only shook her head.

"How about we just ask him?" she suggested. "Easy peasy."

"If we ask him," Raynee said, "then he'll know what we want. But we could ask him about Avarus."

It was worth a shot. We hid while the other students filed in, then, once the lessons began, we searched for Algard. My heart was racing, and he was way too easy to be found. His normally disheveled hair was straight, and his mustache was recently thinned. He seemed unfazed by our approach.

"What's she doing here?" He pointed to Sareya.

"What did Avarus find?" Sareya asked.

Algard smirked, then frowned after a long silence.

"Go home, little girl. As for you two, minus three hundred points for disrespect."

"Did Avarus have anything to do with Heskera?" I knew the question would likely mean the end of my points and a subsequent expulsion. "You visited it before Mordriss."

"A coincidence, and I don't like your tone."

"We searched for Avarus," Raynee said. "But you already knew his name, didn't you? You never planned for us to actually find anything."

"I will have nothing of this sort! You are both expelled—"

Since he'd stated the inevitable, I felt it necessary to deserve it. Raynee was next to me. I took a deep sigh, and knew I could do it. There would be no more questions.

The entire hallway split apart, and the blast from my universe threw the stunned Algard into the foyer. A whirlwind of planets and small supernovas spun before me, taking out everything from the floor tiles to the occasional sofa. Just when he stood, I slammed him back down with it.

He reached a hand out, but Raynee was on him. She resonated him upward, then threw him against the wall while he screamed. With every bit of strength, I pressed my spinning mass of darkness against him. A supernova crashed into him, while Raynee cried as she desperately held him down.

Sareya didn't need the call. She walked nimbly across the ceiling and reached for his forehead.

The headmaster roared, and the wall behind him cracked. "Enough!" he bellowed and the wall crumbled.

Two sudden blasts sent Raynee and me down in succession. In one gesture of his hand, my universe smashed through the opposite wall and disintegrated.

Students were now pouring in around us.

"How dare you!"

"No!" I replied. "How dare you! You knew all along how to stop Mordriss. You *let* him murder everyone. You, the one person who knew the secret to destroying him, let us down."

"I did nothing of the sort. You have no idea. Now get the hell out of here. I never want to see any of you in this school again."

"No," Raynee replied. "My mother, my father, my brother, my entire town died because you wouldn't take a stand. You knew Avarus was the key to Mordriss, but you were too chickenshit to get him."

"Avarus was pursuing something that should never be touched! I'm sorry for your family, I really am, but there are worse evils."

"You bastard!" I added. "You probably set Heskera up. You knew he would attack there."

There were a hundred students around us now, along with all of the professors. The wall to Darstan's classroom had been destroyed.

"And what was so bad that you let that creature murder everyone?" Raynee asked, then pointed at Sareya. "You see this little girl? He tried to kill her yesterday. How do you explain that to her? How is her life not important?"

"You have no idea of the consequences—" he began, but never finished.

A tremendous blast of resonance lifted Algard in the air and pummeled him through three successive walls.

"My wife, my daughter, died!" Darstan screamed at the top of his lungs. "And you did nothing!"

The entire wing of the school burst into cinders and Algard faced off against the fuming professor.

"Keep out of this, Darstan!"

They both fired at the same time, but Algard was a master for a reason. Darstan, against his best effort, flew through the back of Fantasa's classroom.

I didn't wait for him to turn to us.

This time I was the one who roared, then pounded Algard with a fifty-foot tornado of creation. Students dove for cover, while others were tossed aside by the twisting, pulsating mass of stars. Raynee resonated him down, then Darstan appeared from the rubble and added his own fury.

Algard was screaming, but against our combined forces was momentarily helpless. With a wink, Sareya leaped over my whirlwind of destruction and planted her palm on the headmaster's forehead. He roared, but had no power left to resist her.

I felt my entire body weaken from holding up this bulging universe. Raynee, too, was straining.

"I can't hold him much longer!" Darstan shouted. "She needs to find it. Now!"

Sareya lifted her palm from the reddening Algard, then proceeded to smack him hard across the face. The motion stunned him, more for its audacity than its strength. She then shoved her palm against his forehead, and closed her eyes again.

"I got it!" she yelled. Raynee resonated Sareya and me against her, then formed a portal to the meadow with the billion droplets just outside the school's universe.

"It's here," Sareya said, then formed a portal a few feet away.

Seconds later, we were on Earth.

We stood outside what should have been my house. Gone was the jungle complete with tree kangaroo. A young boy and girl played in the front yard, while their parents looked on. Everything looked so familiar, yet so completely different.

"So, how do we find him?" Raynee asked.

There was no time for false leads now. Algard would certainly pursue us, once he dealt with Darstan. Luckily, I'd given this moment some thought.

"We need to find the Khan."

Raynee groaned. "How many damn Khans do we need to find?"

"Just one more. My mother passed on the job to another, a turnip. He terrorized the world. His name was Temujin."

"Do you mean Genghis Khan?" she asked.

"Ummm—"

"You're hopeless, sometimes," she added with her melting smile.

A man passed us while looking at his phone, and Raynee froze him in place for a moment, then released him.

"Your Khan is buried in an unknown location. To keep it secret, he killed everyone who carried his body there and constructed his burial site."

"Well, he sucks," Sareya said.

"We can find him," Raynee added. "It'll just be annoying."

She essonated a portal, and immediately we were standing in the bitter cold, with endless green plains around us. A few inches of stone wall revealed what may have been a palace, long ago.

"Someone knew." She closed her eyes to resonate around us. Within seconds, small bone fragments rose to midair. Sareya and I nodded, and we each took one.

It didn't take long to orasate someone who had met the Khan, but a bit longer for someone alive during the funeral. When we'd located the date the party left, Raynee pulled us away.

"Been studying a bit. This'll be pretty cool."

Raynee reached down and grabbed a handful of dirt, then poured it slowly down. While the grains drained from her fingers, the ghostly mirage of an army appeared. They were mirror images of Sa'ira's troops. There were grim but sad demeanors on each of the immaculately adorned warriors. They weren't fools. This would be their last march.

We watched them march to the wilderness, then moved ahead. Raynee fast forwarded it, and within minutes we were witnessing a swarm of soldiers, a few digging the grave, with the rest laboring to redirect a river over it.

She dropped the remaining sand over the grave, and we stood in a nondescript spot on the edge of nowhere. The river had long ago meandered elsewhere, and there was now no sign that one of the most vicious men in Earth's history was buried here.

Remembering my procedure on the school's founder, I lifted the dried corpse from the dusty earth. Precious few fragments remained of the actual body, but it was enough. All three of us touched him at the same time.

Everything had been orasated blank, save one part near the end of his life. A thick, heavily armored man stood in a vast empty yurt. Not a single object, save the carpets used for floor decorations, adorned the interior. From outside, there was only wind.

"I am now fulfilling your wishes, oh Great One," he said out loud with no one else in listening range. "You made me, on great pain, memorize this until today."

He then proceeded to read out several numbers. When he finished, he calmly stood and walked from the tent. There was no one outside.

Just when I was ready to bang my head in after another useless clue, Raynee sighed in frustration at me.

"They're coordinates." She created another portal.

We were in some jungle. A kookaburra called in the distance, while before us was an endless maze of vines and twisted trunks. She knelt, then lifted a tiny marble. It was another universe.

A single familiar blue planet circled around a very particular sun. It was another Earth clone, but this time without the filler. There were no other galaxies or stars. Only one planet existed in this solar system, and on it was but a single straw hut, standing defiantly on a vast green plain, with empty blackness above it.

The door cracked open when we approached, and a strongly built, bearded man appeared from behind it. Raynee and Sareya both halted with me as I realized the next few steps would change my life forever.

This man had the same brown eyes as mine, but he wasn't smiling. There was a weariness of years across his face. His grim demeanor revealed neither surprise nor anger, only penitence. He was my father.

"We can spare the reunion," he said while I nervously walked forward. "There isn't any time."

I didn't want this to end. Here I had a million questions about my provenance, and his first words were that we had no time.

"Mordriss is coming, isn't he?" I asked.

"Yes. I'm sure you guessed, but I'm Avarus. Your father."

Though he had the countenance of a snarling grizzly, he was still family. I opened my arms and moved to hug him, but he shoved me away.

A tear fell down Raynee's cheek.

"There are some things you need to know. Important things."

Though our meeting wasn't as emotional as I'd dreamed, this was still my father. I had to do something, no matter how small. "Very well." I held out my hand. "I'm Jason."

My hand shook as my father just stared at me.

"No, you're not."

The three of us jumped back.

"That was just a name to protect you, to keep you hidden."

"Then what's my real name?"

"The same one your mother and I gave you before you were born. Your name is Mordriss."

26

THE NAME MORDRISS echoed through my body. My knees grew week and my breathing slowed while I noticed Sareya and Raynee stepping away from me. How could I ever be that monster? And yet there was my father, glaring at me through years of hiding and toil. My dreams of a normal life were destroyed.

It was clear now why Mordriss always wore a mask. He never wanted to reveal to the world that the real culprit was in their midst, so well hidden that even he believed himself innocent. Of course, he had not murdered me with the rest of the villagers. He needed me alive.

"He's not Mordriss," Raynee demanded, but my father didn't flinch.

"That's his name. My wife . . . It was her favorite. But I suppose it sounds different now."

"But I didn't kill anyone!"

"Not yet, you haven't."

The hut was bare, save for a basic cot in the corner. It was surprising that such a powerful man would avalate such simple and filthy accommodations. He peered out the window at the horizon, which formed a bright line where the sun had just set. We wouldn't be alone for long.

"I'm sure you have many questions, but we need to focus on what you need to know. That I'll show you. Only then will you understand."

He sat on the floor and lifted his forehead. One-by-one, each of us placed a hand on top. We were back in the desert world.

It was a bright day, though the sun was obscured by a gray haze over the sands that painted the sky white while the winds skirted the dunes. My father was making the same journey through the desert world that I had multiple times, only this time it was for real.

While I had been greeted by an overzealous Jamol and a pensive Ilyos, my father was instead met by the stench of burning corpses strewn across the remains of the village. Standing in their midst, with her arms held wide, was my mother.

The version I'd met was already weary from years. Here, she was radiant and not much older than I was now. Her eyes glowered at him while her hair was smooth and skin free from years of sorrows. He stopped on seeing her, and from both of their bewildered looks, neither had expected the other.

"What happened to the turnips?" my father asked.

"Practice."

"You're practicing to kill turnips?" he said playfully. "Not much of a challenge, is it?"

"Well." She drew nearer. "If this were a duel. But that's not much fun."

He plugged his nose from the smell, then waved his hand and the bodies disintegrated.

"You have a strange sense of fun." He laughed, but she didn't share it. With a similar wave, she put every corpse back.

He jumped back just as a black stain appeared on the horizon. They poured forward in the thousands. There were shouts and cheers as they advanced. The hooves shook the earth. When they reached her, a lone warrior separated from the mass.

"See what I have done to those who defy me!" she shouted.

She lifted a head and threw it at them. The horseman drew his scabbard and moved to a full charge.

"Are you so foolish as to disregard my wrath?" she called to them while my father looked on with a smirk.

My mother was calm while the warrior's armor gleamed from the dust storm that enveloped him. When he reached her, he lifted his sword for the kill, and she had the widest grin.

One jump was all it took. With an eight-inch stiletto blade she easily somersaulted over him and sliced the marauder from the skull down to the torso. His horse never stopped moving, but his body soon collapsed over the side and joined the others.

The entire army stood in silence, then one-by-one each dismounted and bowed across the sands.

"Fear and loyalty," she said to my father. "Building an empire."

She lifted her hands high, then bellowed to the crowd "Hear me, my soldiers! The world will cower under our steeds. We will topple the empires surrounding us. We will build a force that will be feared for all history, for we are the horde that never stops. A thousand generations will grow up in fear of our names."

"Very impressive," my father said. In complete view of the horde, he collapsed to the sand and bowed. "You have my interest, and likely my heart as well."

This was how my parents met. Normal parents meet on blind dates, parties, and bold approaches at the park. Mine met on a battlefield of corpses and prostrating warriors. I was beginning to long for someone who just watched a tablet.

We were back in Oreca Gifted. My father was there, but stood at the front of the room. He was a professor. The lecture was on the intricacies of time correlation in cenosance. My mother stood at the back with a big grin. While he talked, she danced as if in tune to the mathematics. Several times he had to stop the lesson while barely holding his laughter. This was how I preferred to remember them.

Once he finished and the students filed out, she ran up and jumped into his arms.

"You figured it out, didn't you?"

"Maybe I have." He kissed her. "He's coming."

She grabbed a quick kiss, then essonated away. Algard's gaunt form entered. He wore the same dark suit and looked little changed from the one I'd so recently pissed off.

"I see you're unfortunately making progress."

"That's of no consequence to you," my father replied.

"Oh, but Avarus, it is. You and I both know what waits out there. Your findings *will* be noticed, and then we're all dead. You need to stop this foolishness."

"That's what thin-minded men always seem to think of progress."

"Regardless, I cannot allow it."

My father laughed. "Well, look at you. Receive a promotion and you're all the sudden giving out orders, playing top of the roost. And yet you've forgotten one important thing."

Algard reached out his hand, but my father calmly resisted the blast, then resonated Algard's legs and arms apart until he hung like a toy doll in midair.

"You call yourself a master, but I've always outclassed you, haven't I?"

"You can take the school by force," the catatonic Algard mumbled. "But they'll never follow you. You'll inherit an empty building."

"Perhaps you're right." My father tossed the helpless Algard into a wall.

The poor man struggled to his feet while eyeing my father's hands. It had taken my, Raynee's, and Darstan's best to hold Algard, but my father was playing with him. I looked at my own hands. Was this the genesis of the Mordriss I was to become?

"We all respect your unparalleled knowledge of resonance and cenosance," said the master in a meeker tone. "I don't recall anyone having such mastery of two forces."

My father only nodded while glaring at him.

"But you need to stop this. There are some things not worth doing. I admire your enthusiasm, but there are other aspects—"

"Such as?"

"You're going to draw attention! You certainly must know how much damage that will cause. You don't need the math for that."

"Not possible. You always were inferior at figuring the details."

"Then I have no choice but to ban you," Algard stated. "You will be removed from all records. This school will never again welcome you."

"This school will never be what it was. You want followers, not discoverers."

My father exited the room while continuing to confront the defiant Algard.

We orasated to a bright room. Outside bloomed endless fields of flowers. My mother lay on a couch, her belly bulging and her face sweating despite being a tepid day. She stared quietly at my father, who had worn through the carpet with his pacing.

"I'm so close," he said. "There's just . . . something I'm not seeing."

"You'll find it soon enough," she said. "I know you will."

He stopped, then as if in an afterthought leaned down to kiss her.

"Remember that night in the desert?" she said in a sultry manner, and I looked away. "How I wish to be back there right now. Maybe not the heat . . . but the excitement, the glory."

"No one to tell us what to study," added my father.

"Damn time correlation," she said. "It's not the same anymore."

My father stopped, put his finger on his lips, and stared outward. "Maybe—"

Then my mother screamed.

We orasated to the delivery room. My mother was dressed in a light blue gown while three nurses frantically rushed around her. Her pupils were nearly popping out, her hands still held the torn-out bed bars, and she shrieked a bone curdling cry.

"This isn't supposed to happen!" she screamed.

"What the hell is going on!" my father asked the nurses.

My mother dropped the right bed bar, reached out her arm, and resonated a nurse against the ceiling.

"We don't know," a nurse said frantically to my father. "It's supposed to be painless . . . natural." She leaned toward him. "Something's wrong."

My mother's stomach lifted into the air, nearly bending her into an upsidedown U, and another nurse was pinned to the wall. Her hand was splayed out now, reaching desperately for something, anything.

"Make it stop!"

"Please, Avarus," one of the nurses said while pulling herself together. "Wait just outside."

"This isn't natural," he pleaded.

"Please."

He tore open the wall, then walked through it. From the new hallway, two more nurses charged into their room. Their eyes were blank. None had a clue.

And then came a sound that I'll never forget. My mother echoed a loud piercing wail as the fully grown Mordriss began to rip open her stomach and enter our world. Shrieks echoed through the room and my father collapsed to the floor. His mouth opened to cry but nothing came out.

Her screaming reached a crescendo in a bursting sound, like a moist clam pried open, and the entire wall was coated in blood. She gargled as the blood poured through her throat, and with one last gasp she was dead.

A torn limb flew out of the room while my father only froze in terror.

"What the—!" a nurse screamed, then came the sound of her, too, choking on her own blood. Her head rolled to the doorway before it burst apart.

My father's face was both wet with tears and white with terror as he tried to crawl toward the splattered remains of my mother, but he was unable to move. There were more cries, the crack of bones, spraying of blood, until only one nurse remained. She was backing slowly through the doorway.

Those were the last steps she took. From behind, someone resonated her into the air, then pulled her torso in half. And then I saw him. I saw myself.

My deep brown hair had grayed a bit, and my skin was now poorly shaven with a few wrinkles, but my eyes and physique were all there. Raynee gasped. She was far more used to my movements. I truly was Mordriss.

He glared at the lifeless body, whose head still stared at him as if asking "why."

Mordriss laughed, then incinerated it.

My father covered his head and sobbed.

He wore a suit slightly unbuttoned and without a tie, as if returning from a party. Some of my mother's intestines hung from his shoulder. After a snap of a finger, his suit was new again. Upon noticing the coiled-up man, Mordriss knelt down to him while my father tried not to look.

"Greetings, Father," he said with half a smile.

My father continued to cry.

"Your idea worked, Father. It really did. Aren't you proud?"

"What did you do?" Father in a hoarse voice. "My wife—"

"Poor Father," Mordriss said in a sinister tone. "You really don't know yet, do you?"

For a moment, Mordriss looked at us and smiled. I almost swore he saw us.

"She was a traitor. Tried to stop me." He grabbed my father by the chin and glared into his eyes. "We can't have that now, can we?"

"What do you want?"

Mordriss scanned around. "Well, we'll see, won't we? You taught me everything I know, so I owe you a few minutes." He stood. "I'm going to tidy up a bit here. You stick around, and then we'll discuss how this moves forward . . . or doesn't."

Mordriss walked past my father, who resumed cowering. Just before leaving, he turned.

"And don't go anywhere, *Father*. I will find you, and I won't be patient like I was with Mother."

He left, and my father let out a loud scream while arching his body against the wall. He collapsed, defeated. Then his cries stopped. There was something still in the room. It was moving. Whatever it was, was alive.

After looking back for a few seconds, he crawled through the blood and torn corpses into the delivery room. He kept low not for fear of Mordriss, but to avoid seeing the remains of his wife.

One of her legs dangled by a ligament from the bed, while both arms were splayed off either side. Blood dripped from every end. There was a light cry, then a wail. It was a baby.

I was in the delivery room.

My father shielded his eyes, then sat up slightly and lifted my newborn self from my mother's carcass. He looked around again, then essonated a portal and jumped through it.

We were back in the hut in our own time. My father sat on his cot with his head downward.

"Time travel. . . . I thought everything would be better, but Algard was right."

Raynee stood next to me and grabbed my hand. When I tried to release it, she held on.

"So, he's not Mordriss," she stated out loud.

"It depends," my father replied. "Did he kill all those people? Not yet."

We stood there in silence. The horizon outside turned orange.

"In some other timeline, your mother and I had a baby. You grew up in this world, not on a fake one, and had everything a child in the paramount dimension desired. I solved the mysteries of time travel, and taught you everything. That was a mistake."

"So, what do we do now?" Raynee asked.

"Nothing," my father said glumly. "Algard was right. I thought it was impossible to go back farther than the machine itself, but I clearly miscalculated."

The sky was a deep red now. My father stood and walked toward it.

"We can't kill him," he said. "I just thought you should know the truth, before—"

The plains erupted in fire, and I knew our time was up.

"I'll stay with you, Father. Until the end."

"No, you won't. Your mother and I weren't good people. I know that now. We killed turnips. We enjoyed torturing them. We were arrogant. You're none of that."

"But we're family," I said.

"No, we're not." The fire roared. "You were the single good thing a bad man did in his life. Make what's left of yours into something better. Create new universes. Bring some good into this world that I fouled up."

He lifted his palms, and ten thousand horse warriors appeared before us. They lifted their swords and bows, then charged toward the horizon while shouting in unison.

"This is the way your mother would've preferred," he said somberly, then avalated away the hut.

"We're staying," Raynee said, squeezing my hand.

My father walked through the advancing horde. The entire sky now swirled in fire.

"No, you're not." He essonated a portal and shoved us through, while in the distance, a dark figure appeared from the fire.

Raynee, Sareya, and I stood before the school. Most of the student body was there, looking at us in amazement.

There would be no easy way to do this. Mordriss was coming, and we had no way to defeat him.

27

MY FATHER WAS gone, and our entire adventure was for nothing. There was no secret to stopping Mordriss. We were the same person, I now knew, but from separate timelines. For the last few weeks, I'd desperately wished that I'd been born to the same advantages of everyone else in this dimension, and now I knew the consequences. The version of me that was Mordriss had received everything growing up, and had become the worse for it.

With the demon about to arrive, my thoughts turned to Raynee and Sareya. Mordriss must have reasons to keep me alive, but how would I ever hope to protect them? How could I prevent him from taking absolutely everything?

The entire student body had surrounded us now. Their arms and legs were all spread wide, ready to attack. I glanced behind me, but there was no one. Then I scanned their faces. None were happy.

Raynee stepped back and prepared to counter, but I gently grabbed her hand. There were a hundred of them and two and a half of us, counting myself as the half, of course. We stood no chance against a coordinated attack.

Revis stood at their front with the biggest smirk. I spotted Henry and Sarlat in the crowd and smiled at them, desperately trying to defuse the situation, but all I met were frowns.

Revis stepped forward.

"We had to do it," I stated. "We needed to know—"

"Enough, Mordriss," Revis shouted.

I was stunned. How could they know this? No one here had ever met my father. I glanced at Algard, who had appeared from the shadows and was calmly avoiding my gaze.

"Do you deny it?" Revis demanded.

I shook my head and winced in anticipation of a hundred resonations.

"He's not *that* Mordriss," Raynee pleaded. "That one's from a different time line."

"That's bullshit," Revis said. "We have proof."

Henry stepped forward. "They managed to orasate some of the bodies in Heskera. It took them awhile, but one of them blew off your mask. They saw you, Mordriss."

I paused while wondering how that could possibly be. I'd been nowhere near Heskera. And then it came to me.

"Someone just changed the orasations. The grand master did that when I orasated him to find the school."

"Impossible!" came isolated replies. "He's just making that up!"

"Isn't that true, Algard?" I boomed.

That was a poor decision. After tweaking his mustache, he looked away, then answered. "No. No one can orasate an image into someone else. The math doesn't lie."

He now had his revenge. Raynee and Sareya jumped in front of me, and a hundred students prepared for an assault. Not far away, I knew, was the actual Mordriss, waiting to finish us off.

"He didn't do it!" Sareya yelled, and for a moment they held back.

That was the last time a six-year-old girl would be able to save me. Whatever the reasons, Mordriss wanted to destroy me. The massacre at Heskera had been planned solely for that purpose. I looked down at the bright, blue-eyed wonder who stood two feet shorter than her foes but was still ready to take their best. They were not our worst foe. The real Mordriss was waiting.

"You need to go," I whispered to her.

Raynee turned suddenly, but my eyes said it all. This was for her own good. Sareya needed to survive.

"Not happening," Sareya answered, and stomped her foot.

"I'm sorry," Raynee said with sorrowful eyes, "but he's right."

While Sareya kicked and screamed, Raynee resonated her into the air and gently dropped her behind the crowd. As a temporary truce, the crowd watched her pass, then once two students locked her in a force field to hold her, their gaze returned.

"You, too, Raynee," I said with a tear. "This is on me now."

"I'm not Sareya, so, *not* happening. And you're not making me."

We had no more opportunities for discussion. Immediately, my arms spread wide, my lungs grew tight, and I was thrust twenty feet into the air. Raynee, for her part, screamed while she struggled to resist dozens of resonations. Yet as strong as she was, after a minute of fight, she, too, was hovering next to me, completely immobilized.

I didn't resist. Any attempt to would only make me appear guiltier. With the two of us on display, Revis lifted his arm and let out a war cry. The entire student body roared back. As he approached, I wondered what the plan was. Only Mordriss knew how to kill, and there were no prisons. Eventually, they would have to release us, and then maybe we could have a discussion. Perhaps on that realization, my body slowly returned to the ground.

This was not intentional. A hundred clenched teeth growled around me. They were frantically trying to prevent it, but someone was resonating me down, someone more powerful than the group combined.

Revis collapsed. Against my best efforts, my arm extended toward him while Raynee looked on helplessly above. My mouth was shut while Revis hovered, then was slammed against the asphalt. Mordriss was controlling me. He wanted witnesses to my first murder.

With every bit of strength, I attempted to pull back my arm, but it was useless. Mordriss waved my arm across, and a shock wave toppled the crowd with ease. Raynee fell back and there were groans everywhere, while I continued to torture poor Revis.

He cried and begged for mercy while Mordriss slowly bent his leg in half. Every student tried to resonate me in place, but it didn't matter. The bone took too long to snap, and when it did, I sensed a desperation in my fellow students. There was nothing anyone could do. Revis was going to die, by my hand.

Raynee was now struggling to knock me away, and my fears turned to her. She knew of course that Mordriss was controlling me, but what if his gaze turned to her? He could easily make me rip her apart, or Sareya. I had to stop this.

A dozen students poured between me and Revis, but they were no match for Mordriss. Within seconds, they, too, were sprawled across the ground, screaming in agony while their fingers broke one-by-one. He was toying with us.

Just as Revis' right arm was about to snap, a planet whizzed by my head and a blast knocked me back. With those brief seconds I circled to find my controller, but there was nothing but groaning students and Darstan, standing before me and wielding a maelstrom of a universe.

"Help!" was all I had the opportunity to say before the professor went flying and my arm reached out to finish Revis.

"You have to control it!" Raynee yelled, and my heart sank.

Slowly my arm pulled back from torturing Revis, then turned to a different foe. A single tear flowed down across her perfect skin, and with all my might I held myself back. I tried to open my mouth, scream at her to run, essonate away, get out of here, but she wouldn't have obliged. She knew.

There was another blast from the recovered Darstan, and my

arm held in place from the combined efforts of the other teachers minus Algard, who had for some reason disappeared. Finally, with Mordriss's attention toward them, I managed to scream.

"Stop this!"

There was no response. And then it occurred to me. This would never work. I had to change my tone.

"What do you want?"

The power flew from me like a breeze, then my hands and legs flayed apart from the professors' combined efforts. It felt like my entire body was to be ripped in half, but once they felt satisfied that I was immobile, they released the pressure slightly.

"So Mordriss was with us the entire time," Algard announced, who reappeared suddenly.

There were murmurs from the students, but I noticed Darstan's glance turn. He wasn't buying it. Raynee was beside me again, though twenty hands were pointed her way just in case.

"It's time for a little chat," Algard decreed.

"Are you sure that's prudent?" Fantasa asked, who seemed more than a little smug at my predicament. "We couldn't restrain him."

"Until I helped," he responded with confidence.

Against Raynee's pleading, Algard waved his hands and darkness overcame me. When I awoke, we were back in Fantasa's classroom, filled with a vague emptiness now. I stood at the front, as if ready to provide the lesson, while Algard and the Halloween decoration that was Fantasa were seated. A hole from our recent battle had already been patched.

"Admirably done, boy," Algard said.

I shook my head and struggled to move, but they weren't taking any chances. My feet and hands were glued together. My mouth moved. I could talk again.

"I don't understand."

"Come now," Algard said. "You can't believe us that daft. It's obvious that Mordriss was controlling you."

Instantly my thoughts turned to Sareya and Raynee. I twitched my neck toward the door.

"Ahh, don't worry about them. Farlan and Darstan are still out there. If Mordriss shows up, they can handle him."

"I doubt that."

"Yes, yes. I presume the meeting with your father was fruitful. I was a bit of a weakling back then. You know, I toyed with you and your little girl. Trust me. I can be far more fearsome now. There's a reason Mordriss hasn't shown himself here yet."

"Then why don't you find him, and end this?"

"In due time, in due time." Algard lowered his hands. "First, I need to know some things."

"My father figured it out. But he said you were right. It's possible for people to go back. That's what Mordriss did."

"Yes, that's what I so recently feared." He stood. "I must apologize for sending you on a false errand. While I was correct that Avarus is your father, I didn't tie Mordriss into the equation until you left."

"You mean, you figured out that we're the same person?"

Fantasa's eyes popped open.

"Well, first, you're not the same person. As you know, he's from a different time line. He grew up under completely different circumstances. In no way should you bear guilt for his atrocities."

"Then why didn't you help me back there? You let them attack me."

Algard sighed. "There's no way to reason with a mob mentality. Unfortunately, I was unable to filter the news from Heskera. When crowds are involved, the simplest answer is too often assumed to be the truth. Have patience. Once they calm down, I'll explain everything."

As friendly as Algard was being, this still made no sense. If he had the ability to stop Mordriss, why hadn't he done so long ago? I longed for Raynee. She would have seen what I was missing.

"So." I gave him my friendliest smile. "You have some questions for me?"

Fantasa leaned forward in her chair. Her gaunt face provided little emotion, but I sensed curiosity in those eyes. She was as confused as I.

"Well," Algard said. "Yes, I do." He turned to Fantasa. "Ask away."

She sat there for an uncomfortable moment, as she returned glances between me and Algard. Finally, she spoke in her ghostly tone. "I have to agree with Jason. Finish Mordriss, then tell the truth."

"The truth is, you've never liked Jason much," Algard said.

She stood and her palms moved slightly to her sides.

"From the very first day. I mean, the kid couldn't breathe. It was his first day in our school and you had not an ounce of compassion."

She drew back with a frightened look, and he turned to me.

"Fine, since she doesn't have a question, I'll ask. I have only a single important one. Did you screw her?"

This time I jumped. "Screw who?" I glanced at the gaunt Fantasa and nearly threw up.

"This old hag?" Algard laughed while Fantasa cautiously moved toward the wall. "No one in his right mind would do her. No, I mean Raynee."

Was Algard actually asking this? Fantasa was ready to resonate into the next room, until Algard gently waved his finger. She scowled, then with one flourish created a portal and attempted to jump. It was all over in a second.

Blood splattered across my shirt as Fantasa's throat burst, then her frail body collapsed to the floor. Algard calmly wiped his hands, then destroyed her portal. That's when I knew.

"Damn it!" he shouted. "Here I'd hoped to monologue her, tell her how horrible she was and how much she deserved this. Now look at this mess!" He placed several fingers gently over what was left of Fantasa's head.

"You're orasating her, so everyone will think it was me," I said.

"Very perceptive."

"And you killed Algard long ago. Didn't you . . . Mordriss."

The person I'd previously known as Algard gave a devious smile.

"I knew you weren't that stupid. Father always spoke about Algard the asshole, who terminated him from the university despite being the inferior. I expected you to be happier, but then, you never knew the original Algard. He would never have let you study here."

He stood and turned to me. He waved one hand, and I was facing my mirror image in thirty years. His eyes were sunken from years of hate, and I felt very unsafe when he grinned.

"Answer my question, Young Mordriss," he said.

"I love Raynee." I held out my chest and expected the worst.

"Of course, you love her. I loved her, but I think she always suspected me. Always kept me at a fair distance. So, since we're talking about your dearly beloved here, I'll dispense with the vulgar terms. Did she give herself to you?"

I strongly considered my response. One wrong word and he wouldn't hesitate to kill her.

"No. She didn't."

He seemed to chuckle lightly, and I was amazed by how much of an asshole I was going to be.

"So, what now?" I asked.

"My! I'm continually amazed by how much of a chickenshit this version of me is. What the hell did they do to you on Earth?"

"They improved me. Had I been born here, I would've been like you."

My throat shrank and the air to my lungs ceased. I felt my knees collapse to the floor while the room began to spin.

"How dare you!" he hissed, then calmed himself. "You still think there's an opportunity for you here? You think it was a miraculous fate that got you this far? I could've easily finished you many times."

He leaned down and forced my head up and my eyes open

to stare into that menacing face, which was so familiar yet completely unknown.

"You've done exactly what I needed." He tossed me to the ceiling.

When my body slammed, his gaze drifted for just a second. It was my only chance. With my thoughts on Raynee, I cenosated a whirlwind of a universe and pounded him with it. After a snap of his fingers, it was gone.

"How quaint. You try to compensate your poor ass resonance for cenosance." His eyes narrowed. "I would've never thought of that."

My entire world went black, then a massive burst blinded me before my body felt ripped apart by the expanding universe.

"You see," Mordriss shouted from the darkness, "I'm the better you in every respect."

Each galaxy was like a needle piercing straight through me, and after a few seconds I could only scream while my body felt ready to burst apart. Then the room was bright.

"You disappoint me." He lifted his arms for what I presumed was the end.

The room jolted and a beam of light blasted Mordriss to the wall. Another force held him there as he struggled to push back. I could barely move, but managed to turn my head. It was Darstan and Farlan.

Though Mordriss managed to dispel Darstan's universe after a few seconds, Farlan proved the tougher foe. As much as he struggled with his teeth clenched, Mordriss couldn't break through Farlan's shield. Raynee appeared behind them. She ran to me.

The very essence of the room wobbled, and Mordriss snapped free from the trap.

"Very impressive, Farlan. I always took you for an idiot."

Farlan blasted another wave, but this one Mordriss deflected.

Raynee knelt next to me. "Let's end this," she whispered.

Sareya appeared at the doorway, and Raynee let go a single tear.

Mordriss noticed. "How fitting." He lifted his hand toward those bright blue eyes.

Raynee grabbed my arm and together we jumped at the startled Mordriss. The moment we touched, there was nothing but streaks of light amid the darkness.

It was the last trick Raynee had ever learned from her brother Val. Given just the right balance of resonance and essonance, it was possible to carry multiple people light years away. Since it destroyed all worm holes, it remained an arcane piece of knowledge. Yet in this case it was most effective, and she had delivered a far more powerful dose than Val had ever dreamed.

The three of us were now a hundred light years away, which meant a hundred years in the future.

And there was no way to get back.

28

GIANT ROCKS TUMBLED through the reaches of space. We were spinning in this alien landscape, an endless flow of brown asteroids jostling together in a thick mass of debris. By second nature now, I avalated enough air to breathe in this desolate world.

Raynee still held my hand. Her eyes were wide, but her breathing normal, while she stared at the grinning Mordriss. We had saved them, but doomed ourselves. It no longer mattered what Mordriss did to us. There was no escape from time. Whoever survived this encounter would die of old age before coming across anyone else.

He floated away, and an asteroid briefly rolled between us. When our view returned, he was smiling.

"Val taught you well. But there's so much you don't understand, my love."

"Go ahead and kill us, you asshole," Raynee snarled back. "You'll never hurt them again. And no, I don't love you."

He drew closer, but did not attack us just yet.

"But you did once." Then he was gone in a flash of light.

"What the hell!" Raynee cried as we floated among the debris. She looked around. "What even *is* this place?"

We both scanned the rocks, but Mordriss was gone. He had

simply disappeared. What was more, the landscape made no sense. Our entire universe consisted of a single land mass. There were no asteroids or debris. Someone had done this.

I moved to create a portal, but Raynee shook her head.

"Didn't you hear him? There's something we don't know. We have to find him, just in case there's a way back."

Our hands were drifting apart in this mess. Why had he seemed so smug? The longer we stayed here, the more he could do. I glanced at Raynee, with her fiery brown eyes. A single sun illuminated this part of the paramount dimension, and for a brief moment a beam poured between the rocks and illuminated her face. She turned to me and the light twinkled from a small marble just above her bosom. It was my first universe.

"Do you remember what Darstan said about time correlation?" I asked.

Raynee shook her head violently. She'd already guessed where I was going.

"My father mentioned something similar."

"We have no idea how to do that. It would be crazy. Who knows what could happen if we got it wrong?"

"But don't you see? That's the hidden piece! That's how Mordriss gets around so easy! He time travels, using time correlated universes."

"But this one's only a few weeks old. So, it will only buy us maybe a week."

"And I think he used it."

She stared back at me with disapproving eyes.

"What if he anticipated this? What if he placed other universes around, with different time correlations? He could get back. Maybe a week is all he needs for now."

A gigantic boulder rolled by, and Raynee resonated us to its surface. She stared at me, as if waiting for my next move.

"I know it sounds strange, but I think I know how to do it."

She looked back, and I knew what she was thinking. We could

essonate away here, form our own world, and be free. Mordriss would never find us, nor would anyone else.

And yet there was Sareya. Given it was now a hundred years in the future, she was almost certainly dead. But what if there was a way to get back? What if Mordriss could get to her, and we didn't stop him?

"We need to do this," I said softly.

"For Sareya," she added, then turned toward me. "You know, if this fails . . . we could be separated forever. There are infinite worlds out there, and we'll never find each other."

I took a deep breath, then gently cradled her pendant in my left hand. With my right arm, I reached around her waist and held her tight. She kissed me just when I triggered the jump, and I held her desperately while we flew into the universe, then essonated through its barrier. Regardless whether this worked, it would be our last kiss.

The calculations and precision had to be exact. Imagine having to throw a curve ball through an exact-sized hole from two miles away, then doing something billions of times harder. Only at the exact size, at the exact velocity, and the exact moment of essonation would this work. If there was a single mistake, we were doomed to travel the universes apart forever.

We landed on the same barren landscape, but in a single piece. There was no more floating debris, but instead an unending horizon of jagged brown rock. Next to me was Raynee. We'd made it, though I still had no idea where.

My arm was still holding her, and upon realizing that I'd done it, she smiled. It didn't last long. Before I could grin back, a force ripped her from my grasp and slammed her into a rock.

From out of the air, Mordriss appeared. Immediately I cenosated a universe toward him, but he calmly brushed it away, then lifted me with my legs and arms locked.

"Very stupid move on your part. Why did you follow me?"

He slammed me into the jagged rock so hard that everything

went black, then I resonated to my feet and scanned for Raynee. I only found Mordriss's cold glare.

With my hands free, I recalled my sparring lessons with Raynee, then attempted to knock him down. He only laughed.

"This is so sad. You've got to feel it!"

A surge pulled my body in two directions, and I collapsed to the ground while I felt my veins struggle to remain together.

"Resonation is the force of hate. You have to *mean* it."

My head was lifted into the air, then pounded into the rock.

Now I was getting pissed. Faster than he could move, I ripped my arm forward and tore at his leg. It only wobbled.

"Is that it?" He laughed. "Is that truly all you can do?"

He shut my eyes and immobilized my body in the air. Only through resonation could I see. Mordriss turned to Raynee.

"You see, my dear, in every way, I'm the superior Mordriss."

She had pulled herself up from the original attack, and now stood opposite him. Her palms were by her sides, ready for anything, but they were also trembling.

"Go fuck yourself," she shouted back.

"Not today. In the meantime, let's get rid of this copy. It's been a long time, Raynee, but imagine the world I could give you."

"I want nothing of your world." She spit a tuft of blood at him. "And he's not Mordriss. His name is Jason and you're nothing compared to him."

He resonated her inches from him. Her limbs were locked, and I was seething to escape. Slowly, I opened my eyes, then began to wiggle my legs.

"Shall I force you?" he snarled.

Raynee pulled herself away and her arms flung out. With every bit of force she had, she threw him to the ground. Mordriss's head slammed against the rock, then he lifted his palm and blocked the next blow.

"You always were my weakness," he said softly. "But no longer."

Everything stopped. Raynee's knees fell to the ground, and she reached her hand to her chest. It was covered in blood. Mordriss had torn her stomach open.

Blood poured from her mouth and she looked at me with wide eyes as the life flowed from her.

"NO!" I screamed. Upon seeing her dying, my veins surged and suddenly I felt the universe in every microcosmic detail. I pulled myself from Mordriss's grasp and sent a fury of rocks directly at him.

He parried them to his sides with some difficulty, but I wasn't done yet. For the first time, I could feel every piece of his body. I tore at his back, and my evil copy fell to the ground.

I was now high in the air, hitting him with every form of punch and blast I could muster. Raynee was beside me. She was gasping and choking, her thin hands unable to do anything against the flow of blood that now soaked the rocks in front of her.

Mordriss stood, his teeth clenched and his hair unkempt, then hurled a blast that earlier would have killed me. I blocked it easily. I felt his lungs filling, his heart beating, and every drop of blood moving through his veins. He looked into my eyes, and I sensed the blood rush faster. I knew how to kill him now.

I pulled my fist closed and his right femur snapped. His leg was wobbling, but still Mordriss held his pose while more meekly attempting to fight back. I glanced toward Raynee. Her hand was weakening against her chest, and her body was ready to collapse forward. There was no way to save her. She was going to die, and the best I could hope for was revenge on her killer.

"You lousy piece of shit!" I screamed and one-by-one twisted every bone in his wrist. He only glared at me.

"Why did you do that?" I shouted.

With all my strength, I focused on his healthy leg until blood began to pour out, and Mordriss fell to the ground. Yet there was no look of defeat. He only gave me a blank stare, and stopped fighting back.

Another blast crushed his arm while I hovered over him, then I prepared for the final blow. I would crush his skull and end this. While I resonated him still, I looked out toward the horizon. I would be forever alone here.

Raynee tried to gargle something.

She was nearly collapsed now. Blood covered her entire chest and legs. Those piercing brown eyes I'd first fallen in love with were ready to close. I released Mordriss and moved toward her. Raynee's last gasp shouldn't be alone.

"Break . . . the . . . cycle," she made out with her last words.

From beneath Mordriss's collar came the twinkle of a familiar marble. The woven gold chain was unmistakable, and for the first time I understood my purpose in everything. I knew now that Mordriss had received everything he wanted.

Everything had fallen to his plan. There was a reason he never killed me. It was the same reason I was defeating him just now. He had always planned to lose.

I looked back at the bloody, crawling person that was my future self. This entire thing had been training. Only when he had killed Raynee did I understand the true measure of hate. Only when he took the most important thing away from me could I match him in resonance. He had taught me to time travel. He had taught me to kill. He had placed me in this desolate world where I was destined to go insane from solitude. He had placed the Oreca badge in my pocket and forced me to orasate Sareya. He had made me Mordriss.

With one blast I shoved him over, then I rushed to Raynee. She was pale now, with precious little blood left. I looked down at her wound, but there was no way I could avalate that. She was trembling now, and I gently held her hand and kissed her forehead.

"I love you, Raynee," I said. "And my name is Jason."

The entire life of Mordriss was a vicious circle. He knew my every step, because he had once followed them. This Mordriss, like myself, was born on Earth. A girl named Raynee had found him, and he'd been subjected to the same ridicule as a new student. And then, just when he thought things were perfect, the previous Mordriss had arrived. He taught him the things never mentioned in school, then took away his entire life and left him to seethe in the wilderness.

His anger had only risen in solitary confinement, until a horrible idea had come to light. Since he was Mordriss, he should *be* Mordriss. He mastered the final pieces of time travel, then returned and followed those steps he'd retraced in his head during those many years alone.

The end goal was never world domination. It was an end. This Mordriss wanted to die, and only another Mordriss could kill him. It was impossible to harm oneself with any of the forces. My previous copy was now sprawled across the ground, waiting for me to administer his fate. It was time for me to take his place.

Raynee was falling forward, but I held her up. Her breath was slowing, and with great difficulty she raised her arm. I grasped it, but she slowly wrung it free, then rested it on her pendant. More blood flowed from her mouth while she attempted to speak. She held it toward me.

Time travel would be of no use here. She wouldn't survive the trip. Raynee was falling into my arms, her throat gargling.

No. She wanted to tell me something, and it wasn't time travel. There was no way to save her, but the universe was presenting another option. The cycle didn't have to continue.

Despite being mostly inept at every other force, I was a master of cenosance. Yet only with my thoughts on Raynee could I achieve anything. There was a reason for that.

It took two particles to trigger cenosance. Each had to be in precisely the right dance around the other. I remembered back to the rock fields we'd encountered earlier. Somehow, this landscape was destroyed. Mordriss hadn't done that. I had.

While Raynee drew her last gasps, I realized that we were just two particles in the universe, doing a dance around each other the entire time. That's how she found me, despite the nearly infinite odds against. We were destined to be together. We were destined to create something new, and in all his hate Mordriss had never realized that.

I thought to Sareya. We would never see her again, but she would be safe. There would be no Mordriss for her to ever fear.

I lifted Raynee's chin and stared into her still piercing eyes.

"For Sareya," I whispered, and she nodded in understanding.

The doomed copy of Mordriss screamed when Raynee and I embraced. Around me there was only a sense of great love and awe as our bodies burst to pieces, disintegrating what was left of that evil being, then joining together in the throngs of a new universe.

Our bodies were now nothing as the heavens broke loose and we gave ourselves completely to each other. The forms that used to be Raynee and Jason were no more, but she was closer to me than ever before. We had created something new. And then all went white.

29

THE VAST MAJORITY of hikers never knew there was an alternate path. This trail was famous for its wonderful vistas over lupine covered meadows. Most visitors knew that a true summit trip was not in their plans, but were still satisfied by the views of neighboring peaks amidst the barks of pikas. More than a few spent the day munching on the endless groves of huckleberries.

Yet for a determined few, there was another way. Hidden behind the last trees before the mountain went bare was a steep incline, with only occasional blotches of paint and stacked rocks for guides. This was the direct route. This went to the summit.

She hesitated only long enough to figure out which bush blocked the way. A poor choice could lead her to the wrong cliff, though even that didn't scare her. She knew what she was doing.

The branches gave way and she was soon on a scramble upward. This was her least favorite part. She was still technically on a trail, it was steep enough to slip down, but lacked the standard amount of hand holds typical on a true climb. When the way turned completely vertical, she sighed a breath of relief.

Someone once asked her why she bothered to spend a free day like this. The walking trail took far less time, was considerably less dangerous, and offered nearly the same view. Those points were not incorrect, but she found the true advantage more difficult to articulate. Virtually no one climbed this route. The entire ascent provided solitude, and the summit was hers alone.

It was a warm day, perhaps a bit too much. She sweated profusely, despite an early start designed to avoid the brunt of the sun. Nature always had a way of deterring people from mountains, she thought. During winter, the danger from snow and ice made most ascents impossible, but summer could be nearly as dangerous. There were easier ways to ascend, of course, but the thrill of lifting herself foot-by-foot was the most exhilarating.

She paused a few times to admire the views. At the summit, she would enjoy a panoramic view from one of the tallest peaks, but this one was no slouch. Beyond, the mountainsides were bright red and green.

It had taken until late July for all the snow to melt. The walking trail had been clear since the end of June, but the peak always required a bit longer. The wait had been frustrating. Sure, there were other routes on other mountains, but this one offered something special.

The sky was bright blue, without a single cloud. She would have preferred a few to buffer against this unbearable sun. She slowed her breathing enough to concentrate on a difficult part, then lifted herself to a ledge and eyed the short distance remaining.

Even other climbers had rebuked her for not ascending with others, and going without ropes. Yet the concept seemed simple enough to her. In its essence, climbing was a basic endeavor. One simply needed to not fall, or at least not unintentionally. It wasn't her fault they didn't realize that. Then again, there were many things they didn't know, and it wasn't her job to teach them.

She took her time with the final hundred feet. A year ago, a less serious climber had hurried this section, thinking that it was more of a scramble than a climb. One wrongly placed foot had ended that assumption.

On this particular mountain, the summit was a single flat rock, perhaps six feet square. She'd considered spending the night there more than a few times to gaze at the myriad stars under an unpolluted night's sky, then marvel at the following sunrise. Yet every time, caution had sent her down before sunset.

She reached the top with one hand, then pulled herself up where an endless field of mountains paraded her on every side.

She was not alone.

A young man sat on the middle of the rock with eyes nearly the same shade of brown as hers, and of similar age. His legs were folded and he bore neither signs of equipment, nor of sweat.

She sat across from him. He reached behind his back and pulled out a reddish fruit, then tossed it at her. She caught it, then placed it down with a wide grin.

Her forehead was no longer sweating, and her skin was as fresh as if she had never climbed. He opened his mouth to say something, but was met with hers as she knocked him over, then kissed him until far after the sun set.

ABOUT THE AUTHOR

A New York immigrant to Seattle, Joseph Calev is a proud Luxembourgish-American photographer, traveler, and writer who couldn't focus on one thing if his life depended on it. His novels and photography reflect his passions that include the savannah of Africa, ancient villages of Europe, and astrophysics. The world around us is simply too amazing to only admire one part. When he's not photographing and writing, you may find him in Bellevue, WA, where he lives with his immensely understanding wife and two sons.

Made in the USA
Monee, IL
03 March 2021